T u o +

l

So glad you guys are my
friends!

MY NAME IS
HAMMERFIST

AARON N. HALL

ISBN: 9781654264994

Beta Readers: Conner Van Wilkinson, Skyler Rogers, Gary Hall, Jesse Schumacher

Cover design by Tyler Carpenter | @tyler_c_world

Dedicated to mom and dad

and everyone else who inspired me

to keep writing.

1

On the edge of Citytown, not far from the smog and neon lights and noise, an abandoned hospital rests beneath a deep purple sunset. Ambulances plagued with rust and flat tires occupy a sun-bleached parking lot littered with cracks behind a massive chain link fence. The exterior walls of the fortress are rampant with graffiti and most of windows are broken, regardless of the numerous "KEEP OUT" signs that mark the perimeter.

Inside, it was a labyrinth of decaying walls decorated with rotting posters and safety signs. They connecting operating rooms were mostly ransacked except for some bacteria-infested mattresses and discarded operation tools. The broken windows threw blue moonlight into the halls in patches, leaving much in the shadows. Thick dust and broken glass scattered across the floors where doctors and nurses once darted about. The hospital would have been entirely silent if it weren't for the eerie echoes coming from one operation room—the sounds of clinking glasses and bubbling fluid.

Crack!

In the room, a dark figure muttered an expletive as one of the beakers slipped and fell to the ground. The figure quickly scurried away from the broken glass and grabbed a dustpan. As he swept up the glass fragments, he stared hard at the contents that splattered on the floor: a thick, fluorescent green fluid letting off an eerie smoke. He frowned, knowing how much the fluid was worth.

He threw away the pieces, then went back to his work, clinking and clanking the beakers as he worked in a meditated frenzy. The long table he hunched over was totally packed with these beakers and accompanying notes. His poor posture shrouded his face in darkness. The only light in the room was provided by a single orange lamp in the corner. It threw tall shadows on the wall and flickered in the dark.

Sweat coated his forehead as he went. His hands moved swiftly—decisive, quick, and calculating. After minutes, he held up another beaker to his eyes, filled liberally with the smoking, green liquid. He smiled.

"Just as I remembered," his voice was smooth and dark.

"You know..."

The figure's heart jolted as he flipped about, his eyes wild. Another figure stood in the door frame. An intruder. Uninvited. But when he saw the trespasser, his eyes scrunched in confusion.

The person in the door frame was nothing more than a scraggly hobo, munching on a sandwich with one hand and cradling a dead possum in his other. The two stood there staring at each other, the tension thick as the stranger chewed liberally on his sandwich.

"You know," the hobo continued. "I can smell your boiling cabbage. If you're gonna boil cabbage, you gotta use salt water. That's what the fishes drink. It's good for you. Just ask Reggie here." He held out his possum. "Reggie used to love cabbage before he fell sleep last week. He would--"

The dark figure by the desk didn't wait to hear the dead possum's love of boiled cabbage. He grabbed a shimmering, metal apparatus on the edge of the desk and held it horizontal.

BLAM!

The hobo crumbled the ground, cold and lifeless. The revolver smoked as the gunshot rebounded through the halls. Satisfied that the hobo was dead, he pulled the barrel to his lips and blew out the smoke. Then he set the gun carefully at the edge of the desk where it once was.

The gunshot stopped ringing out. Silence filled the hospital once again, leaving nothing but the soft bubbling of the liquids in front of him.

A soft sigh escaped his lips. "Another mess to clean."

*

In a Citytown high-rise, Herman Fitzgerald tried not to look out the window too much. He couldn't help but notice the smog that so thickly coagulated in the air, hovering between the glass-covered skyscrapers. His leg bounced underneath a table while his palms were on his knees, clammy and cold on top of worn black slacks.

Around him were framed photographs of children smiling, adults wearing branded t-shirts, and people in suits shaking hands. The t-shirts in the pictures all had the logo for Children's Wishes Coalition, the same logo that hung on a massive sign on the far side of the room. The only furniture was a long table and a collection of surrounding grey chairs for meetings and interviews.

A woman sat across the table from Herman wearing an iron grey pantsuit and horn-rimmed glasses. Her long fingernails clacked on the table as her eyes scanned Herman's resume, printed on copy paper. Its contents didn't reach farther than half the page.

"Your resume says you graduated from Citytown Community College with honors?" She asked with an upward swoop in her voice.

"Yes, ma'am," Herman croaked.

"What was your GPA?"

"...two point one."

This caused the woman to cock her eyebrow and glance up at Herman. Herman tried to flush the lump out of his throat, straightening his red tie and smoothing out the shirt he forgot to press.

"The honor was for eighty percent attendance," Herman said. "The Triple C doesn't exactly have a lot of students that are, uh... ambitious. So, they gave me a certificate when I graduated." He paused. "It's the Remarkable Attendance Honor. Otherwise known as the RAH." Another pause, then he said, "...rah!" with a sheepish punch in the air.

The woman locked eyes on Herman and didn't blink. Finally, she sighed and pushed the resume away from her, lacing her hands on the table and pursing her lips.

"Herman," she said. "As you know, Children's Wishes Coalition is a highly-respected nonprofit that exists to grant wishes to children in the last stages of their lives. What makes you want to work here, and why do you consider yourself qualified?"

Herman ran his fingers through his blonde hair then pulled at his collar. His crystal blue eyes went from her, to the window, then to the pictures surrounding him. So many smiling faces. Happy people. People making a difference. He cleared his throat and he stared at the table as he spoke.

"It's because, well…" he sighed. "I just want to help people. I don't want to come to work every day and punch a clock and feel like I'm not making a difference for anybody. I want to do some good—some *real* good. I guess I could find a typical corporate job where I'm at a desk all day trying to trick people into buying something they don't need, but that's not me. That's why I want to be in the nonprofit sector. I want to help people that can't help themselves… you know?"

The woman's face softened. Not only that, but she almost smiled. Herman almost smiled back. She was silent for a moment, thinking, not making eye contact, but then, she looked Herman in the eye.

"Herman, I'd like to offer you this position on our public affairs team—"

Herman's heart leapt into his throat.

"—but I can't."

Then it dropped.

"Your heart is in the right place," she continued. "But you're simply not qualified. Your grades aren't anything impressive, you have no internship experience, no letters of recommendation… you're just not a good candidate for the job. Forgive me for being blunt, but it would be a mistake if I hired you."

"Ouch," Herman couldn't help but stammer. He tried to regain his composure. "Please, Miss—uh, I'm sorry, I forgot your name."

"Lois," she said flatly, her face hard again.

"Lois, please, I promise that if you consider me for the position, I'll do all that I can—"

"Don't make this harder than it needs to be, Herman," Lois said. "I've got a dozen other interviews lined up today with candidates that have real experience in the nonprofit sector. One candidate even helped raise fifty thousand dollars for babies born without elbows. That's a tough act to follow. Please understand that I don't get any pleasure out of telling you no, Herman. I'm sorry."

At that, Herman was silent. His heart was still in his stomach and he wiped his clammy palms on his slacks. After a long, drawn-out sigh, he nodded and stood up.

"I understand. Well, thanks anyway."

"Thank you for your time, Herman," Lois said as she came around the table. As they shook hands, she said, "And good luck. I mean that. I have your resume. If an internship opportunity comes up in the next few months, I'll put you on the list."

"Thank you," Herman said as he was led to the door.

As Herman exited the conference room, he stepped into the lobby for Children's Wishes Coalition. The same red, blue, and yellow logo hung over the reception desk and other job candidates sat in chairs leading to the door. All of them sported crisp haircuts, pressed slacks, and sharp ties—dressed to impress and succeeding.

Herman didn't want to look at any of them, let alone speak to them. He dragged his feet to the front desk and asked, "Do you guys validate?"

The receptionist was a girl in her early twenties with her face buried in her phone. Her thumb scrolled through her feed and she pushed a lollipop to the side of her mouth as she said, "No."

Clearly, Herman thought to himself. *How is it that this brat could get a job at a place like this and I can't?*

"Alright. Well, thanks," Herman said glumly. With that, Herman Fitzgerald was out the door.

The elevator ride down to the ground floor was grim and unceremonious. A beep sounded when each floor was passed, but the elevator never stopped and no one joined him. Herman couldn't help but give another long sigh. As he stared at his dull, slouching reflection in the polished aluminum as he noticed something. He leaned in closer… and closer…

He had a mustard stain on his tie.

"Huh?" Herman said as he brought it to his eyes. "Ugh! Son of a…!"

He fumbled with the knot and threw the tie off his neck about the same time the elevator doors slid open. A trash can right outside the elevator became the tie's new home. Huffing angrily, Herman shoved his hands in his pockets and marched through the lobby. He didn't stop to appreciate the polished marble beneath him or the mahogany front desk. The front door was just ahead.

As he burst out onto the sidewalk, Herman rummaged around for his keys and finally extracted them after pulling some lint and string from the bottom of his pocket. People passed all around him, seemingly ignorant of each other as they jabbered on private phone calls or listened to music in their headphones. Garbage packed the gutters beside parked cars and the neon signs that hung above the tightly-packed stores wouldn't ignite for several hours. Above him, skyscrapers stretched for dozens of stories like towering giants of glass and steel.

Herman approached a clunky white sedan two decades old. It was too old for a key fob, so he had to unlock it the old-fashioned way. He jammed the car key into the lock and had to jingle it just right before the door would creak open. But before he could get in, he noticed a slip of paper pinned beneath his windshield wiper.

His hand reached out and snatched the slip from under the windshield wiper. It was a note from the Citytown Police Department.

"A parking ticket. Because why not?" Herman rolled his eyes as he stuffed it in his pocket. "Glad to know the police in this town are on top of *something*."

"Hey!"

Herman's heart jolted horribly and his head swiveled about. Standing just a few feet away from him, a ragged, unshaven old man approached him. The coat over his shoulders was covered in bits of hair and crumbs and the bags under his eyes were droopy and blue. The unwashed smell emanating from him was pungent and Herman tried not to scrunch his nose for fear of being rude.

Definitely a homeless guy, he thought.

"A dollar for some food?" The man implored through yellow teeth.

Herman tightened his jaw. After briefly looking up and down the old man, he rummaged around in his other pocket and managed to procure two crumpled dollar bills.

"Here you go," Herman said. "It's not a lot. Times are tough all over, you know?"

"God bless," the homeless man gave a little bow before he took the dollars and slipped away.

The car door creaked and slammed shut as Herman plopped into the driver's seat. As he jammed the key into the ignition, he pressed a number on speed dial with his other hand. The car sputtered and churned as it rumbled to life, and finally, Herman pulled out of the parking spot as he pressed the phone to his ear.

Brrrrr... brrrrrr... brrrr—click!

"*Hey honey!*"

"Hey, Aunt Josie," Herman said as squealed to a stop behind another car.

"*How did the interview go?*"

"Same as the others."

Aunt Josie sighed on the other end. *"Oh, I'm so sorry, Herman... I know you're doing your best. Something will come up."*

"I sure hope so."

"If nothing else, you can always move back to Gladview and work at the restaurant with me! Lord knows how dangerous Citytown is. I worry about you every day."

Herman half-smiled. "Thanks, Aunt Josie, but I'm okay. As long as you're in before dark you usually don't have to worry. And I don't think I'm cut out to work at a small town diner anyway. I'm not a good cook."

"What are you talking about? Your toast is perfect!"

"Well, when Mister Beasley is looking to hire a full-time toast chef, let me know," Herman grinned.

Aunt Josie cackled with laughter on the other end of the phone. When it died down, she said, *"You know what I thought of today? How proud your mom would be if she were still around."*

The grin on Herman's face faded as he remembered standing next to Aunt Josie years ago, holding her hand, gazing over a black casket in the middle of a February afternoon. Snow fell heavily all around and the dozens of people who had gathered around the casket, dressed in black. Aunt Josie squeezed Herman's eleven-year-old hand, and that night, he went home to stay with her for good.

"I still miss her sometimes," Aunt Josie's voice trailed.

"So do I, Aunt Josie," Herman said softly.

"Well, I sure do love you," Aunt Josie said. *"Don't give up! You'll find something! Just stay strong and keep swinging!"*

"Thanks," Herman said. "Love you, too. I'll keep you updated."

"Hugs and kisses! Mwah!"

"Mwah."

Boop.

Herman pushed the phone back in his pocket then rested his head on his hand as he cruised through the streets, starting and stopping at nearly every light. The folks on the sidewalk marched quickly and silently, avoiding eye contact with passersby. Occasionally, a homeless person or other bleary-eyed nomad would stake their claim with a cardboard sign, shopping cart, or sleeping bag. At their feet, all sorts of trash scooted along the sidewalks and through the gutters as passing cars kicked them aside.

Herman reached for the radio dial and flipped it.

"—has now ranked Citytown the Most Dangerous City in America according to recent crime statistics. According to the study, Citytown has seen eighteen homicides, thirty-seven armed robberies, and nearly four hundred burglaries since the beginning of this month! Unbelievable... Citytown Police want to assure the public that the rise in crime is being dealt with swiftly and admonish city residents to stay off the streets at night. What do I think? Personally, I never think it's a bad time for kung fu lessons!

"But hey, you people of Citytown, summer is here and it's time to get out for the weekend! Hit those trails! Enjoy our polluted beaches! Show off that sexy summer body! Speaking of which, I'm on a strict diet of fish tacos, beer, and meat lover's pizza—"

Suddenly, the car ahead of him slammed on its breaks.

"Whoa!" Herman jolted.

Herman's car lurched to a halt right before he rear-ended the car in front of him. Ice water rushed through his blood stream and his heart pounded in his chest. Exhaling, Herman slumped down in his seat.

"Freaking idiot…" Herman mumbled.

Green light. Red light. Green light. Red light. Eventually, Herman found himself at the front of an intersection. The car's blinker ticked on and off. A procession of cars came and went through the intersection as Herman waited.

Green light. Herman put his foot on the gas and crept out slowly.

HONK HOONNKK

Herman's head jerked to the right. Like a bull charging through the streets of Pamplona, an eighteen-wheeler barreled through the street, trying to catch the light. Its massive headlights flashed like sirens among the blaring horn filling the buzzing airwaves of Citytown. A large, yellow logo indicating radioactivity was painted on the side of its massive tank.

HONK HOOONNNNKKK

Metal scraped and rubber burned as Herman slammed on the breaks. He was already too far into the intersection. For a split second, he thought of throwing the car in reverse and stomping on the gas, but the thought was all he had time for. The truck's horn continued to rage, and Herman's car stopped dead center of the intersection.

His head jerked again toward the truck. Its tires squealed, sending plumes of smoke onto the street, but it didn't slow. Reflexively, Herman threw his hand up to protect himself.

BLAM!

The truck smashed into Herman's car like hammer into a tin can. The car spun out of the way as broken glass showered him. His body reeled and his head slammed against the window as the car flipped onto its side. As the car scraped to a horrible stop, Herman Fitzgerald lost consciousness.

Meanwhile, the contents of the truck's load—a toxic, green sludge—began seeping toward Herman's car.

2

Herman felt himself drift in and out of consciousness. The first thing he knew was there was a bright light over him, and the second thing he knew was that he was on his back. Voices chattered all around him, severe and hurried.

"Hazardous waste?" A frantic voice said. "Why is a truck driver with hazardous waste trying so hard just to catch a light?"

"The paramedics said he had dozens of lacerations, but I don't see anything," another voice said.

"Oh my, his hand!" a feminine voice whispered in disgust and awe. "I've never seen one that bad before."

"Hopefully he's left-handed," the first voice replied. "If not, he's going to be."

I don't think I am, Herman thought as everything went black.

*

His eyes felt magnetized shut. His whole body ached. He didn't dare move any of his limbs, and even if he wanted to, he didn't have the strength. But he started with his eyelids. With great effort, Herman pushed his heavy eyelids open, trying to decipher where he was.

"Herman?" A female voice sounded foggy and faint.

Herman? He thought. *That's me. That's my name.*

"Herman, can you hear me?" the voice came again.

There was a hand on his arm—he could feel it. Everything was blurry at first and every sound came as if Herman's head were under water. There was a shallow beeping, along with the muted shuffle of footsteps from a nearby hallway. As Herman blinked a few more times, things came into focus: harsh florescent lights above him, stuck amid a grid of ceiling tiles. A television set bolted into the far wall, which only had to be ten feet away.

Memories started flooding back. He didn't know how recent. The car crash. The truck. That's when he had blacked out. Herman coughed, and that's when he felt the plastic mask over his mouth, steadily feeding him oxygen. Blinking became easier, then he was able to force his head to look to the side.

To his left, a window with opened blinds looked onto Citytown. The faint sound of car horns and shouts could be heard from the traffic and bustle outside. An empty chair sat under that window, along with a potted plant that was beginning to yellow. By Herman's left shoulder, an apparatus on wheels hooked a small plastic tube into his arm that beeped rhythmically.

He blinked hard and turned his head. To his right, a woman with crystal blue eyes and thick blonde hair had her hand on his arm. As he blinked more, the stifling worry riddled across her face became clearer, from her crow's feet to the dimples on her cheeks. When she smiled, her eyes squinted into small, sideways crescents.

"Aunt Josie?" Herman uttered. Then he coughed horribly.

"Herman!" Aunt Josie breathed as she put her other hand on his cheek. "I dropped everything came as quickly as I can.

You're at Citytown General Hospital. You were in a terrible accident with an eighteen-wheeler yesterday and the first responders were amazed you came out alive."

Herman exhaled painfully, followed by another hacking cough. "Was that today...?"

Aunt Josie shook her head. "No. You've been under for twenty-four hours. The surgeons worked on you as quickly as possible."

"Surgeons?" Herman said as he tried to scratch his head. "What did they—*huh!*"

That's when he noticed it. His right hand. Gone. In its place, a thick, blunt metal hook protruded from the bandages that encased his lower forearm. He stared at it, his eyes glazed over, his brain still processing it, not believing what he was seeing.

My hand! Herman thought. *Where's my hand?!*

"Fitzgerald family?"

A stout, bespectacled man marched into the room wearing a cozy grin and green scrubs. Under his arm, a clipboard, and in his hand, a jar filled with murky yellow liquid and something Herman couldn't decipher. As he crossed through the door, he caught a glimpse of Aunt Josie.

"Why... hello," he crooned as he gazed upon her. "I'm Doctor Stephenson, the surgeon that operated on your poor nephew. I assure you that we're doing all that we can, miss. He's going to be fine."

Aunt Josie grinned politely. Herman narrowed his eyes. When the doctor saw this, he cleared his throat.

"It took us several hours," he said. "But we managed to attach that prosthetic appendage to the ends of his radius and ulna. It took us longer than expected because his bones are so *dense*—and that made it all the more remarkable because nearly every bone in his right hand was completely shattered. The good news is… you're not losing it!"

That's when he held up the jar. The strange shape inside the yellow liquid was immediately obvious. Aunt Josie yelped and Herman felt as though he might pass out again. The doctor went on as if he didn't notice.

"For whenever someone asks you if you can lend a hand," he chortled before his voice died down. "Adding that to your bill right here…" A few pen scratches on the clipboard, then he looked up. "Anyway, it looks as though Herman is healing up remarkably well. It would be a miracle, but if he continues to recover at this rate, he might even leave the hospital in three or four days. We'll keep a close eye on him, don't you worry."

He winked at Aunt Josie, then he walked off. Herman tried to let out something like a growl, but it turned into a hacking cough again. The gunk in his lungs made his breathing hurt. Aunt Josie squeezed his forearm.

"I'm so sorry, Herman," she said. "And all this—" she looked around the room "—I don't know how we're going to afford this. I don't have much saved up after sending you to school. Maybe Mister Beasley will be willing to cover some of this or—"

Herman reached out and put his one hand on hers just as her eyes were beginning to get misty and her voice was starting to crack. His breath felt warm against the plastic mask.

"Hey," he said. "Look. I'm here. I'm okay. Things are going to be fine. You always say that things come together for good people. Well, you're one of the best people I know. So something will turn up, right?"

A single tear rolled down Aunt Josie's cheek. She smeared it away with one of her fingers and forced herself to smile.

"I'm just glad you're okay," she sniffed.

*

The next forty-eight hours were filled with mystified nurses whispering to each other outside Herman's recovery room. After visiting hours expired and Aunt Josie left, Herman fell asleep again, waking up just a few hours later. His head wasn't swimming like it was hours before. In fact, he couldn't recall feeling so clear. He popped up in bed energetically without thinking much of it, but the nearby nurse greeted this with a scowl and some stern orders to relax.

After a shorter nap, the nurse wasn't around. Herman watched with wide eyes as his skin pushed out the needle that was stuck into his left arm. And a quick power nap after that, he found it in himself to swing his legs off his bed and walk around his recovery room. It felt good to stand up and move around. He managed to hop back in bed and hide the plastic tube under his arm so the nurse didn't flip her lid when she came back.

From that point on, Herman pretended to sleep, but couldn't. All sleepiness had fled from him, night and day, regardless of what he did or didn't eat. In the middle of the night, Herman finally couldn't resist a serious hankering for potato chips. Silently, he got up and began stalking the halls for a vending machine, not wanting to bother anyone. However, his designated nurse caught him in the act. Her shriek nearly woke up the entire hall.

Herman was probably fine to leave after just a day, but the doctors wanted to keep him longer so they could charge more for their services. Or maybe they were concerned for his health.

What took a lot of getting used to was his missing right hand. Herman was, as a matter of fact, right-handed. After several startling gonks on the head, Herman learned to scratch his head with his left hand. Doing simple things like drinking a cup of water or opening the previously-mentioned bag of potato chips became more of a chore as he learned to use his teeth as a tool for grabbing and pulling.

On his second and final night at the hospital, he simply laid awake and stared at the ceiling, occasionally glancing at the hook protruding from his right arm. A fully-functional hand used to be there. A hand that could grab, flick, snap, and grip among other things. How were other simple tasks going to change when he only had one hand? Why did this have to happen?

He didn't sleep at all. The next morning, Aunt Josie collected him from the hospital with a fresh pair of clothes. Not only that, she had even gone out and purchased him a black leather jacket and a bus pass as a couple of get-well presents. Herman wanted to scold her for buying such thoughtful gifts at a time when they had hospital bills to worry about, but he thought better of it.

It was the middle of the afternoon when Aunt Josie dropped off Herman at his apartment complex in the middle of town.

"They have all of the bus schedules with the app, so you'll know how to get around," she said as she straightened the new jacket on Herman's shoulders. "After I save up for a while, I could help you buy a new car. I could also get one of those special handles for the steering wheel."

"One step at a time," Herman said, holding up his bus pass with his left hand. "This will be great for now."

Aunt Josie pressed her lips together. "Okay." Then she paused for a second, staring deeply into Herman's eyes. Her chin tightened. Then she threw her arms around his neck.

Herman staggered a little as her weight was suddenly thrown on him, but he promptly pulled her in and held her close. As they embraced, Aunt Josie sniffled.

"Promise me you'll be safe, okay?" she whispered. "Stay out of trouble. I don't need you joining your mom anytime soon."

Herman didn't hesitate. "I promise, Aunt Josie."

Aunt Josie let go, pulling tightly on Herman's new leather jacket one more time, making sure it was snug. She stepped backward and forced another smile. Her eyes glistened.

"Okay!" she said. "I'm heading back to Gladview but call me if you need *anything!* You've been through a lot, so take it easy as much as you can."

Herman smiled. "I will. Love you."

"I love you, too! Mwah!" she blew a kiss.

"Mwah."

With that, Aunt Josie retreated to her car and pulled out of the parking lot. She waved as she drove by, and Herman waved back. As her car turned the corner and vanished, the smile on Herman's face slowly fell. A sigh escaped Herman's lips as he surveyed the apartment building that he temporarily called home —a large square edifice of cracked, fading red brick. Then he looked at his hook. He rubbed the smudges off it with his thumb before he dragged his feet toward the building.

Herman wasn't in any hurry as he ascended the metal staircase to the top floor. At the top, the number 329 hung above a door—the number 3 dangled on a single rusty screw. He put his hand in his pocket to pull out his keys, then realized that he didn't have a hand on that side. Clenching his teeth, he reached his left hand around to his right pocket and pulled out his apartment key. After unlocking it, he pushed open the door.

"*Hermannnn!*"

Sitting on the couch, a crusty white guy with long, blonde dreadlocks sat in a fading tie-die shirt. In his fist, he clutched the string to with a single "Get Well Soon" balloon. His red-streaked eyes accompanied yellow teeth that stretched in a wide smile as

Herman entered. He leapt off the couch, crossed the room, and threw his arms around Herman. The smell of smoke was thick on his clothes.

"Thanks, Bridger," Herman didn't smile as he sheepishly patted his back. "The balloon is really nice. Are Zach and Adam home?"

"Nah, man," Bridger said as he brushed the hair out of his eyes. "I bet Adam is hungover at someone's house. And I dunno what Zach is doing. Prob'ly shopping for fancy Italian shoes or sweater vests."

"Sounds on brand for him."

Light spilled in from the one window in the room, illuminating the dust particles that shivered in the air. Aside from the overused couch, the only piece of furniture in the room was an impressive flatscreen TV on a rosewood table, courtesy of Zach's parents. A hallway led to their four private rooms on the other end of a modest kitchen populated with piles of dirty dishes and crumb-laden counters.

"*Whhooaa!*" Bridger's eyes suddenly got wide as he saw Herman's hook hand. "You're totally a cripple now!"

Herman deflated and said, "Thanks."

"Do you get phantom itches or whatever?"

"Phantom what?"

"Phantom itches!" Bridger piped. "You know, like, you feel your hand get all itchy but you can't scratch it 'cuz your brain still thinks you have a hand there! I read about it online. That blows, man."

Herman lifted his hook hand and twisted it, rubbing it with his thumb to slick away the smudges again. He pressed his lips together. *Cripple.* This is how things were going to be from now on.

I guess all I need is a peg leg and I can switch my career to piracy, Herman thought dryly.

"By the way," Bridger began as he slowly poked his finger in Herman's chest. "Sorry to be that guy, bro, but rent was due, like, two weeks ago."

"I know."

"Gotta have the moolah soon, my friend."

"I'm working on it. It's hard to find a job."

"Well, I hope you get something pronto," Bridger shrugged. "'Cause you know my uncle owns this place, and he'll kick you out. I don't want that to happen, but he's getting restless."

"I'm telling you, I'm working on it."

At that moment, the door opened. A man walked through with broad shoulders and perfectly parted black hair. He was dressed completely in the clothes of a trust fund kid on probation—designer sunglasses, a designer polo, designer khaki shorts, and designer loafers. A couple of department store bags dangled from his hands.

"Zaaach, *'eeeyyyyy,*" Bridger said with his usual lazy smile.

Zach only acknowledged Bridger with a nod. Then he saw Herman. "Hey. Where've you been?"

"Hospital," Herman said. "Got in a car accident."

That's when Zach noticed the hook hand, which Bridger had started tying the "Get Well Soon" balloon around. His eyes got wide and his mouth opened and closed. It was almost like his mind was looking up what to do when an acquaintance has gone through trauma.

"Whoa," Zach said as his head cocked back. There was a long pause as he took off his sunglasses. "That's... wow. How do you feel?"

Quickly, Herman took another mental inventory. It was probably normal for people fresh from the hospital to spend a lot of time at home doing some additional recovery. They probably needed a lot of rest and someone looking after them.

But honestly, Herman's head was clear and his body felt relaxed and strong, despite the fact that he hadn't slept in two days. No soreness. Not an ounce of fatigue. Not even a headache or a grumbling stomach. Herman's eyebrows furrowed when he realized this.

"Yeah," he said. "I feel pretty good, actually."

Then a wave crashed over him—something like he had never felt before. His eyes went blurry. His head swam. His knees shook and started to lose his balance. But as quickly as the feelings came, they disappeared. He snapped back to total clarity and stability. And with it, a spike of something—like his body just gave itself a triple shot of espresso. He had to get moving. He had to burn off some energy.

Herman swallowed. His eyes darted to either of his roommates. Both of their faces were blank.

They didn't notice a thing, Herman thought. *Was that all in my head?*

Herman blinked and swallowed again. After an uncomfortable pause, he found himself blurting out, "I think I'm going to go on a run."

And just like that, he retreated to his room at the end of the hall, leaving Bridger and Zach exchanging very puzzled glances. He slammed the door behind him and yanked the balloon off his wrist.

The walls of his room were plastered with posters of bands and movies and the fitted sheet was coming off his mattress at one corner. The empty pizza boxes under the bed gave the room a stale greasy odor, and you could see more dirty laundry than carpet. Slowly and clumsily, he single-handedly peeled off his clothes to change into a loose t-shirt and shorts. He did a double-take in the mirror as he did.

"Whoa," he said out loud.

Abs. Six of them. Chiseled and refined like he had done a thousand sit-ups a day. He ogled at them stupidly before poking each one with his hook. Firm and hard. His lower lip tightened before he slipped into another shirt.

Not strange, he thought to himself. *Not strange at all.*

After struggling with tying his shoes for several minutes, he angrily yanked off his socks and decided to go barefoot.

Out his room. Passed a meditating Bridger in the middle of the front room floor, who had surrounded himself with burning incense. Out the front door and into the smoggy Citytown air. Down the rusty stairs toward the apartment fitness center.

As Herman's bare feet flew down the cold stairs and touched the cement on ground level, another person suddenly bumped into him from around a corner.

"*Oof!* Sorry!" Herman said. His face went pink.

It was a girl. Red hair blasted from her head in wavy strands and her face was artfully splashed with a fistful of freckles. Herman would have found her attractive if her pink lips and green eyes weren't compressed into a scowl. She ignored Herman's humble apology and beelined to a nearby door, slamming it behind her. Herman inhaled loudly through clenched teeth and pushed the squeaky metal door to the fitness center.

Luckily, there was no one else at the fitness center because two would have made it crowded. Three treadmills (two of which were functional) were tucked against a wall next to a single rack of dumbbells that rested under a window the size of a trash can lid. Wallpaper peeled from the walls in some places, likely due to the prolonged exposure of severe body odor. Herman hopped onto the nearest treadmill, punched a few buttons, and the belt started to roll.

What's going on? he thought to himself. *I shouldn't feel as good as I do now, and I definitely shouldn't have a six pack. I should have died two days ago! Why do I feel so good?*

The treadmill belt whizzed as his bare feet clapped against it.

What was that truck carrying? It was radioactive or something, wasn't it?

The soft whirring of the treadmill belt sounded as his mind continued to buzz.

And now my hand… how is this going to change things?

At this point, Herman still hadn't broken a sweat. He looked down at the treadmill control panel and was met with yet another surprise. According to the treadmill, he had just run six miles. His eyes popped and his eyebrows nearly touched his hairline.

Six!? He thought. *No way. This thing is broken.*

He gave the LED display a whack. Nothing. So he gave it another whack. Then the numbers on the screen started to flash and spin. After a couple of seconds, they landed back onto the previous number: six miles.

Herman smacked his hand to his forehead, only it was his hook.

"*Ow!*"

He rubbed his throbbing forehead as he stared at the number six, which blinked back at him unchangingly. With that, he turned off the treadmill and the belt gradually crawled to a stop. With his hand on his hips, he kept staring at the display, which now read six-point-one.

I could barely run one mile back in high school! He thought. *What in the world is going on?*

Bzzzzz!

It was at that moment that his phone went off. It took a second for Herman to gather himself before he thrust his hand into his pocket. As he pulled out his phone, he noticed the call was coming from a private number. Herman creased his eyebrows and tapped the green button to answer.

He held it to his ear and said, "Hello?"

"Herman Fitzgerald?" The voice on the other end was a man's.

"Speaking," Herman said guardedly.

"Herman, it's come to my attention that you've been in a terrible accident recently," the voice was rushed, yet professional. "My name is Doctor Sidney Saskatoon. I'm a chemist in the Citytown area. I was referred to you by some friends at the Citytown General Hospital. They alerted me of your strangely fast recovery and I'd love to ask you some questions. When is the soonest you could come by my office?"

Herman blinked, processing everything the unfortunately-named doctor had just told him. He knew about his condition? He might have an explanation?

"Wait," Herman said as he put his hook on his hip. "You have some questions for me? Well, I've got some questions, too."

"Don't we all?" Doctor Saskatoon said. "You've been through a great deal lately and I believe some research on my part could provide some sort of explanation for your peculiar healing conditions. Is that something you would be interested in?"

Herman's eyes darted from his hook, to his feet, to the number on the treadmill display. The absurdity of the situation was laughable, but at the same time, answers were in very short supply.

He scoffed and said, "Absolutely."

The smile on the other end was almost audible. "Excellent! I'll send a location to your phone immediately. I'll be at my office for the remainder of the evening, so come over whenever you can. I'll see you soon, Mister Fitzgerald!"

3

Herman went back up to his room and painstakingly changed back into normal street clothes, but didn't bother to shower. During his run, he hadn't broken a sweat. He was back out the door with some shorts, his jacket, and some slip-on sneakers.

The bus pass in his pocket wasn't going to see any action this afternoon. He pulled out his phone and checked the coordinate that Dr. Saskatoon had given him. The location was just over five miles away.

Well, Herman thought. *I just ran six miles and my heart rate barely picked up. I might as well keep running.*

Out the door, down the stairs, into the afternoon sun. And like that, he was off.

The run through Citytown wasn't as intimidating in the afternoon as it might have been at night. Frankly, Herman had never brought himself to venture out after dark based on the recommendations of locals. But during the day, downtown Citytown was a normal hub of human activity characterized smelly food carts, trendy clothing stores, stuffy hair salons, and loud street performers.

Herman weaved through dozens of people that meandered up and down the street and got the occasional stare at his prosthetic hook. Citytown Central Park passed him on his left as he jogged by—a nighttime hive of staggering drunks, frisky make-outs, and shady exchanges of cash. But during the day, people were throwing frisbees to their dogs and feeding the pigeons amongst the trees and fenced bridges.

Crazy how this whole place changes at night, he thought wryly. *I wonder if any of those homicides happened there?*

After several minutes, Herman had bounded beyond the downtown area and found himself in a crusty, tired industrial district of Citytown. Most of the buildings were warehouses that were obviously full of blue-collar workers decades ago. But now, their walls were coated with rust behind chain-link fences wrapped around lakes of cracked asphalt and cement.

Herman checked his phone as he ran. A beeping point on his display indicated he was right by Dr. Saskatoon's coordinates. As he finally slowed down to a stroll in front of a three-story office building. The tan stucco was obviously decades old, and all the windows had blinds pulled over them. As Herman got closer, he noticed the only sign anywhere was modestly sandblasted onto the glass door entrance.

"*Citytown Applied Technologies,*" he read out loud.

He pocketed his phone and curiously pulled open the door.

A lazily rotating ceiling fan hung just a few feet overhead, which went perfectly with the tan vinyl flooring beneath Herman's sneakers. Dust gathered in the room's corners and the only furniture was a couple of folding chairs and a scratched-up desk that was likely purchased from a thrift store. It's as if the colors of tan and brown had a game of rock-paper-scissors to see who would design the room.

However, Herman's heart jumped when he saw the secretary at the desk. She should have been a runway or in front of a camera instead of behind a desk. Her doll-like face was perched atop a curvy, slender figure, complimented by lush, silky black hair falling down her back. Herman cleared his throat and ran his fingers through his hair before he approached her.

"Hi," He said. "Is this Dr. Saskatoon's office?"

She looked up at him and smiled. He smiled back.

"Yeth, it ith!" She said.

Herman's chest twisted as he tried desperately not to look surprised. The lisp was one thing, but her voice was high and squeaky—like a mouse got in a fight with a broken rubber duck and lost. The secretary's pleasant smile didn't falter in the slightest.

"Ith it Herman Fithgerald?" she followed up.

Herman gathered himself and said, "Y-yes it is."

"I'm Katy!" She said as she thrust out her hand.

"Thanks," he replied. "Nice to meet you, Katy."

She giggled and her hand was as flimsy as a dead fish when Herman shook it. She gasped.

"Oh, you've got thuch a thtrong grip!" She giggled. "One thecond pleathe!"

She thtood up from the dethk and hobbled over to the nearest door as quickly as her pencil skirt could take her. She gave three brittle taps.

"Doctor Thathkatoon!" She said. "Mithter Herman Fithgerald ith here to thee you!"

"Wonderful! Send him in," Dr. Saskatoon's familiar voice came from the other side.

And on that note, Katy the secretary opened the door and motioned Herman inside. Cautiously, curiously, Herman entered. Not much to his surprise, Dr. Saskatoon's office wasn't much different from the lobby. The tan vinyl extended into his office, which was furnished by a plastic folding desk and metal chairs. The only major difference was that Dr. Saskatoon's desk was completely littered with loose papers and there were about a dozen metal filing cabinets stacked throughout the room.

Clearly a low budget operation, Herman thought.

"Herman, my friend!" He said as he stood from his chair. "Come in, come in!"

What Herman saw was a live-action version of a cartoon mad scientist. His white hair sprouted in every direction and massive goggles adorned his forehead, rebounding the florescent light embedded in the ceiling. He even had a white lab coat girt about him with the word "Sid" embroidered on it. He quickly threw off his red rubber gloves so he could shake Herman's one hand with both of his own.

"It's a pleasure to meet you, my young friend!" He said with a wild toothy smile.

"Thanks," Herman said stiffly.

Dr. Saskatoon gasped. "And look at this! Remarkable!"

He grabbed for Herman's hook without even asking for it. He brought it up to his eyes to examine it as if it were a piece of fine china or a rare insect. Meanwhile, Herman stood back as far as he could without being rude. Dr. Saskatoon's eyes, wide and excited, traced every molecule of the hook hand.

"They surgically fashioned a blunt steel hook directly to your ulna and radius?" He said reverently.

"Yeah, that's what the surgeon said," Herman said. "They also said my bones are crazy dense. The densest they've ever seen. They almost couldn't complete the surgery."

"Oh, do tell, do tell!" Dr. Saskatoon immediately retreated to his desk. "Please, sit down!"

Herman slipped deliberately into the folding metal chair across from Dr. Saskatoon's desk. He discretely scanned the room, still getting his bearings. The doctor's numerous college degrees hung from the wall, along with a map of Citytown and framed pictures of Albert Einstein, Alexander Fleming, and Stan Lee. Behind him, Herman noticed a framed picture behind him of a young man with a lab coat and a big smile. He was standing outside of a building called The Genesis Corporation.

Herman turned back around to face him.

"Well," Herman began. "I got into a car accident a few days ago, and that's when it all started. I don't really sleep, but I'm never tired. I even ran twelve miles today and I barely broke a sweat. And I healed really fast from my accident. Like, I should have died, but here I am… without a hand, I guess."

"It is fascinating, isn't it?" Dr. Saskatoon said. "The circumstances are absolutely extraordinary! Do you remember anything strange regarding the accident? Anything at all?"

"Well, yeah," Herman replied slowly while holding his hook. "I was bowled over by an eighteen-wheeler. And I think it was carrying some weird chemical. I remember seeing the radioactive logo on its side before it hit me."

"*Good heavens, Mister Fitzgerald!*" Dr. Saskatoon cried, his face beaming. "If hazardous waste got into your vehicle, it surely must have killed you instead have strengthen you!"

"But how?" Herman couldn't help but ask. "What kind of hazardous waste *helps* people?"

"I simply *must* know," Dr. Saskatoon said. "Herman, if you don't mind, I'd like to take a small sample of your blood. If you allow me to do so, I should be able to pick apart the different compounds running through your blood stream and pinpoint what gave you these side effects. May I? It needn't be a large sample."

Herman gulped.

Let's think about this for a second, Herman Fitzgerald, he thought to himself. *A crazy doctor that you've never met just happens to invite you to his office and says he can figure out why you've got superhuman conditions that you've only had for a couple of days. He seems very eager. He also seems a few bricks short of a payload. Does this seem like a stupid idea? Probably. I definitely should have told Aunt Josie about this.*

The discomfort on Herman's face must have been apparent, because immediately Dr. Saskatoon's eyes softened. He leaned forward calmly on his desk, laced his hands together, and spoke in an even tone.

"Herman, I understand your trepidation," he said. "These circumstances are perplexing, and I know that I come across as a bit eccentric, but I assure you that I am a fully-licensed professional with a vested interest in your wellbeing. I won't force you to do anything. If you'd prefer to walk out the door right now, I won't stop you."

With that, the knot in Herman's chest loosened a little and he pursed his lips. He looked down, tapping his fingers on his knee.

Maybe it's not a big deal, he thought. *Aunt Josie donates plasma twice a week and that's pretty similar. Those samples are taken by strangers, too.*

Herman stuck out his arm slowly.

Dr. Saskatoon grinned widely. He procured a small needle from a drawer, ripped off the protective plastic, swept around his desk toward Herman, and knelt down beside him. He pressed the needle into Herman's skin. Herman frowned as he felt the pinprick try to dig into his arm, but after a few painful moments, the needle broke. The doctor blinked at it curiously, then smiled.

"Ah!" he said. "Your epidermis is remarkably firm. I'll have to use a needle reinforced with a metal compound of my own creation to penetrate the surface and withdraw an adequate sample."

Herman gulped again but didn't say anything. From a drawer, Dr. Saskatoon pulled out a slightly larger needle with a wider canal. He came forward, pressed it against Herman's skin, and after a long, uncomfortable pinch, he broke the surface.

The blood didn't look any different as Dr. Saskatoon extracted it—just as red and runny as ever. It filled a tiny reservoir no bigger than Herman's pinky finger.

When the doctor removed the needle from Herman's arm, a large drop of blood began ballooning where the prick was. Herman watched it as it grew... then stopped growing... then shrunk as the hole closed and the blood was sucked back into his arm. His jaw dangled. No need for a bandage of any kind. Healed in seconds, like it never happened.

Satisfied, Doctor Saskatoon stood up and gingerly placed the syringe back in the drawer. Then he withdrew a red lollipop from one of his other pockets. He pinched the stick between two fingers and held it out to Herman.

"Here you go," Dr. Saskatoon said brightly.

"Uh, thanks," Herman said as he took it. "So, sorry for asking, but what kind of doctor are you again? I'm not employed so I don't have any insurance. I hope that's not a problem, but you really didn't discuss—"

"*Ha!* How silly of me!" Dr. Saskatoon plopped himself back into his chair. "Please forgive me. Doctor Sidney Saskatoon, independent chemist and philanthropist, at your service! You can call me Sid. I have worked for several years as a chemist concocting compounds for various corporations around the country. Recently, I've began my own enterprise. You can only handle the fast-paced corporate life for so long."

"I see," Herman said politely.

"But to be frank, I don't consider myself that interesting. Just an old codger living his dream of working independently as a chemist. Nothing more."

33

Herman stored the lollipop in his pocket. At this point, Sid started drumming his fingers together and swinging back and forth in his office chair. "Herman, how do you plan on managing these new circumstances? You are very unusual, to say the least."

Herman shrugged. "I hadn't thought about it, to be honest."

"Really? Hardly at all?"

"No."

"But—with your extraordinary abilities, you could do just about anything!"

Herman couldn't help but scoff. "Not get a basic entry-level job. By the way, you don't know anyone looking for a public relations guy, are you?"

Sid shook his head. "I cannot say that I do, sorry."

"It was worth a shot."

"But I myself am looking for some sort of help, in a sense, and you might be the perfect fit."

Herman chuckled. "My rent was due two weeks ago. At this point, I'm all ears."

Sid leaned forward and looked intently into Herman's eyes. His voice died down to a whisper and his eyes darted to and from the door before he spoke. "Citytown is a struggling metropolis ridden with crime. And for some reason, it has gotten much worse recently. Very recently. I wish there were something I could do to help, but I'm just a chemist and inventor. What I have in substantial intellect, I lack in physical ability.

"You, however," he continued. "Have boundless energy, no need for sleep, and you heal at an uncanny rate. You are, for all intents and purposes, a *superhuman.* So, if you had the tools to... 'clean up the streets,' so to speak... would you do it?"

Herman's eyes narrowed. "Meaning... like... paid community service?"

"In a way," Sid twiddled his thumbs and his eyes scanned the door again. "More specifically"—he took a deep, excited breath —"fight the hive of villainy and crime that plagues Citytown."

Herman didn't blink, but his eyes stayed locked on Sid, probing and confused.

Fight the hive of villainy and crime? He thought. *I think I know what he means… but he can't be serious.*

"Wait," Herman forced himself to say. "Are you asking me if I want to be some kind of superhero? Or something?"

Sid didn't reply with words—just a big, bright smile and a sheepish shrug.

Herman stared at those crazy, excited, expectant eyes, his own mouth agape. His eyes reeled around in their sockets, analyzing the corners of the room, expecting to find some sort of hidden camera. Maybe someone would jump out of the door behind him and tell him he was on TV. But no. Just awkward, irrational silence courtesy of the local scientist.

Finally, Herman frowned.

"You're joking," he said seriously.

"Herman, you haven't quite thought this through," Sid shook his head at Herman's lackluster response. "You're something far more than human now! You have powers that the average person will never attain—couldn't possibly attain! And you want to just walk out of this office as if life goes on as usual?"

"Actually, yeah. That's exactly what I want."

Sid's face radiated incredulity as Herman's mind reeled. Just start fighting crime on a whim? This isn't a comic book! Whether or not the doctor was joking at this point was irrelevant. The next course of action was obvious. Herman stood from his chair.

"Look, I don't know what you're playing at," Herman said. "But this is *not* funny and I'm not sticking around this stupid office if all you're going to do is pursue this."

35

In two quick, decisive steps, Herman was upon the door. His hand reached out. His fingers wrapped around the doorknob and he was just about to twist it when Sid piped up:

"How does five hundred dollars a night sound?"

Herman froze. His eyebrows scrunched and his shoulders were tense, but he cautiously turned himself about to face Sid one more time. Sid was still behind his desk, leaning back in his office chair, his hands in his lap and sporting the smuggest grin.

Sid's eyes flashed. "Is that reasonable?"

Herman didn't say anything. His eyes stayed narrow.

"I won't stop there as well," Sid said, twisting back and forth in the chair. "I'm sure you have some substantial hospital bills as well. I'll make an agreement with you: fight crime for a minimum of fourteen days and I'll pay those off. Just like *that*." He snapped his fingers. "In addition to the agreed-upon five hundred dollars a night."

Herman loosened his grip on the doorknob and cautiously made his way back toward Sid's desk. Sid's eyes flashed brighter and brighter with each step. Herman's eyes were still as probing and narrow as ever.

"So you're crazy, *and* a liar," he said. "One, there's no way you could afford that. Look at all this furniture—it's like you got everything at the Salvation Army. And even if I wanted to fight crime, what would I use? This?" He waved his hook in the air.

Sid's grin didn't fade. He reached in his pocket, revealed a remote with a big red button, and pressed it.

Boop! Pssssshhhhh!

With a quick rumble and the grind of pulley wheels, the entire wall behind Sid began retracting into the ceiling. Sid pushed himself up from his seat, tossed the remote in the air like a baseball, then caught it and slipped it back in his pocket, all the while whistling amiably as he strolled through the retracting wall.

Meanwhile, the filing cabinets and chairs jittered with the rumbling, retracting wall.

Herman didn't move at first. He was too surprised that the wall wasn't actually a wall. That didn't mean he suddenly liked this situation, though. He frowned. Quickly and guardedly, he followed behind Sid. The retracting wall led to a smaller opening on his left, so the backroom wasn't immediately visible.

But when Herman turned the corner, his jaw fell and his eyes glossed over. The backroom was *nothing* like the rest of the office building. The floor and walls were all coated with a midnight blue metal. In the far corner, a control station with multiple computer screens and a comfy office chair waited with a headset and several opened bags of potato chips. Numerous chalkboards filled with formulas and diagrams were strewn throughout the room, gliding on wheels. A lengthy workbench was completely covered in beakers, bottles, and glasses containing various fluids. In the middle of the room, a single light dangled above a large table big enough for a dozen people.

This wasn't just a workspace. It was a command center.

"Not just a boring office, eh?" Sid chortled to himself.

Herman's response was disconnected but sincere. "No."

"Here," Sid said.

He was standing at a table with his back turned to Herman, working on something. Herman dragged his feet, taking in the surroundings that were only supposed to exist in science fiction novels and action movies.

"I've put some thought into your specific conditions and arrived at a solution," Sid said. "You should be able to fight with this. I'm not much of a prosthetist, but I believe this should do quite nicely."

When Sid turned around, he held a silver apparatus about the size of a football. Herman's palm was clammy as he leaned his face in curiously. It was essentially a giant, metal sledgehammer. The head was huge, but the handle was short.

"I was able to take the measurements of your hook from the hospital and design it to fit a reinforced aluminum alloy," Sid said. "This hammer is impressively light but can deflect bullets. Try it."

He held it out to Herman. All Herman could do was stare at it. He looked at his hook hand, then the hammer, then the hook hand again, then back to the hammer. His mouth felt dry. Inch by inch, he reached his hook toward the hammer until it slipped into a groove carved into the metal handle. As the hook hand rested in the groove, he cocked his forearm forward.

Click.

Just like that, the hammer became a part of him. He held it up to his face and gazed at his warped reflection in the dim metal. It fit perfectly. It felt almost as if all he had done was ball his fist, but it was much bigger.

Holy crap, was all Herman could think.

He gave it a little swing. It was weighted just enough—not too heavy, but heavy enough to pack a wallop. Sid smiled.

"It's yours if you want it," Sid said. "I understand what I've asked you to do is very abrupt. But this city needs someone like you, and you can do things that no one else can. I'll help you every step of the way. Take it. And if you do, take this as well."

Sid held out an oddly-shaped black device no larger than a quarter. A tiny red light danced on its surface.

"It's a communication device that fits in your ear," he said. "It can pick up your voice, too. This is how I'll be your eyes and ears, minding the city's radio frequencies for danger. If you ever want to reach me, put it in your ear and say my name. I'll be contacted immediately."

Herman took it and placed it in his ear. It molded as if it were made just for him.

"Well?" Sid said expectantly.

Herman gazed down at the hammer attached to his forearm and thought of the radio in his ear. He was just a normal, boring guy a few days ago that was trying to find a job and pay the rent —nothing special. But now, he was something extraordinary. And what was he to do about it? Start fighting crime on the whim of an old lunatic he just met? The money is great, and the hospital bills are definitely an issue, but what about his promise to Aunt Josie?

"Promise me you'll be safe, okay?"

On that thought, he popped the radio out of his ear.

"I'm not doing this," Herman said, holding his hand out. "This is crazy. You're crazy. I know I have these powers or—whatever —but this just isn't who I am. This city has police. They can handle things themselves. I'm just one guy."

He kept his fist held out, but Sid just smiled paternally with his hands clasped behind his back.

"Keep it," he said. "The hammer, too. Go home, Herman. It'll be late soon. You can forget this meeting ever happened, but you're passing up an opportunity to help people in a way that will make a real difference. I thought that might be something you'd want. If not, so be it. If you change your mind, you know how to reach me."

Sid cocked his head toward a door against the far wall. Herman frowned, staring at Sid for a long moment. Then, without a word, he pocketed the earpiece, turned about and ran toward the door. He threw it open with his one hand, bursting into the sunset.

The door slammed shut behind him, and a battalion of locks and switches automatically bolted it shut. He picked up his feet and ran. The sun was dipping over the western horizon, throwing splashes of orange and purple into the sky. Meanwhile, his mind buzzed and echoed the words that Doctor Saskatoon spoke.

"You can do things for this town that no one else can."

Yeah, maybe! But that doesn't mean I should! I'm not crazy.

"You have powers the average person will never attain!"

Does that make me obligated to use them in the way you want? I didn't ask for this! This is the product of some freak accident and I'm not about to put my life on the line just because! It doesn't matter how much I need the money!

Police sirens wailed in the distance, reverberating off the skyscrapers as Herman closed in on the downtown area. Cars came and went, flashing him with yellow or red lights as they sped by. The food carts were gone. Shops were closing up. The people walking about were fewer than earlier, and nearly all of them stared as they witnessed a blonde-haired boy with a hammer hand whiz by.

As he ran, three police cars came barreling around a corner, sirens blasting. They dodged the various cars that pulled off to the side, their lights rebounding eyewatering shades of red and blue against the buildings. Herman didn't look at them.

Yeah. This city has police. I'm just going to try to move on with these conditions like a normal person—

WHAM!

At that moment, a large passerby reached out and clotheslined Herman. Herman's head jerked and he landed hard on his back as the wind knocked out of him. His eyes teared up and his hammer scraped against the cement as blood began to dribble from his nose.

The figure laughed and said, "You in a hurry, pal?"

Herman tried to scramble to his feet, but two more figures hurriedly burst out from an alleyway and dragged him back into the darkness. The whole thing happened in only a few seconds. The two figures threw Herman against a brick wall and quickly picked up a couple of crowbars that were laying around. The three figures towered over him, their faces hidden under their hoods.

"Drop the hammer," one said thickly. "Cell phone, credit cards, cash, jewelry. Now."

Herman ground his teeth together. He had remembered learning about fight-or-flight syndrome when a person was in danger. He assumed he'd be the kind of person to fly if ever in one of those situations. But tonight, Herman's impulse to run wasn't there. All he felt was rage—rage that a few strangers would have the audacity to attack him and rob him after the week he's had. His car got totaled. His body is weird. A crazy doctor just asked him to be a superhero. Now this?

Screw this, he thought.

He shot to his feet and wiped his bloody nose. The three men squared up, clenching their crowbars tighter.

"I said drop the hamm—!"

Whack!

The strike was quick. Herman's hammer found the first robber's gut. He doubled over, grabbing his stomach and dropping his crowbar to the cement with a *clang*. The other two took action. The first one lifted his crowbar and gave a swing at Herman. He ducked as felt the whoosh of the crowbar swing over him.

Crack!

Herman's hammer found its mark across the second robber's face. Just like that, he toppled to the ground, out cold. That's when the third robber's crowbar made contact with Herman's back.

Herman yelped before giving a blind swing at the third robber. He got nothing but air, but the second swing was successful. He managed to connect with the robber's crowbar, knocking it out of his hand and sending it flying deeper into the alleyway. This one didn't stick around to get cracked—his feet revved up and he darted onto the street, leaving his last friend to Herman's mercy.

The last mugger remained on his hands and knees, coughing and sputtering. With a grunt, he scooped up his crowbar and lunged at Herman with a mighty swing.

Clanggg!

Herman held up his hammer hand, reflexively blocking the blow. Using his momentum, he followed through with another swing at the robber's hand. Success. The robber's fingers crackled as he dropped his crowbar and cried mightily. As he cradled his broken hand, Herman put his foot to his chest and kicked him to the ground. The robber stumbled as he backpedaled before crumbling down beside a wall. He glared at Herman through gritted teeth, holding his broken hand, incredulous of what just happened.

Finally, Herman was breathing hard, his face hot and his head swimming. He pointed with this hammer and said, "You screwed with the wrong guy tonight, bucko! I've had it up to *here* this week! My car's been totaled, I lost my freaking hand, and now you bozos thought you could *rob me?* You're lucky you didn't end up like thug number two over here!" He pointed to his unconscious friend. "I'm out! You see me again, you better run, princess! *Peace!*"

Herman almost ran out of the alleyway, but decided to give the discarded crowbar an angry little kick before he pedaled off.

It clanged lifelessly on the cement. He made eye contact with the robber again, said "Yeah!" and peeled off.

As he burst out of the alleyway, headed toward his apartment complex, he felt the welt on his back where the crowbar hit. He twisted his shoulders as he ran, trying to soothe the pain. Incredibly, it seemed as though the farther he ran, the more it subsided. By the time he had gotten back to apartment 329 at the tired old brick building, he could hardly feel it at all.

He threw open the door, then quickly remembered the hammer attached to his forearm. He hastily hid it behind his back just in time. Zach was sitting on the couch, wearing board shorts and reading a book. He looked up curiously as Herman exploded into the room.

"Hey," he said with his eyebrows creased.

"Sup," Herman shot back a little too quickly.

Zach was visibly perplexed when Herman powerwalked down the hallway with his hook behind his back. He slammed his bedroom door shut and immediately unzipped his jacket. He threw it off his back, then realized it was still attached to him because the sleeve was too small for the hammer. With a frustrated sigh, Herman grabbed the hammer and yanked it off. It disconnected with a brawny *click*, then Herman tossed it onto his bed.

Herman stalked over to his mirror and stood at an angle to it, arching his head in order to see his back.

Nothing. Not even a bruise—like the crowbar never happened. His body had effectively healed itself from a crowbar strike in a matter of minutes. His nose wasn't bleeding anymore, either. Herman stared at his hook hand, then the hammer laying on his unmade bed. The scuffle began replaying in his mind.

A thug sucker punched him and threw him into an alley with two other thugs. Three on one—all of them with crowbars versus

Herman with a hammer. Somehow, he managed to make quick work of all of them. And what did he have to show for it? Nothing. He should have gotten his butt handed to him, but he didn't. He should have been beaten to a pulp, but he wasn't. There should have been a huge welt and maybe some bruising on his spine from the blow, but his back felt fine. Totally healed. No problem.

"You can do things that no one else can."

The earpiece in his pocket. That's when he remembered it.

Something is running through my veins that is making me like this, Herman thought. *Doctor Saskatoon can figure it out, and he's willing to pay to me to fight crime on the regular until he does. Is that dangerous? Sure. But I got ambushed tonight and I was just fine.*

Herman knew it was crazy to think it, but he thought it.

Maybe this isn't that big of a deal. Maybe I could give it a shot for a while. Those fourteen days to pay off the hospital bills, then that's it. That would be a huge weight off Aunt Josie.

His heart sank.

Aunt Josie, he thought. *She made me promise to stay safe. This is definitely, absolutely, positively not safe behavior. But what else are we going to do? There's no way she can afford the hospital bills, even if Mister Beasley helps out. Now here I am with this opportunity…*

He looked back at the hammer on his bed. His eyes locked with it for a moment, then walked over and picked it up again, staring at his reflection once again on its surface. The hook on his forearm found the lock inside the handle, and it clicked in, once again becoming a part of him.

He twisted it, eyeing it. He gave it a little swing, recollecting the sensation of its edge colliding with the robber's jaw.

With his feet frozen and his eyes baring into his warped reflection, Herman let out a mighty sigh.

Well, he thought. *I think this is my best shot. Aunt Josie doesn't have to know. Not now, at least.*

Finally, his hand dug into his pocket and fished out the earpiece. After putting it in snugly in his ear, he waited a moment.

"...Sid?" he said softly.

Nothing.

After another moment, he said a little louder, "Sid?"

"Herman?" Dr. Saskatoon's voice was clear inside his ear. "Herman Fitzgerald, is that you?"

"It is," Herman replied, still trying to remain quiet. "Look, I—" he sighed—"I've changed my mind. I'll try it for the fourteen days, this whole *crime fighting* whatever, but I can't guarantee how long it'll be for, okay? This whole thing is nuts, and so are you... but I'll give it a shot. For now. But you better work on my blood sample and figure out what's inside me! I want to know what's going on."

Dr. Saskatoon's smile was nearly audible. After a moment, he said, "Fair enough. Welcome to the force, Hammerfist."

4

"You gave me this hammer just so you could call me that, didn't you?" Herman questioned flatly.

The back wall in Dr. Saskatoon's office rumbled and grinded as it retracted into the ceiling. Herman stood shoulder to shoulder with the eccentric scientist, waiting for what else was in store.

"Isn't it *perfect?*" Sid said happily. "Your name is *Herman Fitz*gerald, you have a hammer hand, so you're called Hammer*fist*! You can't tell me that's not pretty neat!"

"It's not."

"You'll get used to it."

As they slipped into the secret lab, Herman said, "Wait, yesterday you said welcome to the *force.* Does that mean there are others like me?"

Sid smiled. "You're an observant one, Mr. Fitzgerald. The others had very similar experiences as you, leading to similar results. The day I met with you is the same day I met with most of them. Very peculiar indeed."

"They had similar experiences as me?" Herman echoed, dumbfounded. "Wait, were they all in car accidents too? With the same toxic sludge? That doesn't seem possible. How does that work?"

"My, so many questions! All will be answered in time, Mr. Fitzgerald. In the meanwhile, I'd like you to introduce yourself to them."

As they turned the corner, Herman noticed three other characters standing around the giant table. The one light above the table cast a dim orange glow, which threw sharp shadows down their faces. Sid strolled a couple of steps ahead of Herman as they made their way to the chair circle. As they approached, the unfamiliar faces caught sight of Herman and stared. Herman swallowed.

"Everyone, I'd like you to meet our latest member, Herman Fitzgerald!"

No one said anything. Herman pressed his lips together and gave an awkward wave with his hook. Sid cheerily marched to the table and drummed his hands on the end before lacing his hands together.

The characters in the circle were a hodgepodge of different features. One was an Asian boy about Herman's age with almond eyes, tan skin, and short black hair. A pair of headphones was slung around his neck and a retro boombox sat right beside him on the table. The second was a gorgeous woman about the age of Aunt Josie, but Aunt Josie wasn't a brunette and she never wore high-end workout clothes. The other was—

"Hey! I remember you!" Herman blurted.

It was the girl from his apartment building—the one with the wild red hair that he ran into as he was walking to the fitness center. Her shoulders rolled forward as she folded her arms. Her freckled scowl wasn't any different than it was yesterday, and she glared at Herman with indifferent emerald eyes.

"You two know each other?" Sid said brightly.

"No," Herman and the girl said in unison. The girl's tone was much darker.

"Well, if that's the case," Sid said. "Why don't we go around and get to know each other? We can say each other's name and something interesting about ourselves."

Herman blinked at Sid. *Seriously? This is just like syllabus week. At least there are only five of us.*

"Ideally, there should be six of us," Sid said as he straightened his goggles. "But Tyler said he wouldn't be available today. He's got other things he prefers to focus his attention on."

What could possibly be more important than this? Herman scrunched his nose.

"Anyway, Mr. Chan, why don't you get started?" Sid continued.

"Hey," The Asian kid said with the smile. "Frankie Chan. From Citytown, born and raised. I study music over at the Triple C."

"I graduated from the Triple C," Herman said timidly. "Public relations."

Frankie scoffed. "Man, that sucks. Their PR program blows."

"I doubt their music program is much better," the beautiful brunette woman squinted at Frankie in Herman's defense.

"Hey, my mom teaches there!" Frankie retorted. "It's not bad, and I get free tuition!"

"My name is Susan," the woman brushed the hair out of her eyes and spoke to Herman, ignoring Frankie. "Susan Terry. Interior designer and mom of two by day, and *this* by night, as of today."

"Did you ever have to pay for college, Susan?" Frankie sneered.

"No," Susan said sweetly. "Soccer scholarship."

Frankie's eyes flashed.

At this point, everyone turned to look at the redheaded girl, including Sid and especially Herman. She scanned her onlookers and her nose bristled as if she were going to snort like a warthog. Her folded arms stiffened.

"Cassie Copland," she said.

Her onlookers awaited more information, but she remained silent. After exchanging a few awkward glances, Sid finally said, "Cassandra, could you tell us something interesting about yourself?"

"There's nothing," she said.

The caliber of awkward in the room stiffly increased. However, Herman had a hard time tearing his eyes away from hers. They were so *green.* Like a grassy meadow got condensed into two little crystal orbs and placed into a pale, slender face. And did they seem even more green because of her bright red hair? Or would they be that green anyway?

"Okay, I have questions," Frankie raised his hand. "So we all got powers, like, recently, right? Can I ask how? I feel like I'm prying. Am I prying?"

"An excellent question!" Sid slapped his hand on the table. "And a fascinating coincidence, I might say. It appears as though all of you…" Sid paused for dramatic effect. "Acquired your conditions during a recent stay at the Citytown General Hospital!"

Herman looked around. "All of you were in the hospital recently, too?" Everyone nodded. "So wait, my powers have nothing to do with the car accident? What about the toxic waste?"

"You were in a car accident involving *toxic waste?*" Frankie cried.

"Good heavens, how are you still alive?" Susan said incredulously.

49

"It certainly is strange," Sid scratched his chin. "But these three and Tyler have exhibited identical conditions such as yourself—limitless stamina, insomnia, rapid healing properties— with no toxic waste or radioactive sludge to speak of. The only consistency is your recent stay at the Citytown General Hospital."

"Which means?" Susan said.

"It means someone in the hospital did something to us to give us these conditions," Cassie said impatiently, her arms still folded.

Sid pointed at her. "Precisely."

"So, wait," Herman said. "Are you positive the accident had nothing to do with it? That just doesn't make sense to me."

Sid shrugged. "I'm as baffled as you are, Mister Fitzgerald! It certainly would seem probable that the car accident and the toxic waste would be the primary factor in your conditions, but how does that explain these individuals?" He motioned to the rest of the group. "They didn't experience anything similar to you, yet here we are. At least—I assume none of you have had recent run-ins with mass quantities of toxic waste?"

Everyone confirmed Sid's assumption. Herman's eyebrows creased and he stared into space as the thoughts raced around his head. *My powers have nothing to do with my accident?*

"Do you think if we found whoever made us like this, they might have an antidote?" Frankie asked while making the motions of plunging an invisible syringe into his bottom.

"We need to find them first," Susan said firmly.

"Agreed," Sid pointed at Susan this time. "And I believe I may have an idea on where to start."

With that, Sid rummaged through a nearby drawer and extracted a copy of the local newspaper, *The Citytown Harold*. He slapped it onto the table. The orange light spilled onto the grey-and-black newsprint. A column on the right had a thick black headline circled in red crayon.

HALLOWEEN IN MAY? COSTUMED THIEVES ROB JEWELRY STORE

The article was accompanied by a low-resolution security camera photo. The figures in the photo were dark and blurry, but it was clear that one of them had a sword and the other was shooting something from his hand. It was a long, craggily white streak that stretched out of frame—almost like a bolt of lightning. Herman's eyes widened.

"I tracked down the jewelry store and was able to hack into their security system to observe the footage," Sid pointed at the photograph. "What you see here are not typical burglars or street thugs. They're different. And this individual here, that lightning isn't coming from a weapon of some sort. It's coming from his *fingertips*."

Everyone leaned in to gaze at the photo. Palms became clammy and there was a mix of coughs and gulps among the crew.

"So... these are other superhumans like us," Herman said in awe. "But bad."

Sid nodded. "And I believe if we can catch one of them, they might be able to give us some answers on where *your* powers came from. By finding *these people*, we not only will get answers about your conditions and who created them, but bring these people and their supplier to justice."

Everyone was silent as they mulled over Sid's proposition. Susan's eyes were like lasers on the newspaper, as if every word Sid said was immediately committed to memory. Frankie drummed his fingers on the table anxiously. Cassie's face was as stony and serious as ever.

"So... how... do we find them?" Herman asked, wiping his palm on his jeans.

"Great question," Susan confirmed. "How do we find two needles in a haystack of crime?"

"I've noticed that these characters have gravitated to establishments nearby Citytown Central Park," Sid said. "I recommend starting there. It shouldn't be difficult. All of you are the protagonists in this strange and eccentric piece of literature, and for the sake of pacing, I'd wager you'll encounter at least one of them soon." He paused, then cleared his throat. "For now, we have other business to attend to! Since you four—and Tyler—will be working as a team moving forward, you should become familiar with each other's powers! And that means an excursion to the practice range! Follow me, everyone! I'll drive!"

Sid was already marching merrily to the door, swinging his arms forward and back as he went. Everyone stood from the table, collected their things, and followed. Herman smirked because of how comical Sid looked, but couldn't help but think, *Why do we need to go to a practice range? What's there to show?*

"So what's your power?" Frankie had swooped up next to Herman and began walking side-by-side with him. He swung his boombox by his side as he went.

"Uh—" Herman stammered. "Same as you guys? No sleep, lots of energy, healing super fast."

"Yeah, but what else?"

Herman squinted. "What do you mean what else?"

Frankie's eyes got wide. "Ooooohh," he cooed. "You haven't figured out your other thing yet!"

"Other thing?"

"Yeah! Your special thing aside from the things you mentioned! I'll show you mine soon. It's pretty dope."

It was still midday when everyone exited the lab and walked out to the dirty Citytown air.

Sid led the pack, followed closely by Susan, who now carried a soccer ball pinned to her hip as she walked. Herman tilted his head when he saw it, puzzled.

She must have had it under the table during our conversation, he thought.

Cassie strode briskly two paces ahead of him, arms folded. Herman tried not to look at her too much. The back parking lot of Citytown Applied Technologies had a four cars parked—three uninteresting cars and one upscale luxury SUV. Considering Sid's fortune, Herman imagined that they would be driving to the practice range in the SUV, but he was wrong.

Sid strolled over to one the most beat-up, rust-crusted old cars Herman had ever seen. The hubcaps barely clung on and one of the tires was a spare that probably hadn't been replaced in months. Sid had to unlock the car manually (much like Herman's old car) then unlock the other doors from the inside. They all creaked as everyone pulled them open and squeezed inside. Herman was right next to Cassie in the back seat.

"Sid," Frankie said. "With all the cheddar cheese you've got, why don't you drive a better car?"

"An automobile is a liability," Sid said as he clicked his seatbelt. "What's the purpose of an automobile, Mr. Chan? To get you from point A to point B, nothing more. Why spend more money than you need on that? It baffles me. You want a fast car? You have to drive the speed limit like everyone else. You want heated seats? Well, that, I may understand but it's not worth the cost of insurance and—"

"Alright, alright, jeez."

"The heated seats are absolutely worth it," Susan chimed.

"Sid, how much money do you make, actually?" Herman asked from the back-middle seat. "Am I allowed to ask that?"

"Certainly, Mr. Fitzgerald," Sid said with a smug smirk as he churned the car the life. "First off, I make less as a chemist than you think. The majority of my fortune is derived from two sources: my trust fund and my family royalties."

"Trust fund?" Frankie repeated.

"Royalties?" Herman echoed.

"Precisely," Sid said. "My great-great-grandfather was the inventor of the steam-powered toothpick dispenser back in the 19th century. A revolutionary product."

"Oh, the Picko company!" Susan said. "I love their products."

"Secondly, my last name," Sid said. "Saskatoon. The Canadian city in Saskatchewan. My ancestors founded that city. Whenever a business attaches itself to our name, they must pay us a yearly royalty."

"I don't believe you," Frankie said.

Sid sneered in the rearview mirror as he slid on a pair of wraparound sunglasses that gave him the aesthetic of an insect. He said, "Sometimes, Mr. Chan, the truth is a little strange."

With that, the car rolled backward and sputtered out of the parking lot.

The practice range was only a ten-minute drive from the office building. The car rumbled and creaked with every bump and pothole it drove over. Most of the time, Herman sat quietly with his hand and hook between his knees. He watched the tan-and-grey scenery of the Citytown industrial district crawl by as he stared out the splotchy window.

At one point, they turned a corner and the car traveled parallel to the Citytown Wharf, which was populated with pleasure boats of all sizes sitting in murky, polluted water.

Beyond the wharf, the afternoon sun blazed in the sky, sending shimmering light down to the water's surface. Eventually, the car slowed to a crawl and turned away from the ocean.

"Well, this is it!" Sid said.

The car pulled through a tall chain link fence that hosted a worn-away sign marked "Citytown Regional Airport." A derelict building that must have been a terminal stood in the not-so-far-distance with murky windows, faded paint, and a mural of graffiti tags. Two hangars were also splattered with graffiti that stood between them and the terminal. Everything else was cracked asphalt, fading paint lines, or loose trash.

Sid rolled the car up to the nearest hangar and the vehicle lurched to a halt. The car doors clicked and squealed as everyone pushed them open. There wasn't anyone else around and a soft breeze came from the ocean that nipped at Herman's nose and fingers, causing him to pull his jacket tighter. Sid bounced out of the car as everyone else filed out. He threw open the trunk and pulled out three boxes with—

"Inflatable punching bags?" Herman asked pointedly. "You're having us demonstrate our powers with inflatable punching bags?"

Sid ignored him and got to work blowing up the first one with great breaths of air. All of them resembled the same thing: a white-faced clown with crossed eyes, buck teeth and a wagging tongue.

"Betcha got these on sale," Frankie said as he leaned against the car.

"Correct!" Sid confirmed as he blew another great breath.

Susan and Herman helped Sid fill the other two, although Herman had a hard time putting the stopper in with his one hand. When he was done, Cassie snatched the punching bag from him and closed the stopper without looking him in the eye.

With all three punching bags inflated, Sid satisfactorily put his hands on his hips. "Wonderful! Now, Cassandra, could you move these out a ways, please?"

When Sid requested her assistance, Cassie unfolded her arms, planted her feet, and held her hands parallel to the ground. As if by invisible hands, the punching bags lifted by their red noses and tongues, then flew fifty yards apart from each other before they toppled to the asphalt. Then they righted themselves vertically.

Herman's jaw fell.

"You moved that with your *brain?*" Frankie whooped. "You have *telekinesis?*"

"Only with things that are red," Cassie replied.

Taking courage, Herman cleared his throat and pointed at her hair. "That's gotta be really helpful when you're doing your hair every morning."

Cassie flipped her hair and glared intensely. "That's the one thing I can't control."

Herman gulped and his cheeks burned.

"That's right! Telekinesis!" Sid clapped his hands. "With some concentration, Cassandra can control any physical object containing a red pigment. Excluding her hair, of course." He laughed uncomfortably. "Frankie, would you please?"

"Awe yeah," Frankie said.

Frankie sauntered up with his boombox in one hand. With his other hand, he slipped his headphones onto his ears. A spark shot through his eyes as his grip on the boombox tightened. Everybody stood back, silently watching as Frankie clicked a button on the device. His toe started to tap. The others could hear thumping dance music starting to build from the reinforced speakers. Then the beat dropped.

Frankie threw his hand forward and percussive waves of air blasted from his palm.

BOOM. BOOM. BOOM. BOOM.

The first clown bag was launched off its base, and Frankie continued to pelt it through the air with each blast, perfectly synchronized to the beat. When he had cast the first one dozens of feet back, he went to the next one, then the next one. Satisfied, he clicked off the music, took off his headphones, and turned around.

"That's not all I can do, either!" He said with a cheeky grin. "That's just one song! And this thing?" He held up the boombox. "It's reinforced so I can swing it around and smack baddies with it. I call it the Bambox. Sid made it for me."

"Well done, Mr. Chan!" Sid said with applause. Cassie went to work retrieving the punching bags like a telekinetic puppeteer. "Music of different varieties affects Frankie in various ways. We're still experimenting, but what we've seen so far is astonishing!" With eyes still glowing, Sid turned to Susan. "Mrs. Terry?"

Susan didn't say anything. She just smiled.

After taking a few steps forward, Susan twirled her soccer ball on her finger, expertly balanced. Then she dropped it and wound up her foot.

Smack!

The force in which she launched the soccer ball was eye-popping. It pelted directly toward a clown at rocket speed, curving through the air before connecting with its face. Bullseye. Then, as if disregarding the laws of physics, the ball bounced back to her. She wound up another kick and launched it at the ball as it returned. It soared into the other clown's face and rebounded back to Susan again. This time, Susan jumped in the air, stopped the ball with her heels, and caught it gracefully in her hand.

She brushed her hair out of her face.

"If only I could do that back in college," she said as she walked back to the group with the ball by her hip.

"Wait," Herman said, squinting his eyes. "It's like that ball knows you... follows you."

"I know, it makes zero sense," Susan said, holding it up. "I can kick it around with absolute precision and force and it always comes back to me. It's not telekinesis or magic music blasts, but it's better than nothing, I guess." She smiled.

Herman looked down. *Yeah, you're telling me.*

"Herman, it's your turn now!" Sid said sporting a sensational smile.

Herman held up his hook and said, "I didn't bring my hammer though."

"Oh," Sid said absently. "Well, hm... well, why don't you just go show them anyway? Just pretend it's there. We'll get the idea."

Herman stared at him for a second, then looked at the nearest clown, then back to Sid. He shot quick glances at everyone else, who were watching him curiously.

"There's seriously nothing to show," Herman shrugged as his face went a little pink. "Sid, I don't have my hammer and I don't have any powers like—"

"Don't be ridiculous, just go on!"

Everyone was still looking at him. Even Cassie's disinterested eyes were on him now. Herman blushed profusely. Finally, he flipped around and dragged his feet toward the clowns. He stared at the ground as he went.

Telekinesis, musical powers, and a super soccer mom, Herman thought. *Then there's me.*

After a few moments, he stood face to face with the inflated plastic shell. The thing ogled at him with googly crossed eyes and a long tongue, silently taunting him. Herman lifted his hook hand and unceremoniously whacked the clown's balloon-like face. The clown leaned back, then silently came up again.

Herman turned around and held his arms in the air, "That's it. I guess that's what I do."

"Well done, Herman!" Sid said positively.

As he walked back to the group, he said, "I did beat up three guys yesterday with my hammer, though. They tried to mug me."

"Seriously?" Frankie's tone rose. "Were they big?"

"Huge," Herman nodded. "And they had crowbars."

"Awesome," Frankie grinned widely.

"You better not be lying, Fitzgerald," Cassie said coldly. "Or you're going to be a liability to us. You don't do anything."

Suddenly, every eye was on Herman again. Something inside Herman's chest shriveled up, like a snail hiding in its shell because it got poked by a stick. His face burned again.

"Look, don't take it personally," Cassie shrugged. "But all of us actually have some powers that will give us an advantage when we start pounding bad guys. All you've got is a hammer that sticks onto your stump hand. That sucks."

Herman's jaw fell. Those emerald eyes held no sparkle—no warmth, no sympathy.

Wow, was all he could think.

Suddenly, Herman had an arm around his shoulders. It was Sid's.

"I'm confident that Herman will be a great addition to our little team," Sid said brightly. "No one here has actually fought any crime yet, so let's refrain on placing value on each other's skills until they're put to the test, hm?" He patted Herman on the shoulder. "Shall we?"

Sid deflated the punching bags and everybody clambered into the car. The doors slammed shut, Sid climbed in, and they drove away.

Herman sat in the front seat, per Susan's insistence. It gave him the chance to stare at the wharf some more as they drove past. As they made their way through the quiet streets of the industrial district, he couldn't take his mind off Cassie's unforgiving comments.

Am I really going to be a liability to this team? He thought. *Everyone's got such awesome powers except me. How am I supposed to help when I'm fighting someone who can shoot a bolt of lightning? Is this all a huge mistake?*

They had arrived back at Citytown Applied Technologies and Sid put the car in park.

"Well, off you go!" he said. "Tonight is the first night, so make sure you get plenty of rest!" He paused. "*Ha!* See, that's a joke, because none of you need rest anymore!"

Everybody piled out of the car and walked toward their own cars. Cassie darted for her car across the parking lot. Frankie said goodbye to Herman and the others before going to his car and starting it up. Herman was about to pick up his feet and jog home when he felt Susan take his elbow. He faltered.

"Herman," she said, speaking softly. "Don't let her get in your head. We all have something to contribute here. She doesn't determine your value."

The knot in Herman's chest slackened a little bit. There was no guile in her chocolatey brown eyes, just sincerity. She pulled the corners of her mouth into a smile and patted Herman on the cheek before she strode over to her SUV. Silently, Herman thanked her.

At that moment, Frankie rumbled up next to him in his car. He rolled down the window.

"Hey!" he said as he poked his head out. "Sorry we forgot to tell you this, but we're planning on meeting tonight at Citytown Central Park at ten o'clock. The bad guys should turn up somewhere around there."

"Is that Tyler guy going to come along?" Herman asked. "The guy that couldn't show up today?"

"Beats me, muchacho," Frankie shrugged. "But hey, I have a biology test to study for tomorrow and Susan has date night with her husband, so it's just going to be you and Cassie. Is that cool?"

No, nothing could be less cool than that.

"I don't know," Herman said slowly. "I don't think she likes me. Like, at all."

"Girls are crazy, man," Frankie said as he swatted the air with his hand. "I never take anything they say too seriously. Especially an angry ginger like her."

"But still."

"I know you'll do great!" Frankie said brightly as he slapped the side of his car. "Go knock some heads tonight! Catcha later, Hammerfist!"

He gave Herman peace fingers as he peeled out of the parking lot. Herman took a look around. Almost everyone had left. It dawned to him that Cassie lives at the same apartment complex as him and didn't offer him a ride home. The only car that was left in the parking lot was Sid's crusted old piece of junk.

I bet he practically lives here, Herman briefly thought as he straightened his jacket. *I guess I should get ready for tonight.*

5

Less than an hour later, Herman was back at home in apartment 329. He would have been home sooner but decided to make a brief stop at a 99-cent store. His goal was to find a ski mask or something similar to cover his face with. After all, superheroes have secret identities, right? Unfortunately, the only ski masks the store had were mauve and seafoam green, so Herman went with mauve. The cashier was understandably perplexed when a one-handed college student walked up to the counter with a ski mask in the middle of May.

"*Heeeeyyy.*"

"Hey, Bridger."

As Herman entered the apartment, Bridger was laying spread-eagle with his face up and headphones on his ears. His eyes were closed and his breathing came in great, slow breaths. Deep, oscillating hums emanated from him with each exhale. Herman hung by the door, teased the thought of asking him what he was doing, then thought better of it and slipped back to his room.

He found his hammer under his bed and clicked it onto his wrist before strolling over to his mirror. He took a good look at himself with a white t-shirt and holey jeans. His nose scrunched. Then he took the hammer off, scooped up his leather jacket, thrust it on, followed by his new ski mask, hammer, and sneakers.

As he stepped in front of the mirror, he gazed at himself up and down.

I look like a B-movie bank robber with a hammer for a hand, he thought with a sigh. *Oh well. Hopefully people who see me can figure out that I'm one of the good guys.*

Knock knock knock

In a flash, the ski mask was off his head and the hammer was behind his back. Herman forcefully cleared his throat and it ended up sounding more like a nervous cough. The door swung open, revealing Zach's liberally moisturized face and crisp haircut. He had one hand in the pocket of his khaki shorts and his other hand on a half-eaten apple.

"Hey," he said as he took a crispy bite. He chomped and talked to Herman simultaneously. "Look, *(smack)* I know life's been kind of *(smack)* crazy lately with your... hand and everything. *(gulp)* Do you like sushi?"

Herman blinked and ignored his thickly beating heart. He said, "It's fine. Never really had any except for some I had at a buffet one time."

"That's not good sushi. Let's go get some good sushi. I'll buy."

Herman tilted his head. "Wait, you're... asking me to hang out?"

"Yeah," Zach said with a shrug. "Don't make it weird. I just want to do something nice because you're a cripple now."

Herman had to stop himself from rolling his eyes. "Yeah, hey, that sounds nice. But I actually have plans tonight."

"Tomorrow then."

"I'm probably busy tomorrow, too."

Zach squinted and took another bite of his apple. "Doing what? *(smack)* You never used to go out, but now *(smack)* you're going on random runs and walking outside at dark? What are you doing?"

This is when Herman's eyes discreetly darted to the discarded ski mask just out of view. Secret identity, right? Don't tell people what's going on. You don't want them to worry about you and your health. Zach's probing gaze become a little much after a few seconds and Herman blurted out the first thing he could think of.

"I'm—uh, seeing someone now," he said.

Zach's eyebrows raised and his posture loosened. "Oh. Cool. What's her name? Or his. I dunno what you like."

Herman had to think for a second. He drummed his fingers on his leg. Then he blurted the first name that came to mind. "Abby."

"Abby who?"

Another pause. "Gale. Abby Gale."

Zach was halfway into another bite of his apple, then he stopped. "Her name is Abby *Gale?*"

"Yep. I know. Crazy, huh? Her mom is kind of a hippie."

Zach didn't move his apple. He just stared. Herman held his hammer firmly behind his back and silently prayed that Zach would just go away. It was answered when Zach, still squinting a little bit, took a slow, final bite of his apple and said, "Okay." Then he crept away.

Herman pushed the door shut again with a *click.* Right as he did, he quietly slipped his hammer and ski mask into a backpack. As soon as he had it zipped up, he slipped out of his room and left the apartment. As his feet reached ground level, he turned to the downtown area and started to jog, but then the thought crossed his mind:

Maybe I shouldn't jog downtown this time, he thought. *I'm going to draw enough attention to myself with my hand.*

The bus stop wasn't even fifty yards from where he was standing—a rusty orange sign with a minimalist bus logo that had been around for decades. Right next to it, a splintery wooden bench, completely vacant—he'd be the only one waiting for the next ride. He gripped his backpack and walked over to it.

He plopped down on the bench as cars passed by left and right, their headlights streaming through the darkness. After a few minutes of staring at his feet, counting the passersby, a tired old Citytown Public Transit Authority bus rumbled up to where he sat. As it squealed to a stop, it flatulated a hydraulic hiss before lowering to the ground and swinging the door open. Herman climbed aboard, flashing his bus pass as he did.

"Well, hello there! I'm Mac! Welcome aboard the 831 bus to downtown!"

Most bus drivers that Herman had met sported a scruffy complexion and the faint smell of cheap alcohol. However, Mac looked like he could have been on a toothpaste commercial. His round belly was covered by a bright teal sweater, his sandy brown hair was parted to perfection, and his rosy cheeks reminded Herman of Santa Claus. He beamed at Herman as he climbed aboard.

"Uh—thanks!" Herman forced out.

"You're not planning on roaming the streets this late, are you?" Mac said. "A *looott* of strange goings on have been going on lately in the downtown area. A lot more robberies than usual. It's best to keep your eyes peeled."

"Yeah," Herman said as he sat down and the doors closed. "I'll try to be careful."

He stole a glance at his backpack.

As the bus hissed and crawled away, Herman scanned his surroundings. In the rearview mirror, he could see there were only three other people on the bus. One of them was asleep, one of them stared out the window, and another one stared at the floor and whispered to himself quickly.

Herman frowned and looked out the window. As the bus rolled and stopped on its way down the street, he couldn't help but notice how different characters were that inhabited the sidewalks at night. The innocent shoppers and college students were gone. Instead, groups of suspicious individuals roamed in packs, glancing around with their hands in their pockets as they went. Some people were leaning against run-down buildings, smoking cigarettes and making shady exchanges out of eyesight. One person made eye contact with Herman as he rode by. He gulped.

What am I doing? Herman thought. *I'm literally going downtown just to pick a fight. What if the other people have guns or something? What if Cassie doesn't show or she's not helpful at all? Will I still heal quickly if I'm mortally wounded? What if—*

"So, you go to the local community college?" Mac said.

Herman yanked himself away from his thoughts and cleared his throat. "Uh, used to. I graduated."

"What did you study?"

"Public relations," Herman said. He paused before he added, "I ended up getting a different kind of job, though."

"Oh? What's that?"

Herman's eyes darted to his backpack, then to the characters that they passed along the street.

He said, "I work for the city. Cleaning up the streets."

"Nothing to be ashamed of!" Mac said brightly. "Lots of people find fulfillment in employment outside their degrees. Look at me! I did lots of schooling and found a cushy job with a fat paycheck. Corporate gig. But as the years went by, I got tired of all the lies and the bureaucracy. Now I drive busses! And that's a-okay."

Mac gave him a friendly grin in the rearview mirror. Herman returned it with a half-smile.

The minutes passed and eventually, the bus rolled to a stop. They were across the street from the Citytown Central Park. The bus hissed, descended, and the doors flung open.

Mac turned around in his seat. "Now, you be safe, you hear? You seem like a good kid. This is a dangerous city, but this part is the worst. Wherever you gotta go, keep your head down and walk fast, okay?"

Herman nodded before he slung his backpack over his shoulder, slipped around the seat, and hopped down the stairs. As he touched down in front of a 24-hour arcade, Mac closed the door and the bus pulled away.

On any other night, the sight of a 24-hour arcade would be tempting, but tonight Herman's heart was racing over impending danger instead of extra lives. He looked over Central Park briefly, hoping to catch a glimpse of Cassie. No Cassie—just one couple making out on a blanket and a couple of guys smoking cigarettes by the pond. There were a handful of other people walking around—probably on their way home—but no shocking burst of red hair to be seen.

He fondled the communicator in his ear. Snug and secure.

"Sid," he whispered. "Sid, can you hear me?"

"Clear as day, Herman!" Sid's voice was excited on the other end.

"I don't see Cassie. Where is she?"

"Hm... the GPS coordinates in her earpiece indicate that she's at Central Park."

Herman sighed. Great. As he surveyed the landscape, Herman spotted a group of bushes tall enough to hide behind. When the nearby traffic light turned red, he jogged across the street, cutting through the stopped cars. As he made it to the other side, the grass beneath his feet muffled the sound of his footsteps.

He dove inside the bushes. Sure that no one could see him, he unzipped his backpack and pulled out the hammer and ski mask. He shoved the ski mask on as quickly as he could, trying hard to pull the holes over his eyes and mouth.

Suddenly, a voice said, "What's with the mask?"

Herman yelped as he flipped around. It was Cassie. She was crouched behind the same group of bushes and Herman didn't even notice her. The mask was only half pulled over his head.

He blinked. "You know... secret identity stuff! They can't know—"

"No one cares, you idiot," Cassie said flatly. "You really think someone is going to try to track you down? We have code names—yours is Hammerfist, remember? Don't use our real names. Put that away."

"No, it's a good idea. I'm keeping this on." He finished adjusting his ski mask and clicked the hammer onto his wrist. "What's your code name?"

"Ginger Witch," she said. "Frankie is Ghetto Blaster and Susan is Soccer Mom."

"Ginger Witch, huh?" Herman grumbled. "That's the best Sid could come up with?"

"It was my idea," Cassie said coarsely.

Herman's cheeks went red. *Man, I'm really a pro at pissing her off.* He said, "Sorry. So... what do we do now?"

"We wait."

"We just wait?"

Cassie nodded. "Waiting for a robbery in downtown Citytown is like waiting for a zebra at a water hole. It'll happen. You scared?"

"No," Herman lied.

"Your knees are literally shaking."

"I'm fine!"

"Okay, whatever," Cassie said. "Just try to keep up. I don't know if anyone's ever taught you how to punch, but it's too late now. Stay out of my way if you can."

Herman frowned. He peeked over the top of the bushes. A slight breeze rustled through the trees and caused the water in the nearby stream to shiver. The only other people within earshot were the two guys smoking by the pond. All the shops surrounding the city block had their neon lights burning brightly, their doors locked for the night, but nothing disturbed them. Most of the stores had bars in the windows and doors.

"Nothing is happening," Herman whispered.

Cassie poked her head up, surveying the surroundings. She frowned, too.

"This area has been getting robbed a ton lately," Cassie said. "Something's bound to—"

Crash! Zap!

The sound of smashing glass was close. Herman and Cassie flipped around to see a massive display window completely shattered outside an upscale clothing store. Even the bars behind the window were blown away. Whatever broke them darted inside quickly. Herman barely got a look at the figure as it pelted inside, but he swore he spotted a cape flapping behind it.

"Showtime," Cassie said, leaping out from the bush.

She darted toward the store without hesitation. It was then that Herman noticed a bright red brick hovering by her waist. Her hand was wide open, guiding it along as if with invisible wings as she bolted to the burglary.

She probably flings it around with her mind, he thought. *That's actually pretty cool.*

Taking a deep breath, he leapt out and ran toward Cassie, who had already jumped through the broken window. His heart pounded and his palm was sweaty as he swung his arms forward, thinking of what was in store.

Will this be an easy fight? Will there be a lot of them? Or just one really strong guy with powers like us?

It was about this time that Herman jumped through the window and came face-to-face with what they were dealing with.

"*You!*" Cassie shouted as she lifted the brick to her eye level, ready to launch. "From the newspaper article!"

"Aha! Indeed!"

Whoever he was, he was standing on the counter as if it were his own personal stage. His face was shrouded by a widely-grinning drama mask that reminded Herman of Guy Fawkes. His outfit was definitely stolen from a Shakespeare production—tights and everything. He did a gleeful little jig on the counter, his hands full of jewels and pearls that had to be worth thousands. When he noticed Herman, he cocked his head.

"Oho!" He jeered. "An angry lass and a hammer-clad lad. A permanent team, or superfluous fad?"

Herman couldn't keep his eyes from squinting through the ski mask. "What the…?"

"It is I," he said with another little jig. "*The Thespian!* Avenger of the arts, crusader of the cast and crew! I recommend you depart, or it'll be *curtains* for you!"

"…Oh wow," Herman said.

"Drop the merchandise and maybe I'll let you off with a warning," Cassie said.

"*Ha ha!*" The Thespian chortled. "En garde, then!"

In a flash, the Thespian dropped the goods and flicked back his cape, pointing his fingers like a gun. Cassie hurled the brick forward and Herman jumped out of the way just in time as a blast shot passed them. He took cover behind a rack of clothes.

"*Son of a—*" Herman shouted as he was sprayed with rubble from behind.

The Thespian laughed maniacally as he prepped another lightning blast. The tips of his fingers sparked as Herman and Cassie scrambled to their feet.

Bam!

More rubble and tile burst from the ground as Herman ran by. He tumbled to the ground as his eyes filled with dust. He frantically rubbed them with the back of his hand. His vision was quickly returning, but Cassie was out of sight. He heard her from somewhere else in the store.

"Try to distract him while I find my brick!" she cried out.

His vision was nearly back. He could see the Thespian to his left. Herman gulped again, took a deep breath, then leapt onto his feet.

Bam! Bam! Bam!

Lightning blasts from the Thespian's fingers hurled toward him, missing him by inches, sending out more rubble and dust. Meanwhile, the Thespian laughed like a loon at the top of the counter. One blast collided with Herman's hammer, causing it to vibrate horribly. But as he ran, he managed to find a single red dress discarded on the floor.

"*Hey!*"

He tossed the red dress in the air. Immediately, from somewhere unseen, Cassie gave it life. It shot over to the Thespian's mask and wrapped itself around his head. Muffled shouts permeated from his lips as his hands clawed at the dress, trying to untie himself.

Herman took courage. His feet slid on the floor as he dug in and bolted for the Thespian. The Thespian continued to grapple with the dress and Cassie ran through the store, looking for her discarded red brick. All the while, Herman had only a few more steps until he was on the Thespian.

He leapt into the air, soaring high. He cocked his hammer back.

"Looks like it's curtains for *you,* Thespian!"

Crack!

The Thespian managed to pull the dress off just in time to see Herman's hammer crash into his face. The villain crumbled and fell behind the counter in heap, his cape over his face, completely out cold. Herman stood over him triumphantly.

"*Woo!*" Herman shoved his fist in the air. "That's right! Did you see that?"

"No," Cassie said, appearing into view few yards away, her eyes scanning the ground. "Ugh, where's my *brick*?"

"*Freeze!*"

Herman and Cassie flipped about to see a mob of police officers by the broken window, guns drawn, lights flashing from their police cars. Herman's heart dropped into his butt and he shot a look at Cassie. In return, Cassie's eyes could have burned a hole through him.

"No, wait, it wasn't us!" Herman shouted at the cops. "We got the real bad guy! He's right here behind the counter! Come look!"

"*Drop the hammer and keep your hands up!*" one officer shouted.

"You've got a ski mask and a leather jacket on, genius," Cassie said with her hands up. "You think we look like the good guys? We gotta run."

"But they're cops!"

"*Come on!*"

"They're guarding the one entrance. So, unless you—"

She was already off, darting through the racks of clothing. Herman growled and scrambled to keep up. The police officers didn't fire their weapons, but quickly poured into the store in active pursuit. Cassie made her way to the back door, kicking the door open and busting the lock off. As they emerged into an alleyway, they spotted a fire escape just within reach.

Down the alleyway, officers were darting toward them. Cassie and Herman jumped for the fire escape and began to climb. They pumped their legs as fast as they could up the metal ladder. Herman struggled to climb with only one hand.

"Sid," Cassie said. "We need evac, pronto!"

"I hear you!" Sid's voice suddenly sounded in their ear communicators. "I already had minicopters waiting by your coordinates. They'll be on the roof. Tell me when you're safely fastened and I'll activate them."

"Got it!"

As they continued to hustle upward, none of the cops opened fire, but they were gaining ground. The rusty fire escape shook and rattled as more bodies began to climb. On the last rung, Herman shot his hand upward to climb onto the platform and dart up the stairs. However, the fire escape shook violently as another officer climbed aboard.

Herman yelped as his fingers grazed the rung. He swung his hammer and managed to hang from the last rung just long enough to grab it with his hand. His adrenaline helped him shoot upward just before an officer could grab his ankle.

Up several shaky flights of stairs, they finally emerged to the roof. There waiting for them were two contraptions that looked exactly how they sounded—mini helicopters. Each rig had a bucket seat with its own safety harness. Chopper blades above each seat began to rev up as Herman and Cassie approached.

Cassie dropped herself into the bucket seat and quickly clicked her harness shut. Herman, however, struggled to click the straps together with his one hand.

"Come on, come on…"

He frantically tried biting the strap and guiding the notch in with his hammer, but it was too unsteady. The cops were just about on the roof. He could hear their footsteps and shouts. Cassie shouted at him angrily. Finally, he threw his arms through both straps and hugged himself as tight as he could.

"*Screw it, let's go!*" Herman shouted.

"Activating minicopter autopilot and cloaking," Sid said in his earpiece.

A burst of wind enveloped Herman and Cassie as the chopper blades picked up velocity and slowly lifted off the ground. Within a few seconds, the minicopters hovered off the roof toward the Citytown Applied Technology building. Blue sparkles enveloped them, and Herman realized that the cloaking device had activated. They glided through the air, Cassie scowling with her arms folded, and Herman holding tight to the safety harness. Beneath them, the lights and rooftops of Citytown skyscrapers crawled by.

Down on the roof, a five-foot-tall police officer glared at the sight of two minicopters disappearing into thin air. The cigarette in his mouth was half-smoked, and the scowl that accompanied his glare was branded onto his face as if he always smelled something rotten.

"Detective Axewielder!"

The officer cocked his eyebrow and scratched his five o'clock shadow as another officer approached him. His stony grey eyes made the approaching officer uneasy. He pulled at his collar before continuing to address the detective.

"Sir, we found another character unconscious behind the store counter, dressed in a really bad stage costume. He claims he was assaulted by those two when he tried to stop them."

Detective Axewielder looked hard at the officer, pulled the cigarette out from his lips and flicked it on the ground. The sole of his boot stomped the cigarette out.

"Bring him in for questioning, then," Detective Axewielder said, his voice like gravel. "It looks like more of these freaks are popping up every night. Tell me what you guys dig up. We'll find them."

6

Clink... clink...

Herman skewered the sausage links on his plate and shoved them in his mouth. He couldn't help but grin as he looked down at the plate in front of him—populated by two large pancakes swimming in syrup, a half-eaten strip of bacon, and a full glass of orange juice. He sat alone at a table by the window that streamed in morning sunlight. The rest of the diner, known as the Snail Stop, was slow and quiet—probably since the semester ended weeks ago. It was the staple restaurant of Citytown Community College, named after the school mascot and poised on the south side of campus.

Clink.

Herman placed the fork on the plate and wiped up his hands with a cotton napkin, staring out the window in satisfaction. He had five hundred dollars in his pocket just a few hours ago, courtesy of Doctor Sidney Saskatoon after a successful night of crime fighting. It gave him enough money to pay back what he was behind on rent and still have enough for a delicious breakfast.

As he looked out on the campus, a figure quickly strode by the window—a figure with shocking red hair, a slender frame, and fair skin. Her eyes were sharp, and she marched up to the door with the singular resolution of a woman on a mission.

Ding ding!

The diner door jingled as she threw it open. She quickly surveyed the diner, then spotted Herman sitting by the window. Her eyes sharpened even more and her jaw clenched. Herman lifted the glass of orange juice to his lips. She stormed toward him.

"Hey, Cassie," He said. "You doing okay? You peaced out super quick last night, we barely got to talk—"

"You *royally* effed up last night, Hammerfist," she seethed as she slammed her hand on the table, causing the fork to slide off his plate.

Herman frowned and put it back. "What are you talking about?" His voice died down to a whisper. "I knocked the guy out cold! He was trying to burglarize the store and we stopped him! Period! What else did you want?"

She counted on her fingers as she went. "The chance to question him, my brick…"

"You can always get another brick."

"I liked that one!"

"How did you know I was here, anyway?"

"Frankie texted me!"

Herman's eyebrows pointed. "Frankie?"

His eyes darted around the diner. There was hardly anyone else there. But after a second, he noticed him by the opposite wall. Frankie Chan had a napkin tucked into the neck of his hoodie, digging into a breakfast special just like Herman was. He waved with his fork in hand when he made eye contact with the two.

"What's up guys!" He said brightly. "Herman, I'm all about the breakfast here, too! These pancakes, right?" Frankie dropped his fork on the plate and scurried over to Cassie and Herman. He was there in a matter of moments, sitting down opposite of Herman. "How did it go last night? I'm gonna fail my exam. Screw summer semester."

At the same time, Herman said "Fine," and Cassie said "Terrible."

"Was it the guy from the newspaper article?" Frankie asked.

"Yeah," Cassie said. "Dresses up like Hamlet and calls himself the Thespian."

"The Lesbian?" Frankie replied.

"*Thespian*," Cassie said curtly. "Like a stage actor."

"Okay, sure," Frankie said offhandedly. "So how did it shake out?"

"Knocked him out cold," Herman smirked.

"Nice!"

"And then the cops showed up," Cassie frowned. "We had to take minicopters off the roof to escape. We lost them, but now they're probably going to be looking for us."

Frankie paused, then said, "Oh. Not nice. But hey!" He punched Herman's shoulder. "Way to knock him out cold on the first night! Last night I got bored of studying and started testing what different songs do to me. I listened to some new age stuff that made me pee my pants and I didn't notice for ten minutes."

Cassie rolled her eyes and Herman smiled.

"Check this out," Frankie said. "You guys made the paper."

He slapped the morning edition of the *Citytown Harold* on the table. Herman and Cassie leaned over its front page to see a column about a nightly robbery that happened across the street from Citytown Central Park. They looked at each other.

"'By June Montague'," Frankie began to read in a hushed tone. "'There was an attempted robbery at Charli's on Main last night shortly after ten o'clock. Three perpetrators made an attempt to steal thousands of dollars worth of jewelry, but Citytown Police managed to catch them in the act. One perpetrator was taken into custody."

"So they got him!" Herman said brightly. "There we go. We did some good."

Cassie glared.

"Whoa-whoa, wait," Frankie continued. "It says… 'thousands of dollars of damage were still struck on the property, including merchandise and fixtures. Citytown residents are asked to report any knowledge they might have to the police.' Then there's a phone number. And a couple security camera pictures of you guys! They're super blurry, though."

"Secret identities!" Herman said as he jabbed their pictures. "I'm telling you! We should start wearing masks! So, we still did a bunch of damage to the store. It could be worse, right? We still helped the cops get the guy responsible."

"Ten bucks says that wacko already escaped," Cassie said coldly.

Frankie shrugged. "Yeah, you might be right. The cops in this town aren't exactly world-class."

"So, if he has, we take him down again, right?" Herman said. "It wasn't that hard. And we *are* the protagonists of this story, so that's a huge advantage. On a random note"—he pointed at the newspaper—"*Herald* is supposed to be spelled with an 'e' and an 'a'. They spelled it like the name Harold instead."

"This city was founded by morons, like, two hundred years ago," Frankie said with a smile. "The original creator of the newspaper probably didn't realize they had different spellings. And it just stuck." He paused. "Oh, Susan wants to do a late-night dinner with all of us during our shift tonight. She says it'll give us a chance to all get to know each other better." He shook his head. "She's such a mom."

"No one cares," Cassie said.

Herman said, "What time and where?"

*

"You guys have classy taste," Herman said several hours later.

The four of them sat on rickety wooden chairs surrounding square wooden table. The table itself was plagued with multiple scratches, grease spots, and flecks of fortune cookie dust. All around them were decorations that looked like they were purchased at a discount party store for Chinese New Year, including old paper fans and dragon puppets that hung from the ceiling with fishing wire.

Beneath the table, a collection of backpacks rested by their feet that carried their crime fighting gear. At the end of the table, a pimply teenager dished out menus to the crew.

"Welcome to Won Ton King Kong, rated the best fried rice in Citytown two years in a row," he said mechanically as he sniffed and wiped his nose. "What can I get you to drink?"

Everyone said water was fine.

"'Kay," the server slouched off, discarded the extra menus onto a counter, and disappeared behind a corner.

"It's not the cleanest place, but the fried rice here *is* very good," Susan said as she perused the menu casually.

"The service sucks," Cassie scowled.

"But everything sucks to you, Cassie," Frankie sneered.

Cassie ignored him and opened up her menu.

Frankie scooted his chair closer to the table. He leaned in closely, his voice down to a whisper. "Hey guys, have you wondered why we, you know... eat?"

Everyone returned his question with blank stares.

"Just think about it," he continued. "It doesn't make sense. Why do all animals eat? To get the energy from food, right? You know, proteins, carbohydrates, vitamins, whatever. When you don't eat enough, your body gets tired, right? Well… none of us get sleepy. Like, ever. So why do we eat if we never get tired? It's not like we need the energy."

Everyone blinked and looked at each other, stupefied. It was at that moment when the pimply server was at the table again with four glasses of water.

"You ready?" he said dully.

Susan folded up her menu and said, "Four orders of the fried rice, please."

In a few minutes, everyone was reminded that they all still ate food because it's an enjoyable thing to do. The chatter died to a minimum as the sounds of clinking dishes greeted the oriental music playing over the intercom.

"So," Herman said with a mouth half-full. "How long do you guys plan on doing this? Like, fighting crime and stuff. *Wow,* this is good."

Susan was the first one to reply. "Just long enough for us to find who's responsible so we can find an antidote. I don't need the money—I just want to go back to normal. I have a family and a business to run."

"Yeah," Frankie said. "The money is great, but I think we all just want to find out what's inside us and get a cure. I gotta be honest, I think Sid is kind of a nut. He's got a good heart or whatever—encouraging us to clean up the streets—but this whole situation is pretty bonkers."

Herman smiled. *Glad I'm not the only one.* Then he remembered. "Wait! What happened to you guys… exactly… when you got sent to the hospital? I'm sorry if I'm being too personal."

"Gunshot," Frankie said nonchalantly.

Herman nearly choked on his rice. "You were *shot?*"

"Yeah!" Frankie said. "Right in the shoulder!" He jabbed his shoulder with his chopsticks. "It had to have been a driveby. Maybe I was wearing the wrong thing or they thought I was a member of a gang or something, because someone just drove by me as I was walking down the street, honked their horn, yelled something, and *bam!* Crazy, huh? Someone called an ambulance and they got me to the ER before I lost too much blood."

Everyone stared at Frankie incredulously as he casually dug into his rice. He looked up from his bowl, curiously scanning the stricken faces of his comrades before asking, "Herman, what happened to you? Wasn't it, uh...?"

"Car accident," Herman said after he got his composure. "Got hit by an eighteen-wheeler. Nearly all the bones in my right hand got fractured, which is why I have this now." He waved his hook in the air. "What about you, Susan?"

"Inguinal hernia repair," she said as she dabbed her lips with a napkin. "Sorry if that's too much information. My husband was shocked when I was completely healed the next day. I was supposed to stay away from the gym for several weeks."

"Cassie?" Frankie said. "We always ask you things last because you're so snarky and cynical."

Cassie didn't answer right away. She said, "Fell off a building. Woke up in the hospital."

"You fell off a building?" Herman muttered quietly.

"Did I stutter?"

Herman went back to his rice.

"Does anybody know what happened to Tyler?" Susan asked as she placed the chopsticks in her empty bowl.

Frankie shrugged. "Dude, none of us know anything about him. He met Sid like once and hasn't shown his face since. Apparently he's got a communicator, though."

Herman hummed in recognition. "So... no toxic waste involved in your accidents? Just mine?"

"Guess so," Frankie said with a shrug.

"That's so weird that it would have *nothing* to do with what I'm feeling, though," Herman said.

"Maybe it does and we just don't know it yet," Susan said as she folded her arms and rested them on the table. "There's still a lot we don't know about our conditions. Either way, you should be grateful that you came out alive. That must have been terrifying. I can't imagine what your family felt when they heard about it."

Immediately, Herman thought of Aunt Josie. Her admonition that she gave before she dropped him off at his apartment. *Be safe.* His heart sank as he looked at his hook hand and thought of the hammer in his backpack.

Over Herman's shoulder, Frankie spotted something through the window. He sat upright, staring intently, narrowing his eyes. His face suddenly became hard.

"Guys," he said, pointing out the window. "It's one-thirty in the morning. That place should definitely be closed."

They all turned around to see a giant electronics store right across the street, and the lights inside were definitely on. At least three shadowy figures crept their way through the store. A set of iron bars covering one of the windows had been bent open, and the glass of the window had been shattered. Everyone exchanged glances, then grabbed their stuff from beneath the table and darted for the entrance.

Just as they all dashed out the door, Susan remembered to swing by the table and drop some cash.

As they all burst onto the street, getting their weapons ready, Cassie shot a look at Herman and said, "If we can catch one, *catch one!* These guys have the same conditions as us, so they probably know where they're coming from! *Got it?*"

"Al*right!*"

"We probably have about five or ten minutes before the cops get here," Frankie said as he stuffed in his earpiece and threw on his headphones. "So we gotta make this quick and crush these clowns. Everybody ready?"

"It's game time!" Susan said with soccer ball in hand.

Frankie sneered at her. "Really? You have a *catch phrase* now? And it's something as cliché and character-appropriate as 'it's game time?'"

"Shut up, let's *go!*"

7

As everyone gathered around the base of the broken window, Frankie hunched down and reached into his hoodie.

"Hey, Sid took Herman's advice and decided to make masks for all of us."

Given Sid's resources, the others expected some sort of high-tech face molding device or multi-colored helmets, but this wasn't the case. What Frankie pulled out from his pocket was a wad of random fabric samples bunched together in a ball. Everyone dove their hands in and retrieved a different color, but they were all just strips of craggily-cut material with holes snipped out for the eyes.

"This looks like something for a homemade Ninja Turtles costume," Cassie said coldly.

Herman dangled his mask from two fingers. The description was pretty accurate. It was easy to picture Sid running to a craft store and picking out the four fabrics at the lowest price. The fabric Herman pulled out had a yellow-and-blue paisley pattern. He pressed his lips together.

Everyone had already tied their masks around their head. Herman looked around sheepishly.

"Uh, could somebody—"

"Here," Cassie said.

She swung over, thrust the mask over Herman's eyes, and abruptly tied a knot around the back of his head. Herman winced as she tightened it. The knot pinched the strands of his hair.

"Hopefully these are temporary," Herman said as he pulled the holes over his eyes.

Susan and Cassie were the first to creep through the broken window and into the electronics store. Herman and Frankie followed silently behind. Whoever had decided to rob the place decided to turn on the lights, illuminating the congregation of electronic gadgets and overpriced computer peripherals. Everyone tensely exchanged looks as they hid behind the aisle closest to the window.

The problem with the broken window, though, was that there was broken glass strewn everywhere. And the problem with *that* was that crunching glass on laminate flooring wasn't quiet.

Cr-r-acckk

"*Who's there?*"

It was a man's voice. Nobody moved. Crouched behind an aisle divider, Frankie cranked up the volume in his headphones. A small display between the speakers bounced with light with every beat. Cautiously, everyone else got their tools ready.

They heard creeping footsteps begin to spread out across the store. There had to be three—maybe four perpetrators. They whispered to each other seriously, but Herman and the others could still make out what they were saying across the room.

"Chet, is it the cops?" A woman's voice said.

"No way, Nikki," Chet said in response. "They'd already have their guns out if it were. Probably those kooks from the other day."

"Let them come," a new voice said. It sounded like a teenager.

Behind the aisle divider, Susan tapped the others to get their attention. She mouthed the words, "Let's sneak up on them," while making a walking motion with her fingers. Frankie wasn't paying attention.

"*Ha!* The intruders shall be dealt with swiftly!" The unmistakable voice of The Thespian called through the store.

That was when Frankie took action.

"*You're one to talk!*" He shouted.

Frankie leapt out from behind cover as a burst of energy erupted from his palm. It shot through the air like a visible beam of sound. The intruders on the other end of the store scattered. An aisle divider crumpled and tipped over from the impact of Frankie's blast, followed by the hissing and sparking of severed wire. Susan and Cassie both jumped to their feet.

"You're killing me, Ghetto Blaster!" Susan growled. "We had a chance to—"

"I've got the Thespian!" Cassie said.

"*Ugh!* I've got the kid!" Susan said.

"Hammerfist!" Frankie grabbed Herman's shoulder. "We'll take the others!"

Frankie grabbed a fistful of Herman's jacket and yanked him to his feet. They pelted through the aisles of while Susan and Cassie bolted the opposite way. Herman caught a glance of Susan's high-tech soccer ball rebounding off the walls and Cassie's new brick rocketing toward the Thespian.

Herman tapped his earpiece. "Sid, are you there?"

"I read you, Hammerfist!" Sid replied in his ear. "What's the situation?"

"Four of them in a huge electronics store on 13th Street. One of them is the Thespian from last night."

Sid was absolutely giddy. "Excellent! Capture one of you can! We need answers!"

Why is he always so excited about this stuff? Herman wondered incredulously.

Frankie's Bambox swung by his side as he ran, his headphones tightly wrapped to his head and his free hand pulsing with energy—he had to clench his fist to contain it. Herman couldn't see it, but Frankie was still smirking.

"This playlist really gets me going, man!" He said. "Let's nab one of these—"

With one swoop, they were trapped. A man and a woman had leaped around either side of them, giving them nowhere to run.

They weren't the least bit theatrical like the Thespian. Both of their appearances screamed that of advanced gym memberships. Their bodies were covered from head to toe with thick muscle and fake tans. The guy's jaw couldn't get much squarer and his black hair had at least a fistful of hair gel in it. The woman's bleach-blonde hair was pinned back in a ponytail and her lips had clearly had a Botox injection. On top of it all, they both wore top-of-the-line tank tops, shorts, and lifting shoes.

What the...? Herman thought. *Does every superhuman burglar in this town have a theme?*

Frankie squinted his eyes. "Gym closes at midnight, douchebags."

Chet laughed as he gazed down on Herman and Frankie. "Look at his leather jacket! That's so gay. I bet you don't even have a motorcycle."

"That's a really insensitive use of that word," Frankie sneered. His free hand was sparking. "Your mom didn't teach you to be very polite, did she?"

Chet sneered. "No. But I could tell you what *your* mom taught me."

Nikki laughed. "I think he wants to whack you with his hammer, Chet!"

Frankie's hand twitched. "I'm the one you should worry about."

Bam!

Frankie fired a blast, but Chet dodged with lighting speed. The blast exploded a light several yards away and Chet lunged forward, thrusting out his arm and grabbing Frankie by the wrist.

Frankie struggled to break free, and as he did, his eyes grew wide. A shimmering silver liquid was growing on Chet's arms, starting at his knuckles and moving upward. The liquid hardened and glimmered in the fluorescent light and didn't stop until it reached his elbows.

That's when he smirked at Frankie. Frankie gulped.

Wham!

The uppercut launched Frankie over Herman's head. He crashed into a shelf, sending boxes flying and bending the metal shelf in half. Herman's eyes popped.

Metal hands, he thought. *Okay, good to know.*

Suddenly, he heard Nikki heave from behind him. He ducked reflexively and felt a whoosh just inches above his head. He spun about to see Nikki half-crouched with the same metallic substance coating her calves and feet.

Metallic feet! He thought. *Also good to know!*

"Hey!" Frankie shouted.

Frankie had recovered. Herman dashed aside just in time for one of Frankie's blasts to slam into Nikki, sending her hurtling into Chet. Together, they toppled into a shelf, gathered themselves, then darted off in separate directions.

"Whoa, they're fast!" Frankie said, scrambling to his feet. "Look alive, HF!"

"*Jeff?*" Herman repeated.

"No, HF! Short for Hammerfist!"

"It sounds like 'hey Jeff.'"

"*Oh my gosh, who cares?*"

Meanwhile, Cassie and the Thespian were duking it out by the television sets. As Cassie controlled the hovering brick with her mind, the Thespian rebounded every attack with tiny electrical bolts.

"Must we both fight and give battle like so? There are other paths to adventure, you know!" The Thespian jeered as he blocked another blow. "Thy fire of combat is bright in thine eyes! Join us instead, and to hell with *those* guys!"

"Hard pass," Cassie seethed as she launched another attack. "I'm a lot of things but I'm not a criminal. Tell me why all of you are working together and maybe I won't smash your face. How did you get your powers?"

"Aha, but my child, we have only begun!" The Thespian parried again. "Keep up this fight, and we'll have us some fun!"

Suddenly, the Thespian ducked from Cassie's hurtling brick and shot a bolt directly at her. She cried out as the lightning seared her shoulder. Reeling backward, she clutched her arm as she fell onto her back.

The Thespian readied his finger gun one more time, pointing it at Cassie's heart, sparks beginning to ignite from his fingertip. Cassie discretely jerked her fingertips, which pelted her brick to the back of his head.

Crack! The Thespian's body slackened and he slumped to the ground, unconscious.

Massaging her rapidly-healing burn, Cassie got to her feet and said, "Sparring is such sweet sorrow."

Several yards away, Susan was dealing with problems of her own.

"Don't you have school tomorrow?" she said with a raised eyebrow.

"*How dare you speak to the mighty Demonspawn with such flippancy!*"

"Uh-huh?"

He only had to be about fifteen—the boy staring her down. He brandished a novelty shop katana in both hands, then crouched down and scowled with the utmost intensity. Black, greasy hair fell to his eyes and his pale, stringy body was bare except for some baggy black jeans with a chain hanging from the beltloops.

"You should put that down," Susan said, pointing to the katana.

"Do not underestimate me," the kid uttered dramatically.

He lashed forward, swinging the katana. It failed to connect with Susan on the swipe. Instead, Susan spun out of the way and shoved her knee into his stomach. He loudly coughed before doubling over, his katana clanging to the ground. Susan scooped it up.

"*Hey!*" he yelled. "That was, like, eighty dollars!"

"This thing isn't even sharp," she said as she held it up to her face. "Who are your parents? Go home, kid."

"I am the master of my own destiny," Demonspawn clenched his fist. "And you will pay for your insolence!"

He inhaled sharply, his lungs inflating like balloons. Susan dropped the katana and planted her feet, unclear of what to make of this move. Then Demonspawn roared.

A jet of fire erupted from his mouth. She gasped and she rolled out of the way, tossing the soccer ball at Demonspawn's stomach. The ball connected excellently, cocking Demonspawn's head forward, making him cough.

The ball found its way back to Susan and she said, "Looks like somebody forgot to brush."

Outside aisle twelve, Frankie sent blasts through the air toward Nikki, who was effortlessly dodging and deflecting each blow with her metal legs, making shelves and lights explode across the room. As she was upon Frankie, she threw a punch that he narrowly blocked with his Bambox. He kept his momentum and spun around, shooting her with another blast. Finally, he landed a shot. She soared a dozen yards away and painfully toppled behind the front counter, metal legs flailing.

Chet continued to pommel Herman in short bursts—quick punches aimed at the face or stomach or kidneys—and Herman barely deflected each strike with his hammer. Chet began laughing before each hit, throwing in taunts whenever he could.

"Not doing so hot, Hammerhead!" "Come on, fight back!" "Take that back to the hardware store!"

Herman growled and bore his teeth. *How am I supposed to beat this guy? Even without his metal fists, he's freaking huge! All I've got is my one hammer to block his punches, there's no way I could—*

It was then, just over Chet's shoulder, that he noticed a blur quickly advancing on them. The surprise on his face must have been evident, because it made Chet turn around.

Whoosh!

Chet tripped and belly flopped onto the floor, letting out a painful cough. Herman's eyes darted about, looking for the blur, but he could barely see above the aisles.

Whoosh!

There it was again! This time, the blur stopped in front of him —but it was a person. The kid had to be his same age. He had dark brown skin, thick, black hair in a buzz cut, and the darkest of brown eyes. Aside from that, he wore high-top sneakers, jeans, and a t-shirt that read "Mama G's Thrift Shop".

His eyes scanned Herman up and down before saying, "Hm. So this is what he's got you doing?"

Whoosh!

The kid was gone. In his wake, Chet's hands were tied behind his back and a rope around his mouth kept his lips from moving. Within a matter of seconds, yelps were heard around the electronics store from Nikki, Demonspawn, and the Thespian. All of them had been bound and gagged; out of commission and restrained.

The blur shot across the room and out the broken window. The scuffles stopped. No more fists connecting, smashing metal, or broken glass—just the eerie quiet of a devastated electronics store, thinly tainted by the muffled complaints of B-class supervillains.

Herman's mouth was agape. "That was Tyler, wasn't it?"

"Was it? I don't know," Frankie said as he pulled the headphones off his head. "But if he was super fast and wasn't one of the bad guys, it probably was. Probably thinks he's too cool for us. He sure made things easier, though."

Herman blinked a couple of times. Tyler had been here and gone in a matter of seconds, and he did the work so much better than all of them combined. He was *fast!* Add that to the list of special powers that Herman didn't have. He couldn't help but look down at the hammer attached to his wrist. It had several scratches in it from blocking Chet's fists. Herman traced a couple of the scratches with his fingernail.

"Hey!" Frankie said as he lifted up Chet by his hair. "Let's interrogate some fools before the cops show up!" He dropped Chet's head to the floor. Chet let out a muffled whine. "I bet they'll be here any minute."

"Oh, right!"

Everybody dragged their bounty to the center of the floor and propped their backs up against each other. After briefly debating who the victim should be, everyone agreed that the teenager would be the best bet. Susan ripped the rope off Demonspawn's mouth. The kid gasped and coughed before glaring at his conquerors.

"I shall have my vengeance!" He cried.

He sharply inhaled and his chest grew as much as the ropes allowed. Before he could finish, Susan slammed her soccer ball in his face. A few wispy flames fell from his lips.

"*Ow!*" he whined.

"Try it again," Susan lobbed her ball in the air casually.

Cassie grabbed Demonspawn by the collar. "Where did you guys get your powers?"

Demonspawn said nothing. He simply glared, eyes full of fire. Cassie bristled.

"*Where?*" she bellowed as she leaned her face mere inches away from his. "Was it someone at the hospital? How long ago? *Tell us!*"

"You don't know who bestowed your gifts upon you?" Demonspawn's words slithered from his lips. "Such a shame... not knowing... it must be killing you..."

Susan rolled her eyes. "Almost as much as your theatrics."

Cassie flipped around to face Herman, then said, "Smash his face."

"*What?* Come on," Herman said, taking a step back. "He's defenseless right now! I'm not going to hit him."

As Cassie and Herman vigorously debated the moral and ethical implications of assaulting an unarmed criminal, Frankie's eyes jumped between the two of them. He looked at his watch, then glared at Demonspawn, who readily glared back.

Frankie smiled. He stepped forward and slipped his headphones onto Demonspawn's ears, making sure they were nice and snug. He turned on the Bambox, clicked a few buttons on his playlist, and cranked up the volume.

For a few seconds, Demonspawn held a fiery gaze. Then he started to sweat. Then he bore his teeth. Then he started to squirm. Then he started to sweat and grimace and squirm harder. Sounds that were somewhere between a growl and a moan impulsively escaped his mouth.

This caught Cassie and Herman's attention. Frankie casually held his Bambox in both hands just a couple feet away. Susan was already looking on with a cocked eyebrow. She drummed her fingers on her soccer ball.

She said, "What are you doing to him?"

"Honestly, he's just listening to bluegrass," Frankie shrugged. "He didn't seem the type, and *oh boy* was I right."

"*I will not betray Alpha Master!*" Demonspawn finally shouted. "Stop this accursed, twangy torture or you will die slowly by my blade!"

"Alpha Master, huh?" Frankie said as he turned up the volume. "That's a cute nickname. Tell me more."

Demonspawn howled. "He gives us the Green Juice! *Now unhand me* before I rip out your beating heart and devour it—"

"Now that's just uncivilized. How about that Green Juice, though?"

"You've got company!" Sid hollered in their earpieces. "The police will be there in approximately sixty seconds! Time to leave!"

"But we've barely got anything from this guy!" Herman shouted and pointed to Demonspawn.

"Don't be stupid," Cassie shot. "Let's *go!*"

"*You're* the one who wanted—!"

95

"Let's *goooo!*"

They all darted for the broken window, weaving through aisles and jumping over the broken electronics strewn throughout the floor. One by one, they slipped gracefully out of the window and touched down on the sidewalk—all except for Herman, who fumbled to the cement. He hustled back to his feet and followed the others as they quickly climbed a fire escape on a building just less than a block away. The bars and steps clinked and clanked as they ascended, and from the rooftop, they saw everything.

The police showed up with red and blue lights barreling down the street. Half a dozen cop cars screeched to a halt and officers began piling out with guns drawn. Several officers went in to investigate, and after a minute, began dragging Chet, Nikki, the Thespian, and Demonspawn out of the building.

One of them started to struggle, then another, then the others. The baddies managed to get the ropes off their bodies and several officers tried to take them down. Shouts echoed off the surrounding buildings. Cops were thrown dozens feet apart like ragdolls. Some officers opened fire, and it was then that all four of the baddies managed to slip away and peel off, disappearing into the night. Most of the cop cars went after them with sirens blaring while a few stuck around to investigate the scene and help the injured. It all happened in a matter of minutes.

"You know," Herman began. "I kind of feel bad for breaking all that stuff. The baddies were probably going to steal a lot of gear, but we made the store a wreck. Maybe we did more bad than good."

"Dude, don't think of it like that," Frankie shook his head. "We got the information we need to help us shut them down. We're one step closer."

"I guess," Herman said quietly. He was silent for a second before he added, "The cops couldn't handle those guys at all."

"That means they'll keep looking out for anyone with powers like them," Susan said. She turned to the others. "Including us."

"And what about this Alpha Master guy?" Herman said. "And the Green Juice?"

"You don't know it's a guy," Cassie said.

Herman didn't say anything.

"It doesn't matter if it's a guy or not," Susan replied firmly. "But whoever they are is clearly the distributor here. Alpha Master and the Green Juice must be behind our conditions as well somehow. It's obvious. We find Alpha Master and let the police can crack down on him *or her*"—Cassie glared—"then we can go back to our lives."

"Okay, yeah, but," Frankie said. "How are the cops gonna handle this Alpha Master character if they can't handle a bunch of amateur villains like these guys? Are we gonna have to take him down ourselves?"

8

It was nearly three o'clock in the morning, and not a light was on in apartment 329. Milky white moonlight slid into the room through the cracks in the blinds. Outside, the soft noise of a restless city filled the streets. The soft clomping of footsteps could be heard just outside the door. They gradually came closer, and after a few moments, a key was inserted into the lock and the door slowly creaked open.

Dusty orange breezeway light seeped into the living room as Herman Fitzgerald crept inside. The door inched to a close behind him and he gingerly twisted the door handle to make as little noise as possible. An old backpack containing a detachable hammer and a flimsy mask was slung over his back.

Click. "Hey, Herman."

Herman nearly jolted out of his skin. A lamp on the opposite side of the room had suddenly flipped on as soon as the door had closed. Next to it, Zach sat on the couch, the lamplight throwing harsh shadows across his face. Herman's heart was still thumping loudly, but he tried to sound collected.

"Zach. Hey. What are you doing up so late? It's like, three in the morning."

"I was about to ask you the same thing," Zach said. "Where were you?"

Herman paused. "I was just down in the fitness center, doing some running."

"Wearing a leather jacket in the middle of the night?"

"I like the resistance. And I couldn't sleep anyway."

Zach's eyes continued to dig into Herman. "How's Abby?"

"Who?"

"Your girlfriend!"

Herman's mind was blank. He imagined himself holding hands at some romantic restaurant with a frizzy, red-haired girl with pale skin and freckles. Then he remembered the awkward conversation he had with Zach just recently.

"Oh, right! Abby Gale!" Herman stammered. "Uh... yeah. She's good. We're good. She's great, actually."

Zach's eyes dug harder and his face creased into a skeptical scowl. He twiddled his thumbs as his hands sat in his lap. A cold sweat started to form on Herman's brow.

"What were you guys doing?" Zach probed.

What would a guy normally be doing with his girlfriend this late? Herman thought. There was only one thing that came to mind, and it definitely was not what he was doing. But he decided to run with it anyway. He pulled his face into a frown and flared his nostrils.

"None of your business," he shot coarsely.

Instantly, Zach's demeanor changed. "Whoa, hey man," he began. "I'm sorry. I didn't know you were so touchy about your love life—"

"*Touchy* about my *love life*?" Herman said. "You think that's funny, don't you?"

Zach's face burned red. "Wait, no—I didn't mean it like—"

"You're a piece, you know that?" Herman scoffed. "I'm going to bed."

On that note, he stormed off. It seemed like an opportune moment to escape. Down the hall, smoke was wafting slowly from Bridger's room and Adam's room was unoccupied as usual. The door to his room slammed shut as soon as he crossed through the threshold.

Herman let out a mighty sigh. The room was dark and his feet caught a lot of dirty clothes as he pushed them across the floor. He flipped the blinds shut before he threw his backpack at the foot of his bed and single-handedly changed into some pajamas. He threw his discarded clothes, which were untouched by sweat, on the ground before he collapsed onto his bed in a heap, staring at the ceiling.

At this point, any normal person would fall asleep in a few seconds, but Herman's eyes didn't get heavy. They remained locked on the beige ceiling, his hand and his hook resting on his chest.

Okay, Herman, let's reflect for a minute, he thought. *It's been a couple days. You told Sid that you would give this a shot for a little while. And what's happened? You've had a few fights. Did they go well? Yeah, I guess. I mean, I didn't get badly hurt or anything. But that's hard with this condition.*

What about the baddies? Did you manage to stop any? Well, no. They all got away each time. I only stopped some that first night when those guys tried to mug me. But these other guys from the other two nights are just like me. They have powers and everything. And they're coming from something called Green Juice being made someone named Alpha Master.

Whoa, he sat up in bed. *I really am a superhero right now. I mean, there's even a supervillain and everything! And I'm fighting his cronies on the regular and coming out alive each time! This is insane!*

He smirked about it, and then the smirk dropped as quickly as it formed.

This is totally insane. Is all this really worth it just to pay the rent and get the hospital bills paid? Aunt Josie would be mortified to hear about this. She wouldn't care about the money —she would just want me to be safe.

His heart dropped into his stomach at the thought.

Where is this going to end, then? What if I get killed? But could that really happen? Would it?

He rested his head back on his pillow and pulled the blanket up over his shoulders. But he didn't sleep. All he could do was continue to stare at the ceiling, wondering.

*

In his hand, Herman carried grocery bags filled with cookies, potato chips, chocolate milk, candy, and one bag of baby carrots. He figured that if he didn't need nutrients and energy that comes from eating food, he might as well eat whatever he wanted. As soon as the sun rose, he put on some decent clothes, grabbed some cash from Sid's latest payout, and took the bus to the nearest grocery store.

The climb back up to apartment 329 was quiet and unassuming. Herman found himself looking around a lot more when he was home at his apartment complex. Mostly to see if Cassie was around anywhere. Not surprisingly, she was never anywhere to be seen.

She definitely seems like the type of person that avoids other people, he thought.

Herman transferred all his grocery bags to his hook as he fumbled in his pocket for his keys. As he unlocked the door, he looked down at the hook, which currently toted about eight grocery bags, and smiled.

Silver lining.

He pushed the door open. All of his roommates would be gone this morning, which means he would have the place to himself. And that was something he was looking forward to. But when he opened the door, he instantly stopped. He couldn't help but stare with incredulity at the figure that was sprawled across his couch, wearing a hoodie and a brand new pair of Jordans. As soon as the door was fully opened, the person on the couch sat up with glee.

"Hey, big guy!" Frankie Chan said happily. "Check 'em out! The Retro 1's! I could never afford these kicks until I started doing this!"

"Frankie, how did you get in my house?" Herman accused.

Frankie scratched his head sheepishly. "The window. I found a song that makes me hover really slowly, so I just let it carry me until I reached the top. Hopefully no one was watching. *That* would be weird to see."

Herman's eyes darted to the window. The third-floor window was open with the blinds in disarray. He shook his head. "But how did you even know where I *live?*"

"Come on dude, you know our earpieces have trackers in them. I guess you decided to leave yours at home when you went shopping." Frankie glanced at the groceries hanging on Herman's hook. "Now *those are* the spoils of a man who knows what he wants."

Herman couldn't help but smile as he closed the door. "I'm running to test to see if I can get fat while fighting crime."

Frankie laughed. "Hey. I've got an idea. I asked Susan and Cassie if they wanted to come try this thing with me tonight and they said no. Cassie has to study for a quiz and Susan is just responsible and intelligent."

"When have we ever done anything that isn't responsible or intelligent?"

Frankie leaned forward. "You and I? We're going roof jumping tonight."

*

The sky was splashed with dark hues of purple and green, painted by a waning sun over a city rife with air pollution. The glass skyscrapers skewed the view of the sunset, which would have been a lot prettier if Herman knew it wasn't caused by all the strange chemicals in the sky. Car horns, police sirens, and shouts echoed distantly off the walls of Citytown.

He sat on the sidewalk and drummed on his legs, paying little attention to the people who entered and exited the Burger Boy food shack. A shiny new watch was slung across his wrist—an apology gift from Zach for the night before. As he sat on the curb, he noticed how scuffed and dirty his sneakers had gotten in the past week and wondered how much worse they'll get. He looked at his watch, which read 8:55. Frankie said he'd be off at nine.

He continued to drum on his legs. The smell of bacon burgers and cheesy fries was tempting to his nostrils but didn't make his stomach growl. He would have bought a meal in a heartbeat if he had remembered to take any of his cash with him.

At length, Frankie Chan threw the door open from the kitchen, exiting into the smoggy night air. He swiftly untied his apron and stuffed it in a backpack, which also housed his

Bambox. He saw Herman and did a swift upward nod of recognition.

"Hey, Lefty!" he said. "Sorry I couldn't get off sooner. We got busy."

"It's okay."

Instead of walking out to meet Herman, Frankie dipped back inside. Herman blinked. After only a few seconds, Frankie emerged again with two small baskets of cheesy fries in hand. He trudged over and handed one to Herman.

"Share my spoils," he said.

They started walking down the street and Herman devoured the fries in just a couple of minutes. They were perfectly salty, cheesy, and crispy. His forearm had to cradle the basket against his chest while he ate with his left hand. "These are really good. Do you get them for free?"

"I get two food items free every time I have a shift," Frankie said as he licked his fingers. "Anything but the daily specials or the triple-double pepper jack and bacon jalapeno burger. So, I eat free, like, three times a week."

"Why do you still work here?" Herman couldn't help but asked as he threw his empty fry basket in a nearby trash can. "It's not like you need the money right now." He wiped his salty fingers on his jeans.

"Yeah," Frankie replied thoughtfully. "But I'm also not going to be super forever. I'll still need a job when I stop knocking heads every night, right?"

Herman hummed. "I hadn't thought about that."

Frankie ate slowly as they walked side by side, savoring every fry's flavors. Herman's one hand remained in his pocket while his hook arm swung by his side. The homeless urchins of downtown Citytown were starting to set up camp for the night, huddling into corners with their sleeping bags and shopping carts full of discarded treasures. Herman tried not to stare at them as he thought of people staring at his arm.

"So what's your deal, Herman?" Frankie said as he deposited his empty fry basket into another passing trash can. "Where are you from and what brought you to Citytown?"

"I'm from Gladview," Herman said. "It's just a small town a couple of hours away from here. My aunt helped save up what money she could so she could send me to college after my mom died. She's a waitress, so that wasn't much. That brought me to the Triple C."

"I'm sorry man," Frankie said, looking into the alley ways as they walked by. "What about your dad?"

"I've never met him. My mom got pregnant with me on prom night of her senior year. I think his name was Ryan or something."

"And he didn't want to step up and be a dad? Wow. That's why you keep your pecker in your pocket, dude."

Herman smirked. "What about your family? I know your mom teaches at the Triple C."

"Yeah. My dad is a stockbroker and my mom teaches music history. I'm a third generation immigrant from the Philippines."

"Cool."

"Thanks," Frankie said. "Here. This one looks good."

Immediately, Frankie veered into an alleyway, headed straight for a fire escape that ascended the height of a small building only a couple stories tall. The fire escape shook and creaked as Frankie started climbing. Herman looked around. No one was watching. And honestly, if they did, people probably wouldn't care anyway. He followed Frankie's lead and climbed the fire escape to the top.

When they reached the top, Frankie stood on the edge of the building and looked down to the alley below. Herman straightened his jacket and asked, "So… is roof jumping like one of those cop chase things from a TV show? Like, jumping from roof to roof?"

Frankie didn't take his eyes off the ground. "Nope."

Herman stared quizzically for a moment before Frankie gave him a snide grin. Frankie asked, "Have you ever broken a bone since the accident?"

"I don't think so," Herman said.

"Good."

With that, Frankie jumped.

"*Whoa!*" Herman shouted before he darted to the roof's edge. He reached the edge and looked down just in time to see Frankie hit the pavement. He didn't collapse in a heap, but landed feet-first, staggering a bit before steadying himself on a wall. He hopped around for a bit as if he twisted his ankle.

"*Ooowww!*" his whine echoed off the walls.

"Are you alright?" Herman hollered down.

"Yeah, I'm fine, I just landed weird!" Frankie said. "But that's two stories! You could never have done that a couple of weeks ago! You try!"

Herman shook his head. "No way."

"Come on!"

"Pass."

"But I already did it!"

"I don't care."

"Don't be a wuss!"

"Omigosh, *fine!*"

Herman put his hand on the edge and took a deep breath, staring down at Frankie's expectant eyes two stories below. He mumbled the word "idiot" to himself before he planted one foot on the edge, heaved, and jumped.

It was exhilarating: gravity greedily pulled his body toward the earth's surface, air snapping through his hair and jacket. The sensation would have been terrifying last week, but since he knew he probably wouldn't get hurt, it was nothing but thrilling.

After a few euphoric seconds, Herman's feet touched ground. The impact rocked his knees and ankles and his bones felt as though they might buckle, but they stayed as rigid and rock-solid as ever. He staggered briefly before falling backwards onto his butt, looking up at Frankie and laughing.

"That was awesome!" Herman said as Frankie helped him up. "We're going to do that again, right?"

"Oh yeah," Frankie said. "But this time, we're gonna find a *three*-story building."

They progressively found taller and taller buildings as the night went on, jumping off and marveling at how quickly they recovered from their falls. On the six-story building, Herman landed wrong and finally broke his ankles, but Frankie shoved them back into place and he was walking on them after a couple minutes of tearful, teeth-gritting pain.

At the seven-story building, Frankie learned how to slide down adjacent alley walls to minimize his fall. Herman followed suit. They finally stopped at a ten-story skyscraper, especially since they noticed Citytown Police officers walking down the street just below. Frankie and Herman both sat at the top of the building with their feet dangling over the edge.

"You know," Frankie began. "I don't think these powers are all that bad. Like, we never could be doing this as our normal selves. Yet, here we are. Sometimes I have these moments where I don't even want the antidote."

"I thought you totally wanted to go back to normal?"

"Oh, for real, I do," Frankie continued. "But the perks with these powers are pretty dope. Never falling asleep in class, never getting hungry, *jumping off buildings*... there is one thing I miss, though."

"What?"

"Dreaming."

Herman stared. Frankie's eyes were distant as he stared at the ground below, his hands stuffed in his hoodie pockets.

"Isn't it crazy what your brain does when you're sleeping? Your mind makes things *on the fly* that could never exist, and you're right in the middle of it. It's like your brain is sending you on mini adventures and you have no idea how it's going to end. You can hang out with people you've never met, go places you've never been to, even see people that have died... and it's all in your head. But it only happens while you're asleep." He paused. "I've missed that."

Herman just nodded. After a moment, he said, "Yeah."

"I still want a cure, though," Frankie shrugged. "I'll probably take the antidote when Sid figures it out. Or whenever we find Alpha Master, if they actually have an antidote."

"How long do you think that'll be?"

"Beats me," Frankie continued. "But the goons can't hide everything from us for long. We'll figure it out." He looked at Herman. "What do you think of the others? Do you like our team?"

"Yeah, I like them," Herman said. "We're all so different, but we get along. Susan is really nice. I'm still trying to figure out Cassie, though."

"She's a stone-cold ginger, man," Frankie said. "I've tried hanging out with her like this so I could get to know her, but she's turned me down every time. No lame excuses or anything —just no. She just likes to keep to herself do her own thing. She also doesn't like telling people about herself."

"Mmhm. So what do you think it would take to get on her good side?"

Frankie shrugged again. "I dunno." He smirked at Herman. "You're into her, aren't you?"

Herman flushed bright red. "What? No! I mean, I barely know her."

"It's okay to admit it, homie!" Frankie said. "Your secret is safe with me. I'm down with redheads, too."

"You're an idiot," Herman said as he shook his head, avoided eye contact, and tried not to smile.

"You should take her on a date. But ask her when I'm there. I want to see her face."

"I told you, I'm not into her."

"You're lying, though."

"I'm gonna push you off this building."

Frankie laughed. Still trying not to smile, Herman swung around and retreated from the building's edge, headed toward the fire escape. The sunset had long gone and the sky was filling with endless black. The neon lights of Citytown were lit up below them. Herman took a deep breath as he soaked it all in, knowing that there might be some store getting robbed as they speak.

"I'm gonna get going," Herman said. "I promised my roommate that I would go with him to get some sushi. But you've got me in your earpiece. Give me a buzz if you want me to come help fight crime later tonight. I should be available in a couple of hours."

"Cool."

With that, Herman started descending the fire escape. But before he could get too far, Frankie said, "Hey, Herman."

Herman looked up. Frankie still hadn't moved from where he was, overlooking the city, sitting over the edge of the building. He looked directly at Herman as he spoke.

"All of us on our little superhero squad have always kind of done our own thing. Cassie's totally antisocial, I know I can be kind of annoying, and you seem like a more quiet kind of guy. Susan is just a mom. But what I'm saying is that even though we're all different, we've got each other's backs. You don't ever have to feel like you don't have anyone, okay?"

Herman looked down, then looked up, and said, "Thanks Frankie."

Herman descended the fire escape at his own pace. He waited until he had climbed a few stories down before he jumped off.

9

"Hello, Herman!"

"Hi, Mac."

Herman plopped down in the seat behind Mac the bus driver. It was already ten o'clock, so he was late to meet up with the others for crime fighting. The backpack containing his hammer rested by his feet under the seat. It clanked on the floor, and silently, he hoped Mac didn't notice and get too curious.

"Off to the arcade with your friends?" Mac asked.

"Yep. You got it."

Herman had gotten into the habit of slipping into the arcade whenever the 831 bus dropped him off downtown. He would wait until the bus pulled away before leaving the arcade and trudging across the street for Citytown Central Park. Truthfully, he had never spent a dime in that arcade. He just didn't want to have to tell Mac what was really going on.

"If you don't mind me asking," Mac began as he looked at Herman in the rear-view mirror. "Is it hard to play those games with your hand?"

Herman thought about it, then shook his head. "It's not bad. It's just pushing one button at a time."

"I used to hold the high score for Bone Crunchers back in my day!" Mac said.

"Retro! Very cool."

Frankly, he looked forward to these laidback chats with Mac the bus driver every night. It was a refreshing release from the danger that he knew he faced around the corner. And it was hard not to feel comfortable around Mac with his colorful sweaters and parted hair.

Finally, the bus screeched to a halt and flatulated its hydraulic hiss as it sunk to the ground. The doors flung open and Mac wished Herman a good night. Herman returned the gesture and hopped off the bus, headed straight for the arcade. The bus didn't linger once Herman stepped off. It lurched to a crawl and quickly picked up speed as it merged with the rest of Citytown traffic.

Inside the arcade, Herman hovered around the machines for only a moment as he watched the bus elevate and roll away. Satisfied that it was out of sight, he crossed the floor and put his hand on the door.

At that moment, an associate at the counter said, "*Ugh*, are you ever going to play anything?"

Herman glared at him. He looked exactly like the pimply dull server from Won Ton King Kong a few nights before. But he didn't care. Herman pushed the door open and exited into the polluted Citytown air.

Less than a minute later, Herman was striding across the green grass of Citytown Central Park. His eyes darted about. Nothing unusual so far, just some drunken wanderers and a homeless man laying out by the pond with his pack. Herman found a tree to lean against and tapped his ear. "Hammerfist reporting."

"You're late," Cassie said irritably in his earpiece.

"Cut him some slack, Ginger Witch," Frankie's voice chimed in. "If you've got beef, you can *hammer* it out with him later."

"GB, you're cute sometimes, but that joke got old days ago," Susan's voice came in his ear.

"Aaww, Mom, you think I'm cute?" Frankie said. "If it doesn't work out with you and Clint, I'm all yours. HF, I'm sitting on the bench about fifty yards away from your nine o'clock."

"I see you. Anything suspicious yet?"

"Negatory," Frankie said in response. "It's been surprisingly quiet. Then again, most of these places have gotten broken into already. Maybe the Green Juice goons have gotten smart and are looking for other targets."

"Guys, I think I see something," Cassie's said. "The alleyway by the nail salon. East side."

Herman's eyes darted to that direction to see three large characters in hoodies lurking at the mouth of an alleyway. They leaned against the brick walls, puffing cigarettes and looking around suspiciously.

Herman's eyebrows furrowed. "I've got a visual." It was at that moment that an innocent passerby in a tan trench coat strolled by the alleyway, his face to the ground. In a flash, the three thugs struck out from their perch and grabbed the man, dragging him into the alleyway.

"They grabbed the guy!" Herman said, ripping the hammer from his backpack. "Omigosh, I think those guys tried to mug me last week! I'm gonna get them!"

"Wait!" Susan said. "We should wait for one of the Green Juice guys! This is small game! And you haven't even put on your mask yet!"

"Crime is crime, Susan!" Herman said, clicking his hammer onto his wrist.

"I'm coming!" Frankie said. "There might be more of them."

"On my way," Cassie said.

"Fine!" Susan conceded.

The four of them converged just before they bolted across the street, weaving through cars that wailed their horns at them as they went. Cassie's brick floated inches from her hand. Frankie's Bambox bumped jams into his headphones. Susan juggled her soccer ball as she sped across the asphalt.

As they busted into the alleyway, they saw the three thugs and the victim several feet away, but the victim wasn't being beaten, threatened, or robbed. He stood with the three thugs, staring intently at the mouth of the alleyway, almost like they were awaiting something. They continued to stare as Herman and his friends approached.

Herman narrowed his eyes. "What the—?"

Then, in a flash, all the thugs and the trench coat man whipped out handguns from their pockets and pointed them at Herman and the others. The one in the trench coat bellowed at them:

"*Freeze, CPD! Put your hands where I can see them!*"

"What is he—" Herman began. But before he could finish, blue and red lights flashed into the alleyway. He and the others flipped around to see nearly a dozen more police officers at the mouth of the alley with guns drawn, all pointed at them. Herman exchanged glances with them. Frankie was flabbergasted while Susan clenched her jaw and shook her head. Cassie could have blown steam out of her ears. Defeated, all of them dropped their weapons and slowly raised their hands in the air.

"Sid," Herman whispered. "We've got a problem."

*

"Don't mention your real names. Find your communicators and weapons asap, but wait for my signal. I'll think of something."

Those were the instructions that Sid gave to the crew before they were all handcuffed and shoved into police cars. All of them were separated and stayed separated after they all arrived at the 12th Citytown Police Precinct. As the police cars barreled through the streets, sirens blaring, Herman's heart couldn't stop pounding.

Holy crap, I just blew it big time, he thought. *Arrested! Prison! What are they going to have me for? Destruction of private property? Trespassing? Assault? All the above? I knew this was all a big, stupid, freaking mistake. Aunt Josie is going to be devastated when she hears about this...*

The car screeched to a halt in front of the police station and Herman was hoisted out of the car. An officer forced him forward by the handcuffs while a few more officers followed behind and watched closely.

They pushed their way through an overcrowded precinct, overflowing with criminals big and small. Loads of officers and felons alike stared at the hammer attached to Herman's wrist as he was forcefully escorted through the building. The white noise of shuffling paperwork and keyboards typing were everywhere, accompanied by the chattering of police officers and blaring phones ringing. The aroma of donuts and stale coffee was pungent in every room.

A lot of things happened in a short period of time. Some officers took his picture and collected fingerprints and asked him for his name. After refusing to say his name several times, they noticed the communicator in his ear. They yanked it out, grabbed his arms, and hauled him away to somewhere else.

The last place Herman found himself was a small brick room with a large window and a metal table bolted to the floor. In the corner against the ceiling, an old tube TV set was fastened into the wall. He was commanded to sit down as an officer handcuffed him to the table. The officer unclicked his hammer carefully after he did so, placing it on the opposite end of the table along with Herman's in-ear communicator. Herman stared at it, then stared at his reflection in the window. He knew there had to be officers watching him on the other side.

How in the world is Sid going to get us out of this mess? He thought.

"The detective will be in soon," the officer said. "And he's gonna have a lot of questions for you, freak."

Herman didn't say anything. The officer slammed the door as he left the room.

He looked down at his handcuffs. One was around his left wrist, but the officer had to loop the other end through his prosthetic hook. Could he break them? Maybe. Best not to try it, though. There would be dozens of cops in here within seconds. Have to wait for the signal.

Then he gazed at his reflection in the one-way window. His crystalline blue eyes were a little harder than they used to be. But were those the eyes of a criminal now? All he was doing was trying to do was help people and pay off his hospital bills so his aunt wouldn't have to worry. He was just trying to get by. Was that so wrong?

That was when the door unlatched and flew open.

A man with stony grey eyes marched in, his tie loose and a handgun holstered by his hip. His grisly five o'clock shadow wrapped around a strong jaw and his face scowled mightily. Thick blood veins stretched around his burly forearms beneath his rolled-up sleeves. Everything about him would have screamed intimidation if he weren't five feet tall.

Blam!

He kicked over the chair on the opposite side of Herman's table, sending it toppling across the room into the brick wall.

Herman eyed him. He had never been face to face with such an angry cop before. The officer saw Herman's hammer at the edge of the table and picked it up, swinging it around curiously. He glared at Herman.

"You must think you're pretty hot stuff, swinging this around every night, smashing up those theatrical bastards, don't you?"

Herman said nothing.

Blam! The officer slammed the hammer on the table.

"So why?" he continued. "Do you just like beating up kooks? Think it's fun?"

Herman still said nothing. The cop leaned in.

"I'm Norm Axewielder, but you can call me *sir*," he said slowly, the veins in his neck popping. "I've been in the service for over twenty years and I've never seen a group of freaks like I've seen over the past month. We've got fighting stage actors, hip hop nerds, and now a cripple that swings around a prosthetic hammer.

"One thing I've noticed, though," he continued. "Is that not all of you freaks are bad. There are some that try to steal stuff, and others that try to stop that from happening. You're one of the good ones."

Again, Herman didn't open his mouth.

"I have security footage of four perps breaking into an electronics store two nights ago to steal a bunch of goods... but you and your friends stopped them," Detective Axewielder said.

At that moment, he pulled a remote from his pocket and clicked a button. The tube TV flashed on. Then Herman watched clips of security footage from the electronics store the other night. The footage was fuzzy, so you could hardly make out faces, but he could figure out who was who as he watched fights unfold. He watched as Ghetto Blaster got launched a dozen feet in the air by Chet's punch. He saw Demonspawn breathe fire at

Soccer Mom. He saw Ginger Witch knock the Thespian out cold. He watched himself parry and dodge Chet's blows as his fists crashed into the store shelves.

"You damaged *a lot* of private property," Detective Axewielder continued. "But I can see that you all are trying to do a good thing. And that's why I'm willing to drop your charges if you're willing to cooperate."

Herman looked into his eyes. Detective Axewielder's stony greys were still as stony and grey as ever, probing, trying to read what was going on in Herman's head. Herman's eyes were cold as they fixed on the detective.

"We can't find your prints anywhere in the system," Detective Axewielder said. "Facial recognition isn't working either. The photos of your mugshots keep deleting themselves as soon as we upload them. I don't know how you're doing it, but everything we have on you and your little friends is gone—like you never existed. That's why I'm prepared to keep you here for as long as I need... and you're going to answer some questions."

Herman scrunched his eyebrows. *I don't exist? Nothing on Herman Fitzgerald? That means they have no idea who I really am or where I live. This is actually great for now. Sid probably managed to get into their system somehow.*

Detective Axewielder leaned forward and his tone became deathly. "You're going to start by telling me exactly who you are."

Herman paused, then, with a smirk, said, "I'm Hammerfist."

Detective Axewielder paused in response. Herman continued to smirk. He didn't have much time to relish in the situation, though.

Click. All the lights went out. Even through the thick metal door, Herman could hear disturbed chatter coming from around the precinct. It would have been pitch black except for the static on the TV throwing a dim blue light into the room. The TV hissed and crackled until, suddenly, an image appeared.

It was two sock puppets. One of the sock puppets had a little police hat and badge and the other was unaltered. The footage was obviously taken with a home video camera and the lighting was very unprofessional.

"Hello!" the one with the badge said. "My name is Officer Picklechips!"

"And I'm Super Steve!" the other said.

"What in the name of—" Detective Axewielder began.

Both of the sock puppets' voices were obviously made by the same person, but one was high and raspy and the other's was low and droopy. Both voices were clearly variations of Doctor Sidney Saskatoon.

"Super Steve," Officer Picklechips began. "I won't let you help my smelly old city because I'm selfish and incompetent!"

"Oh, Officer Picklechips," Super Steve replied. "You're so well-intentioned, but your precinct is a mess and you smell like week-old coffee. Give us a chance!"

"TURN-THIS-OFF!" Detective Axewielder bellowed as he pounded the buttons on the remote control.

Herman smiled. *Yep. This is definitely the signal.*

While Detective Axewielder was distracted by the television, Herman gave the handcuffs a mighty yank. *Snap!* Another whack on the table and the one bracelet was off his hook. He leapt up from his seat, grabbed his communicator and hammer, and clicked his hammer onto his wrist.

Detective Axewielder shouted for him to stop, but Herman was too quick. His superhuman legs carried him across the room, where he busted open the door and darted out. As he ran down the darkened hallway, he shouted as quickly as his lips would move, "I'msorryDetectiveIhopeyoustillthinkI'magoodguy!"

As he peeled through the hallway, he touched the communicator in his ear and said, "Nice one, Sid! Where are we heading?"

"I've already got our stuff in a duffle bag," Cassie said. "I had to take out a few officers. They're unconscious, but they'll be okay."

"Everyone rendezvous in the alleyway across the street!" Sid said. "Do whatever you can to get there! Herman, I have a surprise waiting for you. For everyone else, I've got minicopters waiting to take you back to the lab. Get going, and good luck!"

"*Hey!*"

Herman was suddenly face to face with an officer. As the officer reached for his baton, Herman cracked him across the face. The officer fell to the ground.

"Sorry!" Herman said through his teeth. "Thanks for all that you do for this community!"

He darted down another hall. Doors lined each side of the hallway with a single door at the end. Herman thought to himself that the door on the end had to lead to the front lobby. He blasted down the hall and threw open the door.

Nope. It was then that he was met by the faces of eight police officers, standing alert after the power outage, all of them with their hands on their holsters.

Herman gulped. An uncomfortable pause. Then he bore his teeth in a foolish grin and slammed the door shut.

Slam! He bolted back up the hallway, followed by orders to stop as police officers threw open the door and poured into the hallway. He heard guns cock.

Herman slammed through a door on his left, toppling to the floor just as bullets started spraying through the hall.

Herman scrambled to his feet. A window was on the opposite side of this very small room. He slammed the door shut and propped it shut with a wooden chair, hoping to slow down the officers. He ran to the window, shielded his face, and jumped.

Boonnnggg

He found himself toppling back to the floor again. *Crap! Of course the windows would be reinforced!* A stampede of footsteps advanced through the hallway as officers hustled to the door. Herman jumped back onto his feet and repeatedly slammed the window with his hammer as hard as he could.

Bam! Bam! Bam!

The window started to crack. The shouts of officers were getting clearer as they got closer. Herman tried not to look back.

Bam! Bam!

"Come on come on come on..."

There it was. With one final smash, the window cracked and weakened like a spiderweb of broken ice. Herman hurriedly took a few steps back and ran to the window, shielding his face.

Many things happened within a fraction of a second. The door behind him crashed open. He busted through the window, showering glass on the alleyway below. Gunfire opened up, whizzing past him. Amidst it all, he found himself landing in a dumpster several feet below, covered in greasy garbage bags and discarded glass bottles.

Herman shook his head and stumbled out of the dumpster, irritably brushing a banana peel off his shoulder.

"I'm out!" he said as he bolted to the alleyway's entrance. "Where are you guys?"

That's when a shadow lurched out to the entrance of the alleyway. A short shadow. A short shadow with a gun and a scowl of the fiercest caliber. He raised the gun to Herman, who slid to a halt.

"I wanted to reason with you, Hammerfist!" Detective Axewielder growled. "We could work together! But you've turned yourself into a villain!"

"Detective!" Herman raised his arms in the air. "I have nothing but respect for you, but you're in over your heads with these guys! We don't even know who their leader is! You have to let us go so we can—"

"It's *my* job to protect this city, not yours!" Detective Axewielder barked. "Now hold still! I'm only going to shoot your —"

Bam!

A red duffle bag came hurtling from out of sight and slammed into Detective Axewielder, knocking him to the ground. The duffle bag remained suspended in midair as the figure of Cassie Copland emerged to the mouth of the alleyway. Detective Axewielder, however, didn't move.

"I'm getting real sick of carrying your weight, Hammerfist!" She said as she darted across the street.

Herman couldn't help but laugh as he ran behind her. His heart twanged with guilt as he ran past an unconscious Norm Axewielder. The guy was only trying to do his job. He *did* say he was going to shoot him, though. That made Herman feel a little less sorry.

"Mom and I are on the roof!" they heard Frankie shout in their earpieces. "Be there in a second!"

Cassie and Herman reached the mouth of the opposite alleyway and flipped around just in time to see Susan and Frankie leap off the precinct roof. Officers burst onto the roof right as they jumped off. Susan and Frankie careened through the air, their legs flailing as they sailed toward the ground. When they landed, they landed right next to Herman and Cassie, but not without repercussions.

Snap!

Frankie let out a yelp as he toppled to the ground. He landed wrong and his right ankle was bent unnaturally to the side. Cops began stampeding from the precinct's main entrance. Frankie rolled on the ground, baring his teeth and cradling his foot.

Herman didn't hesitate. "I gotcha!"

Swiftly, he hoisted Frankie over his shoulders and sprinted down the alleyway, amazed at how fast he was running while carrying a human body. He and the others spotted the minicopters halfway through the alley. Herman darted to the closest one and threw Frankie inside it like a sack of potatoes.

"*Ouch!* Watch it—"

"Shut up!" Herman shot. He grabbed Frankie's foot and snapped it back into place. Frankie howled but managed to get back in control and click the harnesses together. Susan and Frankie's minicopters revved up and hovered off the ground before the cloaking functions activated, leaving Cassie and Herman stuck in an alleyway with cops rapidly advancing.

"Sid!" Herman said, his heart pounding. "A little help here!"

"It's under the tarp to your right!" Sid responded hurriedly. "There's a holster for your hammer. Insert your hammer into the holster then slip your hook into the loop on the right handle, then twist your wrist to accelerate!"

Herman spotted the black tarp to his left and yanked it off. His jaw dropped.

There, against the brick wall, was one of the most beautiful motorcycles he'd ever seen. Its black paint and chrome pipes screamed masculinity, and a silver hammer emblazoned on the leather seat assured him that this hog was made just for him. A key was already in the ignition and a helmet hung on the left grip. The best part is that the right grip was replaced with a steel loop just big enough for his prosthetic hook.

"I call it the Leftybike," Sid said in his earpiece. "It has a cloaking function just like the minicopters. Get going and meet us back at the lab!"

Herman jumped on, holstered his hammer, threw on the ignition, and the bike roared to life. Officers were nearly upon them. Cassie hopped onto the bike, shoving the helmet onto Herman's skull and wrapping her arms around his torso.

"Do you know how to ride one of these?" She yelled over the engine.

"Nope!" Herman said.

Braaaaapppp!

They were off. He twisted his wrist and the back tire spun, spitting a plume of grey smoke and blasting them both with the potent smell of burnt rubber. The Leftybike peeled out of the alley just as a set of police officers had their hands on them. Cassie held Herman tighter.

The Leftybike burst onto the street and Herman veered a right. Just then, two police cars turned a corner in front of them, lights flashing and sirens wailing.

Herman yanked on the handlebars, spinning the motorcycle into a complete one-eighty before rocketing away in the other direction. The cop cars followed in hot pursuit. The neon lights of Citytown streamed against the night sky as they sped by. Herman gunned the throttle and weaved through cars that blasted their horns at him as he went.

"Sid," he said, his heart still racing. "How about that cloaking device?"

"It seems to be malfunctioning," Sid said worriedly. "Just hang tight! It should be back up in a minute!"

"*We don't have a minute!*"

"Watch out!" Cassie bellowed.

They ran a red light and a car pulled out in front of them. Cassie and Herman yelled as he yanked on the handlebars again, missing the vehicle by inches and weaving through the car behind it. The second car honked its horn angrily as they sped by.

"Sorry! Sorry!" Herman said.

More cop cars appeared behind a corner one block ahead of them, blasting past traffic to head them off. Herman growled. It was then that he spotted an alleyway to his right. He took it.

The Leftybike's tires screeched as Herman made the turn, then fishtailed and straightened as they barreled through the alley. The tires kicked up loose trash as they went, and manholes let out geysers of steam. Cassie clutched him tight as the wind snapped at Herman's jacket. The roar of the engine reverberated off the walls like a cavern. It would have been more exciting if they weren't terrified of getting arrested again.

At the end of the alleyway, two police cars rolled up, blocking their path and throwing light into the dark alleyway. Trapped.

"Crap!" Herman said as he began to slow down. But then he noticed something—a bright red sheet of metal at the end of the alleyway, leaning against a wall. He gunned the throttle again. "Cassie!" he said. "Do you see that? Make a ramp!"

Cassie barely had enough time to react. She thrust her hand forward. The metal twitched. She grunted and stretched her fingers harder. Then the metal speedily dragged along the ground and tilted up just as the first wheel touched it. Cassie couldn't keep the ramp steady as the Leftybike roared over it. The ramp dipped, causing the bike to land on the hood of one of the cop cars. The Leftybike stammered as it hit pavement, leaving a trail of sparks, a dented car hood, and a handful of very bewildered police officers in its wake.

Herman couldn't help but whoop in celebration as they blasted through the street. Cassie smiled behind him and held him tighter. It was at that moment that blue sparkles started to envelop them and the Leftybike.

"Finally got the cloaking back online!" Sid said in their ears. "You're invisible to the naked eye now. Make your way back to the lab and try not to make a scene."

"You don't have to tell me twice," Herman said with a sigh.

10

Unconscious, face-up on the cement, Detective Norm Axewielder began to stir. His eye twitched. Then his fingers. Then he pushed his eyelids open and put his hands on the cement. Sitting up was hard, but so is life and taxes. His head swam.

His eyes darted about him. The flashing neon lights of Citytown were harsh on his eyes as they adjusted. He scowled harder. The sound of a roaring motorcycle engine was distant. Then he remembered Hammerfist and the other freaks. He scowled even harder and pushed himself to his feet.

"Sir! Are you alright?"

Detective Axewielder turned to see another officer sprinting toward him from the precinct's entrance. His eyes were wild.

"Sir, they all escaped!" the officer said. "All four of them! We've sent a patrol to go track down two of them—they left on a motorcycle—but the others just disappeared. Would you like us to send a public release to the local stations about their arrest? Get citizens involved?"

Detective Axewielder creased his eyebrows, thought for a moment, and said, "They've got someone who was able to access our system and erase all their information. We've got nothing on pictures, fingerprints, anything... which means we've got homework to do. Track down the security footage of places they've been and see if we can get some clear faces we can show the public. Contact the *Citytown Harold.* We're gonna find these freaks and throw them behind bars where they belong. Do whatever it takes." He straightened his tie before adding, "Nobody makes a fool of Norm Axewielder."

*

Herman sat with his head propped in his left hand, his face glazing the glossy pages of the first comic book he had ever cracked open. He couldn't help but frown as he soaked up the illustrations and comic-sans typeface.

What kind of psychos go through traumatic things and decide to fight crime as a release? He thought. *Get some therapy, you morons.*

The Citytown Community College library wasn't large—just one level. Shelves of books were everywhere to be seen about every topic under the sun (allowed in a public institution). At the front desk, a dowdy librarian pinched her lips as her eyes trickled through a book called *Primal Desire.* Several students silently poured over books at tables and chairs throughout the room. Herman inhaled deeply and let out a sigh, the memory of last night's escape fresh in his mind.

As he turned the page, someone came up, pulled out the chair next to him, and sat down. Herman glanced at them out of the corner of his eye, then he sat up straight.

"Cassie!" He whispered. At the sight of her wild red hair, hard green eyes and neutral face, he went back to reading his comic book. "What are you doing here? It's almost June."

"Summer semester. Why are you here? You graduated."

"My alumni card lets me use the library," Herman said. He paused. Then he said, "Sorry you had to save me from Detective Axewielder last night. I know… you're always carrying my load."

"I'm not."

Her voice wasn't unfeeling or impatient. It made him take his eyes off the page and stare at her. She held her backpack on her lap with both hands and made infrequent eye contact with him.

"You're not?" Herman said, raising an eyebrow.

Cassie nodded. "That was a good idea last night. The ramp. I had to save you from getting shot, but after that, you were fine. You carried Frankie to his minicopter. You got us away from the cops. You actually did good."

Herman paused, letting that sink in. Cassie was actually *complimenting* him. Whoa. He cleared his throat as his cheeks went pink. "Thanks. You're amazing every night."

Cassie didn't reply right away. Instead, she just unzipped her backpack and pulled out a stack of textbooks.

"I'm going to study here," she said flatly as she dropped her textbooks on the table.

"'Kay," Herman said.

They sat in silence for a long moment, neither of them looking at each other, each of them buried in their books. Herman still couldn't get into the comic book he was reading. This one was about a high school sophomore who got bit by a radioactive chimpanzee and decides to avenge his dog by finding the local gang responsible for its death.

"Look at the front page," Cassie said.

She pulled a copy of the *Citytown Harold* from her backpack and slapped it on top of Herman's textbook. On the cover, there was an image of a cheerful, portly man with a big grin by a hot dog stand. Herman bent his eyebrows and quietly began to read aloud.

"'Bucky Stark of *Phony Bologna Dogs and Franks* opens his twentieth hot dog stand today, celebrating nine years of—'"

"*No,* the thing next to it."

"Oh, the little box near the bottom?"

"Yes."

"'Four perpetrators escaped Citytown Police custody last night that are believed to be connected to several burglaries in the downtown Citytown area. Although pictures are unavailable at this time, citizens are asked to provide any information on characters fitting the following description...' Then it goes on to describe each of us and what we were wearing last night. What the-- *they called me a cripple!*"

"What do we do?" Cassie said.

Herman leaned back in his chair. "I don't know. There aren't any pictures so that helps us. I doubt many people will notice. After all, what's another burglar in Citytown? We should try to figure out a way to get on the police's good side, though. They know we're trying to help. Detective Axewielder said it himself."

"That's something we need to figure out without going to jail," Cassie said severely.

Bzzz! Bzzz!

Herman's phone vibrated in his pocket. He extracted it and glanced at the screen. There, a picture of a lovely blonde-haired woman in her mid-forties was making kissy lips at him. He tapped the green button on his screen and pressed the phone to his ear.

"Hello?" He whispered.

"*Herman!*" Aunt Josie was so chipper on the other end that her greeting came across as a yell. Herman flinched and held the phone away from his ear. "I wanted to surprise you but I couldn't wait—"

"Aunt Josie, I'm in the library!" Herman hissed. The librarian looked up from her book and glared at him from across the room.

"I want to visit you in Citytown tonight!" Aunt Josie said. "It's been over a week since your accident and I wanted to check up on you! Let's go get dinner!"

"Sure, Aunt Josie. That sounds great."

"And if you want to bring some friends, feel free to invite them! I don't know who you're spending time with nowadays, but I'd love to meet them!"

Herman glanced over at Cassie. "Okay. What time?"

*

"You have a job now? That's so exciting! Why didn't you call me to tell me?"

"Sorry, Aunt Josie," Herman rubbed his neck. "I guess it slipped my mind with the accident."

Herman sat in the passenger seat of Aunt Josie's old Toyota as they cruised through the Citytown streets. Frankie and Cassie sat in the back. Frankie tried not to smile, slightly amused at the situation, while Cassie stared out the window.

"So what is it you do? Where is it? Does it pay well? Do you like it?"

"Aunt Josie!" Herman tried not to laugh from the barrage of questions. "Uh... I work for Citytown Applied Technologies. They have an initiative to help the city... like a sort of local cleanup, philanthropy kind of thing. It's temporary, but it's still a job."

Cassie and Frankie looked at each other.

"Well that's great!" Aunt Josie's eyes sparkled. "It sounds like exactly what you were hoping to do! Help people and all that. I'm so proud of you!"

"Yeah. Thanks."

"So this part of town is dangerous, right?" Aunt Josie asked as she scanned her surroundings, her hands firmly on the wheel.

"Most of Citytown is dangerous, honestly," Frankie interjected, giving Herman a break from all the questions. "But we should be done before sundown, which is when most of the crime happens."

"Where are we going for dinner, anyway?" Herman asked.

Aunt Josie flipped around in her seat, making eye contact with all three of her guests. "We're getting pizza! Does that sound alright to you guys?"

Everyone replied politely in the affirmative.

"*Absolutely,*" Frankie smiled wide. "Pizza sounds great. I'm so hungry right now!"

Cassie and Herman slid him looks. Frankie sneered in return.

"Here we are!" Mr. Fitzgerald said as they turned into a parking lot.

When Herman saw the restaurant, his heart dropped into his butt. The exterior of the restaurant was more of a fortress, painted powder blue. On the top of the building, a giant animatronic rat waved at the parking lot with a big, buck-toothed grin. Above the doors, zany letters spelled out the words "WHEEZIE'S CHEESES" in a font that no one had thought of since 1999. Frankie and Cassie shot Herman amused, flabbergasted looks. Herman didn't say anything.

"You all get as many tokens as you want!" Aunt Josie said excitedly as the car parked and she unbuckled her seat belt. "Those prizes aren't going to win themselves!"

Herman tried not to sigh loudly. Everyone piled out of the car and made their way to the entrance, Aunt Josie in the lead. Herman kept his arms by his side and stared at his feet as he dragged them across the asphalt. Behind them, Frankie nudged Herman's arm.

"Dude," he whispered. "Don't be so embarrassed! Free pizza and arcade games! There is literally no downside to this. Just enjoy it."

"Free arcade games, yeah," Herman whispered back. "If you're okay with hanging around screaming kids. Also, the pizza sucks and you know it. It's a steamy, greasy circle of disappointment."

"Your aunt still thinks you're five," Cassie said with her lips pressed together. It was the first time that Herman had see her do anything remotely close to smiling. And she was suppressing a laugh at him. He flushed pink.

As soon as they crossed through the automatic doors, they were hit with the smells of burnt cheese, musty carpets, and freshly-sterilized vomit. The buzzing chatter of children and beeping arcade games filled the airwaves. To their left, the restaurant portion with dozens of square tables that hadn't been wiped. To their right, the arcade portion with an army of flashing lights from metal towers competing for attention. Small children screamed and chased each other like an anarchist colony of munchkins.

Again, Herman tried not to sigh loudly.

"I'll go get a table!" Aunt Josie said, her face beaming and made her way to the left. Everyone followed behind a few paces.

Frankie leaned toward Herman and spoke lowly. "Dude. Your aunt is hot."

"Shut up, Frankie."

The carpets and tables clearly hadn't been replaced in a couple of decades. On the far end of the restaurant, a stringy, pimply teenager stood at a counter and punched orders into a cash register. He looked exactly like the kid from Won Ton King Kong and the downtown arcade. As they all made their way to that counter, Herman shot glances at the squealing children and irritated parents that populated the tables.

There was one table in particular that caught his attention. There, a beautiful woman with brown hair and brown eyes sat with another man her age and two young boys. Herman recognized her immediately but didn't say anything. Frankie, however, wasn't so tactful.

"Hi, Susan!"

Susan looked up and stiffened at the sight of her colleagues. Her eyes seemed to accusingly say what-are-you-doing, but Frankie walked up to her and began to chat as if it were no big deal. Awkwardly, Herman and Cassie followed behind. Aunt Josie continued to the counter to order.

"Is this your family?" Frankie said delightedly.

The man sitting next to Susan was remarkably handsome with symmetrical features, a crisp haircut, and broad shoulders. He looked like a collegiate athlete that went on to become a movie star. He eyed Frankie before saying, "Honey, who is this?"

"Uh," Susan stammered. "Clint, this is Frankie, Cassie, and Herman. They... volunteer at Citytown Applied Technologies. The organization asked me to do some work for them recently."

"Oh, they were remodeling?" Clint said. "Susan is so talented. She's remarkable at what she does, isn't she?"

Everyone awkwardly agreed.

"And who are these?" Frankie was on a roll. Herman and Cassie exchanged looks.

"This," Susan said, putting a hand on her first boy's head, "is Alex. He's eight. He loves soccer almost as much as mommy does."

Alex didn't look up from his pizza. His black hair exploded from his scalp in a wavy mess as it cascaded down his head, stopping just below the cheekbone.

"And this," she said, putting her hand to her second boy, "is Cam."

"I'm five," Cam said firmly as he looked the strangers in the eye and raised his hand. Immediately after he greeted the guests, he went to work cutting his slice of pizza with a knife and fork.

"Cam is *very* tidy and organized," Susan said. "He insists on eating his pizza like that."

Herman tightened his lower lip as he watched this five-year-old child carve into a pizza like a businessman at a five-star dinner. Inwardly, he wondered what side of the family he got that from. After a sufficiently uncomfortable pause, he said, "Well, it was good to see you! Nice to meet you, Clint. And, Susan, thanks again for the couches. And the plant. It's a great plant. I like the leaves."

Susan nodded her head slowly as she concurred with Herman's fictitious fixture. Herman slipped away and the other two followed suit.

"Dude, you're an idiot," Herman said as he shook his head.

"What? She was cool about it!" Frankie said defensively.

"You made it weird," Cassie said. "Don't do anything that dumb for the rest of the night."

"You know I can't guarantee something like that."

After half an hour, the pizza was ordered and delivered. It wasn't long before everyone agreed that the pizza was just as Herman described—a steamy, greasy circle of disappointment.

As dinner progressed, Herman noticed that Frankie was a little looser than usual. His eyes had slightly dilated and he would yammer on with pointless stories at every opportunity. A few of his fingers would twitch ever-so-slightly as he went.

"And that was when I decided to study music," he said at one point with wide eyes and a mouth half-full of pizza. "Because music is my heart and soul and my stomach all at the same time —like, it's *every part of me*. It flows through me like a river... a river of notes and time signatures and ledger lines and staffs. Have you ever wondered why they call it a staff? It's because musicians are *audio wizards.* Yeah. Think about it. They know exactly what frequencies to put notes in to make an emotional reaction from the listener. That's hardcore. *By my staff you shall succumb to my power—*"

"Frankie, you need to slow down," Herman said as he chewed.

Aunt Josie continued to chew on her pizza, pretending to listen intently to Frankie, meanwhile shooting looks at Herman. Herman would send back concerned, puzzled glances. Even Cassie couldn't help but stare.

"Frankie," Herman said. "I think you've had enough pizza. Let's go play some games. Aunt Josie, we'll be back before you know it."

"Okay, have fun..." Aunt Josie said as she eyed Frankie.

The three got up from the table and made their way to the arcade, where the electronic sounds and flashing lights of video games got louder and more intense. Cassie and Herman stood to either side of Frankie.

"Frankie, are you feeling okay?" Herman said as they marched toward the arcade.

"*Yeah!*" Frankie said a little too loud. "Super good! Mega great!"

Herman spoke to Cassie. "I think someone messed with the pizza."

"No," Cassie said. "If someone did, we'd all be feeling loopy. Frankie is the only one."

"Good point," Herman said. "Well, we should definitely keep an eye on him."

"*Noooo,* you guys go on ahead!" Frankie said with the same wide eyes and crazy smile. "I'm gonna go play all the games at the same time! *Woooo!*" He broke away and began darting for the nearest machine but turned around. "Besides, I think there's something blooming here—" his fingers waved between Herman and Cassie "—blooming like a blossom in the springtime. Yoink!" His fingers danced through the air before he tossed up two fingers. "*Peace!*"

And there they were. Frankie staggered into the arcade like a drunken man, leaving Herman's face burning and Cassie avoiding his gaze. Herman swallowed.

"So," he began. "Death Soldier Ultimate is pretty good. And there's co-op."

"Fine," Cassie said as she folded her arms.

The two wandered around the arcade playing various games for about half an hour. Cassie actually out-shot Herman on Death Soldier Ultimate, a rail shooter about a zombie that becomes an operative for the CIA. When it came to a one-on-one fighting game called Sacred Samurai, Herman beat Cassie three times before Cassie used her powers to make Herman's red joystick go haywire.

As Herman's digital samurai fell to his death, Cassie shot him a smirk and said, "Looks like you're losing a step, Fitzgerald."

"Real mature," Herman narrowed his eyes. "Using your powers to beat a cripple at a video game. It's hard enough with just this." He waved his hook.

"Play the victim and you'll be the victim," she said. Her eyes reeked of satisfaction. She flipped about and marched around the corner to the next game, her wild red hair bouncing as she went. Herman followed behind her, smiling absently.

Across the room, by the edge of the restaurant section, a man with a red tie sat at a table with a copy of the *Citytown Harold*. Herman noticed him right before the man looked up and made eye contact. The man looked up to him and Cassie, then back down to the page, then looked up again. He squinted and his eyebrows furrowed.

Herman ducked his head and slid behind a video game tower. "Don't look, but I think someone over at the restaurant knows who we are. He's reading the paper right now."

Cassie followed and peered out from behind a machine. "The guy with the red tie?"

"Yeah."

"What do you think we should do?"

"I don't know. It's not like we can just run for it. We can't just leave Aunt Josie here."

"Right. I could threaten him?"

"That definitely wouldn't help."

"Wait. Hold on."

She stepped out and looked at the man head-on. Herman's blood chilled. The man across the room stared at them with laser eyes and reached into his pocket. He pulled out a cell phone and started to dial. Cassie smirked. Then she waved her hand.

Thud!

In a flash, the man's red tie yanked down, slamming his face into the table. The force was so hard that his head rebounded backward, facing upward. Unconscious, his mouth dangled open and the newspaper sat on his lap like he had merely fallen asleep. No one around him seemed to notice. Herman snorted through his laughter.

"You're amazing," he said, wiping a tear from his eye.

Cassie smiled. She actually smiled.

Frankie, however, wasn't doing quite as well. When they turned the corner to explore more games, they found him laying face-up, staring at the ceiling with wide, ecstatic eyes and mouth agape. A constant note like a soft moan emanated from his lips. A few small children were huddled around him, staring curiously, but Frankie didn't seem to notice.

"What the...?" Cassie muttered.

Herman pushed through the kids and fell to Frankie's side. "Frankie! Frankie, are you okay?"

Frankie's eyes slowly panned in his sockets until they locked onto Herman. The moaning stopped. The two held a long, uncomfortable moment of eye contact before Frankie got completely serious. His body arched upward, focused on Herman. He grabbed Herman by the collar and said, "Herman, I am the master of my own destiny and I sail this ship to forgotten shores. *I will be the mightiest audio wizard the world has ever known.*"

Herman sealed his mouth shut, forcing himself to suppress another chuckle. Then it hit him. The problem wasn't the pizza. No one had done anything to sabotage their evening. Herman's eyes darted about and he realized they were surrounded by dozens of beeping arcade games, each singing their eight-bit siren songs. And what was Frankie's power derived from?

When Herman made his discovery, he turned back to Cassie and said, "I'm taking Frankie outside." The next sentence was a whisper. "*I think the arcade music is making him loopy.*"

Cassie's pink lips couldn't press together any tighter and her emerald eyes couldn't have gotten any wider. She composed herself just enough to say "Okay" and walk away.

Herman hoisted Frankie onto his feet and guided Frankie outside like a wounded soldier, all the while conducting small talk to keep Frankie alert. When they crossed the automatic door into the muggy summer evening, Herman plopped Frankie down on a nearby bench and looked at him intensely. "Frankie, are you back on earth?"

Frankie blinked a couple of times and cleared his throat before putting his hand on his head. "Dude," he cleared his throat again. "That was a trip. My mouth is weirdly dry..."

"Looked like it!" Herman said. "You should log that away. No arcade music for you, GB."

"You said it," Frankie said. Then he sneered. "So, did you and Cassie have fun?"

Herman rolled his eyes. "Wow, you're still on this?"

"Everything was really fuzzy, but I could tell that she's been hovering around you all night!" He said. "Can't you see that she likes you? She's still an angry ginger with a chip on her shoulder but she's warming up to you! If I were your chemistry teacher, I'd give you both an A." He winked.

"Both of you have been gravitating to me tonight. My aunt is paying for this whole evening, genius."

Just then, Cassie came through the automatic doors. She took a good look at Frankie and said, "You done being weird? Good. Hey. I told your aunt that Frankie isn't feeling well. It's a good reason to get out of this garbage palace."

"Thank you so much," Herman said with a sigh.

As if on cue, Aunt Josie came out to the night air. She slung her purse around her shoulder and said, "Are you feeling alright, Frankie? Cassandra said you've been feeling a little sick."

"Uh—" Frankie stammered as he grabbed his stomach. "Yeah! I forgot to mention that I'm lactose intolerant. *Ooohh* my stomach…"

"Alright, let's just head back to the car. It's a good time to leave anyway. A single dad with some big sideburns started talking my ear off after you all left."

The drive home was quiet. Frankie played the lactose intolerant card as hard as he could and Aunt Josie dropped him off at the Triple C library so he could "find a bathroom", leaving Herman and Cassie alone to be dropped off at their apartment complex. When they reached the facility, Aunt Josie told Cassie how nice it was to meet her before she hurriedly left the car.

"Thanks. Bye, Herman."

Aunt Josie blinked as he watched Cassie escape. "She doesn't like people very much, does she?" She turned to face Herman. "So you're feeling alright, sweetie? Nothing strange has happened since the accident?"

"Nope," Herman shook his head stiffly. "Speedy recovery. I feel great."

"That's so odd," Mrs. Fitzgerald said. "You healed so quickly. I'm so excited, don't get me wrong, but it just blows me away."

"Yeah," Herman said. "The doctors at Citytown General really have a good thing going."

Aunt Josie's tone darkened. "Speaking of which, I don't know what I'm going to do when the hospital bills start to come in. I haven't seen anything yet." She paused. "Are you sure you're okay, kiddo? You seem kind of… jumpy."

"There's just been a lot on my mind lately," Herman replied. "With the accident and everything. But I'm fine. Really. I'm glad I have a job now and I have some friends, so that's good."

"As long as they're helping you stay out of trouble," Aunt Josie smiled.

Herman smiled and nodded and hoped she couldn't hear him gulp.

"Hey," Aunt Josie said while putting her hand on Herman's face. "I love you. So much. Just keep swinging, okay? I'm so proud of you."

"I love you too, Aunt Josie. Drive safe."

Herman slipped out of the vehicle and Aunt Josie began her drive back to Gladview. He climbed the stairs slowly, thinking of how he got arrested the other night. What if Aunt Josie found out? Or worse, what if he got killed?

He opened the door to his apartment and closed the door behind him. He caught Bridger in mid-meditation, planted in a firm handstand as whale song played from a stereo. Amazingly, Adam was sitting on the couch clicking away on his phone. His burly, football player frame filled up nearly half the couch and his face was adorned by a shaved haircut above his stony face and square jaw.

"Adam!" Herman said. "It's been a while since I've seen you!"

Adam didn't say anything. He just gave a little nod, acknowledging Herman's presence.

"Herman," Bridger said softly as his feet found the floor. He had no shirt or shoes on, just a pair of sweats that had been pushed up to his knees. He lumbered over slowly to Herman and wrapped his arms around him in a firm embrace. Herman blinked twice and patted him on the back.

"Uh," Herman stammered. "Good to see you, Bridger. Everything okay?"

"All is well, my friend," Bridger said as he brushed his dreadlocks out of his eyes. "I'm trying to embrace others more so I can experience an intercourse of energy with other life around me. All life is part of a greater circle, an enclosed ecosystem of peace and harmony if we accept it."

Herman nodded. "Noted."

"By the way, your girlfriend wants to talk to you about some stuff."

Herman remembered Abby Gale better this time than he did last, but he didn't remember describing her to any of his roommates. Herman said, "Yeah? Where is she?"

"She said she'd be on the top of the roof," Bridger said. "Her hair is *wild*, man! I didn't know you were into that! It's red and big and frizzy like an electrocuted mermaid—"

"Alright, thanks Bridger. When did she say she'd be there?"

"Right now."

11

Cassandra Copland sat with her feet dangling off the edge of the apartment building. Her hands were flat on the brick as she stared down at the street below, watching cars crawl by, honking at each other. The orange glow of passing headlights were soft on her fair face.

Meanwhile, Herman Fitzgerald slowly climbed the fire escape on the opposite side of the building. Cassie wanted to meet with him about something. But what? Did it have to do with Sid and their nightly missions? Was she quitting the team? Did she figure out something new about the Green Juice and Alpha Master?

As Herman reached the rooftop, he saw Cassie on the opposite side, her back to him and her face staring at the passing cars below. Herman straightened his jacket and walked up to her slowly, his hands in his pockets. The skyscrapers of Citytown seemed to tower over them like steel giants—almost invisible as thousands of windows reflecting an endlessly black sky.

"Hi," he said as he slid down beside her, his own two feet dangling over the edge.

"Hey," Cassie responded.

Herman paused before he said, "Everything okay?"

Her gaze stayed fixed on the ground beneath her. "Yeah."

Silence. Herman nodded and stared out over the city. He took a deep breath and said, "The past week has been crazy. I never thought in a million years that I'd be bludgeoning bad guys with a prosthetic hammer. It's hard to believe that we're doing any of this."

"Yeah."

Another little silence. So Herman continued. "I wonder how much longer it's going to take before we find Alpha Master and get a cure. But I don't even know if we can go back to our normal lives after this. Especially with what's been happening with the police and stuff. Sometimes I wonder if this is all worth it, but then I remember that Aunt Josie would have no way to pay off my hospital bills if it weren't for this."

"Yeah."

Herman paused again, then swallowed. "Sorry, you probably wanted to tell me something."

"It's okay."

She didn't say anything else. Herman shifted uncomfortably as he shot a glance at Cassie, who had never once removed her gaze from the street. He frowned.

"Are you sure you're okay?" he said. "Bridger said that you wanted to talk but you don't really seem like it."

"I do," she said. Then she paused again before adding, "But I don't. It's hard."

Herman blinked a couple of times and said, "Okay…"

Another strange silence was filled by the white noise of the city around them. Cassie brushed some of the hair out of her eyes. Herman scratched his neck.

"What happened the day you went to the hospital?" Cassie finally asked, still not looking at him.

Herman rubbed his hand on his knee. "Well, I had just left a job interview that I totally bombed. I remember coming into an intersection and I was getting ready to turn, then an eighteen-wheeler ran a red light and crashed into me. I also remember that I put my arm up really fast, like some part of my brain wanted to stop the truck from hitting me. That's how I got this." He twisted his forearm. "Before I passed out, I saw green sludge come from the eighteen-wheeler's tank and it was moving toward my car. Then I think I woke up the next day at the ICU with Aunt Josie sitting next to me."

"Your Aunt Josie is really nice," Cassie said. Then she added, "My parents weren't at the hospital after I fell."

"Really?" Herman said darkly.

"My mom is a stripper in Reno and my dad is in jail," Cassie said nonchalantly. "I haven't seen them since I was four. I hardly talk to any of my foster parents either, so there's no way they would have known about my accident."

Herman's heart sank and his face softened. Somehow, Cassie's hair and eyes seemed different now. They were no longer the attributes of an angry girl—they were the features of a warrior. A survivor. Someone who had learned to take the trials of life and beat them down with anything she could. He wanted to wrap his arms around her and squeeze away the pain, but he thought better of it.

"Cassie," Herman said. "I'm sorry."

"Don't be," Cassie said with a shrug. "I don't lose sleep over it."

"That's definitely true as of late," Herman said. Then he realized the bad timing of the joke. "That's still hard, though."

"Life is hard for everyone. It's not like I'm the only person who deals with this."

"Tell you what," Herman said. "You can share Aunt Josie with me. She'll probably take you to Wheezie's Cheeses all you want."

Herman teased a grin. Cassie didn't pull a smile, but her eyes gleamed a little bit. She looked over at Herman, the reflection of the city lights on her face.

"You're a nice person, Herman," Cassie said. "Actually nice. I can tell when people are fake nice."

Herman wasn't quite sure what to say at this point. After stealing a glance at his shoes, he sheepishly thanked her. He turned away and looked out over the city, watching the cars pass below them and listening to the sounds of honking horns and car alarms. He didn't know what else to say, but maybe Cassie didn't need him to say anything. Just be there. After another silent moment, Cassie spoke up again.

"Do you want to know what happened the day I went to the hospital?" she said.

"I thought you said that you suffered from a fall?"

"I did," Cassie said. "I jumped off a building. This one."

Herman's mouth went dry and he stared at her, jaw dangling. She didn't look at him. She just kept staring at the ground beneath her. Herman again found himself at a loss for words. She continued:

"I was in a dark place. I thought really hard about it and felt like it wasn't a big deal because life is an endless struggle and no one would miss me anyway. So why not? Just jump. Some people say they care, but they don't. They're just nice to look good. What difference does it actually make to them if I'm alive or dead? So I tried it. It didn't work, though. I woke up in the hospital later that night."

"I'm glad."

Cassie looked him in the eye. Herman stared her down.

"Look, I know you hate most people, but I think you're freaking awesome," Herman said. "You're one of the coolest and strongest people I know. I'm glad that I met you and I'd be super sad if you were gone."

Cassie didn't break her gaze. Her eyes became misty, but she forced herself to keep a straight face. Her lips didn't even twitch.

"I don't think you should be so quick to judge your worth," Herman continued. "Like, I'm sure you have lots of people that care about you, but it's just hard to see sometimes. I don't know how it was before, but you've got me and Frankie and Susan and Sid now. You're a part of our group and you belong. It wouldn't be the same if we didn't have you."

Cassie's eyes were still misty, but not a muscle on her face moved. She broke her gaze, looked back out over the city and said, "Thanks." Then she paused and said, "I haven't told anyone else about what happened. If you blab, I'll murder you."

Herman smiled. "Understood."

Cassie sniffed, her face hidden behind her mess of hair. Her hands were still resting on the brick beside her. Herman eyed her right hand, took a deep breath, wiped his palm on his jeans, then reached out and took it.

Her hand was surprisingly warm. She twitched slightly as Herman held it, but she didn't take it away or recoil. She just continued to stare out to the city—disconnected and deep in thought.

"I'll never understand everything you've gone through," Herman said. "But you don't have to face everything alone anymore. Okay?"

He smiled. The muscles in Cassie's face pulled like she wanted to smile but couldn't bring herself to. She was still a caged animal, treading cautiously. She let Herman hold her hand for just a moment longer, then took it back. She rubbed her palms together. When she spoke again, she still didn't look at him.

"Thanks," she said. "I want to be alone now."

"Okay," Herman said. He felt like he should say something more but couldn't think of the right thing. As he got up, he said, "Goodnight, Cassie." Then he walked away.

Cassie didn't move as he made his way down the fire escape, his feet clanking against the metal steps as he descended. Herman's mind raced with everything he had just heard. He felt like he had a much better understanding of who this girl was and his respect for her skyrocketed, but his heart twanged with sadness hearing about her recent accident. It's no surprise that she's as closed off as she is.

The last thing she said also plagued him.

She wants to be alone right now? Herman thought. *What does that mean? Does she just want some time to be alone and think? If that's what she wanted, why didn't she just go back to her apartment? Does she mean that she wants to be "alone" alone? Was it too forward when I held her hand? So she's just not into me at all? Or maybe she just needs some more time?*

He tried not to get too enveloped in his thoughts as he entered his apartment. He made it to his room uninterrupted and changed into some pajamas, throwing his clothes into a pile. As he lay down on his bed, he noticed his in-ear communicator on his nightstand was blinking with a tiny green light. He scratched his head then put it in his ear.

"You have one new methage!" the unmistakable lisp of Katy, Sid's secretary, sounded in his ear. "To play new methajith, thay 'play.'"

I didn't know these things could do that, Herman thought. "Play."

There was muffled silence for a short second, then the voice of Frankie came in his ear.

"Herman, it's me," Frankie said. "Susan and I managed to gather some intel tonight. We think we've figured out where Alpha Master is hiding; it's the old abandoned hospital at the edge of town. We're going to infiltrate it tomorrow night. Let's meet at the lab tomorrow at five to go over it. I got the word out to Cassie and Tyler—hopefully he comes—but we're gonna need all hands on deck for this one. See you tomorrow!"

"End of methage!" Katy's voice came again. "To delete, thay 'delete.' To thave, thay 'thave.' To—"

"Delete," Herman said.

He took the communicator out of his ear and set it back on his nightstand. That was a lot sooner than expected. It sounds like they're going to meet the creator of their powers within the next twenty-four hours. All their questions should be answered. And maybe the police would let them off easy for turning in Alpha Master. Maybe things could go back to normal after all.

Herman glanced through the cracks in the blinds, wondering if Cassie was still sitting on the roof.

12

Saturday. Herman knew that he had reason to be stressed with the Alpha Master operation that night, but until then, he decided to spend his morning in the best way he knew how.

He sat in his favorite pajamas, sprawled out on the couch with his head on the armrest. Sugar-Coated Hyper Bombs swam in a bowl of milk, their crispy little bomb-shaped surfaces seeping refined sugar into the milk's reservoir. Herman went to work excavating them from his bowl. Drips of milk fell from his lips as his gaze remained fixed on the TV. He had to put the spoon in his mouth sideways since he was laying with his head down.

On the current channel, the movie adaptation of Death Soldier was playing. The movie was much like the game—the story of a zombie named Duke Blownapart that becomes a CIA operative through a series of supernatural events. In this scene, he wore a blood-soaked tank top and scowled as he cocked an unusually large revolver. The man on the receiving end was a simple thug with a gun to a sexy damsel's head. He scowled back at Duke.

"I'm gonna tell you once and only once, punk," Duke said with clenched teeth. "You let her go, or your head gets blown off like Mount Saint Helen's."

"I'll never surrender!" The thug said, cocking his pistol. "Surrender is for the weak!"

"Then welcome to Washington, bucko," Duke said.

Boom! The thug toppled back, a clean headshot from Duke. The sexy damsel scurried over to Blownapart and collapsed into his arms.

"Oh, Duke!" she said, clinging to his neck. "I'll never let you go!"

"I gotcha, baby," Duke said. "It's you and me forever."

Herman stared intently. *Movie adaptations for video games usually suck, but this is so bad… I can't look away.*

Knock knock knock.

Herman frowned. *If it's Frankie again, so help me.*

He placed his bowl on the coffee table and pushed himself off the couch, munching quickly as he made his way to the door. He swallowed just as he put his hand on the handle and pulled it open.

There, standing in the doorway, was a dark-skinned boy of about eighteen, wearing faded blue jeans and a t-shirt. It didn't even take Herman a second to register who he was.

"Tyler!" he said.

"Hey," Tyler said, his hands in his pockets. "Sorry, I know this is kind of out of the blue. I probably could've reached you through the communicator, but you probably wouldn't have it in on a Saturday morning. So, you know… here I am."

Herman wiped the milk from his lips. "Yeah, uh, you can come in if you want. Sorry, it's not clean."

"No worries," Tyler slipped inside with his hands still in his pockets. He didn't make himself at home, though. He remained by the door as Herman closed it.

"So," Herman began. "You got Frankie's message from last night, right?"

"Yeah."

"Are you coming?"

"I dunno. Haven't decided."

Herman deflated. "We could definitely use your help, you know. This is Alpha Master. The big enchilada. The source of our powers. Kind of a big deal." He paused. "Did you use the communicator to find where I live?"

"No. I ran to Sid's hideout and looked through some forms," Tyler shrugged. "His security is pretty tight, but when you have superspeed it's no big deal."

"Figures," Herman replied flatly. "That superspeed would be a lot more convenient to have during fights every night. We've been working hard to find the source of our powers while stopping these goons from terrorizing the city."

"They haven't been terrorizing the city," Tyler raised an eyebrow. "It's just a bunch of petty burglaries, that's all."

"Okay, whatever. But why don't you come fight with us more?"

"Because this city has bigger issues," Tyler said. "Those are what I've been working on."

Herman frowned. "Like what?"

Tyler pulled a set of keys out of his pocket and said, "You got an hour free?"

"I guess."

"Then you'll need some closed toe shoes. And you'll probably want to change out of your pajamas."

Herman only looked at him for a second before he turned to retreat to his room. Before he went, he held up his hook and said, "Is this going to be a problem?"

Tyler shook his head.

After a minute, he emerged wearing some sneakers, a t-shirt, and a pair of jeans. They left his apartment and Tyler led him down to the parking lot where his car was parked. All the while, Herman curiously followed behind with his hand in his pocket, not saying much.

Tyler clicked a button on his key ring and the headlights flashed on a shiny new luxury sedan—nothing like the sputtering mess Herman used to drive. They popped open the doors, slid inside, and were greeted by a sleek black interior. The stitching on the leather seats and chrome dashboard detailing were particularly impressive.

"This is much better than what I used to drive," Herman said, fastening his seat belt.

"That motorcycle is pretty cool, though," Tyler said with a little smile. "That's thoughtful of Sid to put that together for you."

As the car backed out and pulled out of the parking lot, Herman rubbed some smudges from his hook. Tyler didn't say a word. To dispel the silence, Herman asked, "What's your story? Where are you from and everything?"

"I'm not from around here," Tyler shrugged. "My dad's a lawyer. My mom stayed at home raising me until I went off to school. Now she sells scented candles and volunteers with different charities. I'm on an academic scholarship at Citytown State, but I'm going to transfer to an even better college when my general ed classes are done."

"So what do you like to do?"

"Help around."

"But not us?"

"No need to get defensive, man. You guys are managing things just fine. It's barely been a week and you've figured out where Alpha Master is staying."

"What about that one night at the electronics store?" Herman asked. "You came in and tied up everyone in about five seconds. You made things way easier."

"You would've been fine," Tyler replied. "I was just in the area. I wasn't just going to leave you hanging. That wouldn't be cool."

Herman thought for a second and said, "You don't seem to care at all about where we got our powers, do you?"

"No."

"Don't you want to be cured?"

Tyler scoffed. "No! These conditions allow me to get so much more done! Why would I want to go back to being average again?"

"I dunno," Herman said. "It's just weird. I think average is just nice."

"Well, that makes one of us. We're here."

The sedan rolled into a parking spot next to a massive church. The gothic architecture, with multiple towers of stone, felt like a stoic and weathered gnome among giant robots as it stood surrounded by Citytown skyscrapers. Not a single neon light was to be seen. All there was in front of the castle-like edifice was a large sign designating it as The First Baptist Church of Citytown. And the sign itself obviously hadn't been changed in decades, apparent from the rusty weather stains.

That wasn't the first thing that caught Herman's eye, though. A line of homeless people—scruffy, unshaven, unkempt—lined the sidewalk in front of the church. They all carried backpacks, plastic bags, or anything they could find to help carry their shabby belongings. They looked around with bleary eyes and couldn't help but stare when Tyler's car rolled up.

When Herman and Tyler exited the vehicle, Tyler didn't bother locking the car. Many of the homeless people seemed to brighten at the sight of him, and it was reciprocated.

"Come on," Tyler said as he beckoned Herman to follow.

They strode around the long line until they reached a door leading into the basement of the church. As they went, several people greeted Tyler by name. He would kindly say hello in return.

As they crossed the door's threshold, the smell of freshly-cooked chili enveloped them. Several men and women scurried about with disposable aprons, gloves, and hair nets. The line from outside filed into a large florescent-lit room with a low ceiling. Here, the homeless waited patiently with disposable bowls and spoons. Among them, stations with apron-toting volunteers dished up chili from massive, steaming pots.

It's a soup kitchen, Herman thought.

"Here. You'll need these."

Tyler's outstretched hands contained a hairnet, one glove, and a disposable apron. As Herman put on his glove and hair net, Tyler circled around the back of him and tied his apron for him. It was at that moment that a large woman with horn-rimmed glasses approached them both.

"Tyler! Early as usual, God bless you," she said. "And who's this?"

"This is my friend Herman," Tyler said as he fastened his hair net. "He's gonna help us today."

"Nice to meet you, Herman!" the lady shook his gloved hand. "Tyler, you can take table duty. These people could use your bright smile. Herman, are you alright to serve? It shouldn't be hard with one hand."

Herman said that would be fine, and immediately he was led over to the start of the line where a giant pot of chili was waiting for him. He replaced an elderly gentlemen with a hunched back and a big smile who greeted him as he walked away.

He thought to himself, *All these people seem so happy.*

As the homeless filed through, Herman carefully slopped a mighty ladle full of chili into each bowl. Nearly every time, he received a sincere thank you. There was only a handful of people that would stare at the bowl gruffly. But for the most part, Herman heard a lot of "thank you" and "much obliged" and "God bless you".

He stood there serving chili for nearly an hour. When his pot would run low, some apron-clad do-gooder would swiftly bring a new one, filled to the brim. As Herman served Citytown's homeless, he couldn't help but feel a small glow inside him.

He looked over at Tyler, who was busy wiping plastic picnic tables populated by those with bowls of chili. He was talking and laughing with those around him, sharing his beaming, perfect smile and listening politely as people asked him questions or told him stories.

This is great and all, Herman thought. *But does this really mean that he doesn't have time to help us?*

Before he knew it, an elderly woman was tapping him on his shoulder. Herman turned around to look into those same horn-rimmed glasses from earlier. She said, "We're just about to close up, Herman. You and Tyler can go now."

Part of Herman was disappointed. It felt good to take some time out of his day to help those in need and he wasn't quite ready to go. Regardless, he took off his hair net and discarded his apron and glove. After just another minute, Tyler was there by his side, throwing away his things as well.

"What do you think?" Tyler said as he pushed open the door.

"I had a really nice time," Herman said as they walked out into the sun and the sounds of the city enveloped him. "It felt good."

"This is only one of the soup kitchens in the city, too," Tyler said. "There are dozens of others. The thing is that not all of them have the resources to feed everyone that lines up outside their doors. Look."

The line of remaining homeless dissolved as the news spread that the kitchen was closing. Everyone dejectedly walked away, some of them travelling in small groups. Tyler and Herman made their way to Tyler's shiny black car.

"A lot of these people are on their way to the next soup kitchen," Tyler said. "There's another one at Mama G's Thrift Shop just seven blocks down. But Mama G usually doesn't have a lot to go around. This is the biggest one. They definitely need the most donations."

"How often do you do this?" Herman said as he opened the door and slid into the passenger's seat.

"It used to be a couple of times per week," Tyler said as he snapped the door shut. "I used to just go to this one. But since my accident, I volunteer at four kitchens *every day*. Yeah. I have time to go to class in the morning and afternoon, soup kitchens in the evening, and do homework in the middle of the night. It's perfect. That's better than beating thugs with my fists."

Herman was silent and a knot tightened in his chest. He thought to himself, *Four soup kitchens every day still isn't a big deal for someone who has superspeed and endless energy. He could definitely be out with us every night. This is a good thing to do, but that excuse just doesn't hold a lot of water.*

"Now you see why I don't really care about the burglaries," Tyler said as he pulled out and started driving up the street. "It's all just stuff. Stuff is replaceable. When I hear that a bunch of stuff has been stolen and a window or two were broken, I think, who cares? I was always taught growing up that even though my family always had more than enough to get by, stuff is replaceable. People aren't. That's why when you see a person suffering, you gotta help. No question."

Herman hummed and nodded his head but didn't say anything.

After a few minutes, they rolled up to Herman's apartment and Tyler put the car in park. Herman didn't get out immediately. On the drive home, he couldn't help but think about the night that was ahead of him. Frankie said that they needed "all hands on deck," and that included Tyler. It was going to be big.

"I know you think what we're dealing with isn't important," Herman said. "But the rest of us want to get back to our normal lives as quickly as possible, and that means tracking down Alpha Master. This person put these conditions upon us, and we didn't ask for it. That's wrong. Whoever Alpha Master is, they need to be stopped. We need you."

Tyler inhaled deeply and sighed. He shook his head and said, "I don't think so, Herman. Maybe you guys just need to be honest with yourselves and accept that these powers are a part of who you are now. There's nothing wrong with them. My focus is helping those *really* struggling every day with the essentials. You guys will be alright."

"It would seriously only take a few minutes out of your night. We need you, Tyler—"

"I'm telling you, I *don't care.*"

Tyler's dark brown eyes were dead serious. Herman's gaze fixed on them for a second, then he pressed his lips together and slipped out of the car without another word.

He tried not to slam the door. They had *no idea* what was waiting for them at Alpha Master's compound. There could be dozens more like the goons they fight every night. Tyler has the capacity to do away with all of them in a flash, and he couldn't take one night to help? Tyler's self-righteousness made Herman's blood boil, and he was about to storm off until Tyler unrolled the window.

"Herman!"

Herman turned around. Tyler was leaning toward the open passenger window, his hand still on the wheel.

"I'll have my communicator in tonight," Tyler said. "If things get too crazy, hit me up, okay?"

Herman nodded a little bit and said, "Thanks. See you."

Tyler backed his car out of the parking spot and pulled away as Herman began the ascension to apartment 329. He cracked his knuckles as he pressed his fist against his hip.

The rest of the afternoon was uneventful. He had missed the ending of Death Soldier, which he couldn't care less about. He read a book, watched some funny internet videos, and took a shower. By that time, it was 4:30. Nearly time to head out.

He threw on his jacket and slung his backpack over his shoulder as he made his way down the hall. Thankfully, no one (Zach) was in the living room as he made his way to the front door. He checked his pockets to make sure he had his keys to the Leftybike. He threw open the door and stepped outside.

His heart jumped when he found Cassie face-to-face with him. Her arms were folded and she leaned against the doorframe as if she had been there for hours.

"Hey!" Herman said. "I thought you'd already be at the lab?"

"I need a ride," she said. The statement came across more like a demand than an actual request.

"I thought you had a car."

"It won't start."

Herman frowned sympathetically and pulled the keys out from his pocket, telling her that a ride wouldn't be a problem. Just as they were about to walk down the stairs, Herman remembered something.

"Oh! I need to grab my helmet. Give me a sec."

He opened the door and left it open just a crack, expecting to be in and out in less than a minute. He also expected Cassie to wait outside by the door. But she didn't. She followed him through the living room, past the kitchen, and down the hall to his bedroom. Her arms stayed folded and her face remained as blank as ever. Herman looked back at her curiously.

"Don't judge me," he said as he crossed into his bedroom.

With his clothes strewn across the floor, junk cluttering every flat surface, and his bed unkept, it definitely wasn't ready for the presence of a desirable female. Cassie's eyes darted about the posters of movies and bands tacked up on the walls. She carefully stepped between the discarded clothes and plopped down on the bed as if it were her own.

"Wow," she said. "This place is a disaster."

"I said don't judge me."

"Too late," she said. "How do you find anything in here?"

"It's an organized mess," Herman said pointedly. "I still know where everything is. Like I know that I left my helmet right here… wait. No. Maybe it's over… nope—"

"Maybe you should ask those five empty pizza boxes where you put it."

"Ha ha, you're hilarious. *Ah!* Here it is. Let's go."

Herman ducked out of the room, helmet in hand, but Cassie didn't follow. It wasn't until he was halfway down the hall that he realized she wasn't behind him. He stopped, then backtracked to the bedroom. He found her not just sitting on his bed, but laying over his strewn-out comforter, staring at the ceiling. Her hands were behind her head.

Herman leaned against the door. "You okay?"

Cassie didn't look at him. "I think so."

The springs creaked as he sat down on the corner of the mattress. Her eyes panned to his, as if expecting him to say something. Thinking it over, Herman thought he might know what it could be.

"I'm sorry about last night," he said. "I know you're not a touchy person, so I'm sorry if that was a little weird. You know, with the hand holding... or whatever. I was just trying to show you how I feel. I understand if it's not... the same."

Cassie continued to stare into Herman's blue eyes, then her gaze traveled down his arm and rested on his hook. She sat up, making the bed springs creak again. She reached out and took the hook, bringing it up to examine it.

Herman's heart rate picked up and he swallowed. She was sitting close. Her fingers traced the edges of the cold, metal hook—no nerve endings in Herman's prosthetic to reciprocate her touch.

"Are you used to this yet?" She purred.

He shook his head. "No."

Herman could feel her exhale on his arm. It gave him goosebumps. Then she put down the hook, gazed Herman in the eyes, and said, "We're all a little broken, aren't we?"

They stayed like that, suspended in each other's eyes, for a long moment. Herman's heart rate didn't slow down and he swallowed again. Her face was close to his. He couldn't help but look from her eyes, down to her freckled nose, then to her lips, which were so soft and pink. When he looked back into those glowing emeralds, she was already pulling herself away—not willing to take a chance, not willing to put herself on the line.

"Let's go," she said. Then she leapt off the bed and stormed out the hallway.

Herman took a deep breath to collect himself. He glared at the hook protruding from his right forearm, took another breath, grabbed his helmet, and followed.

13

Katy led Cassie and Herman into Sid's office, and from that point, they knew how to get into the lab. They found the red button in Sid's desk drawer and clicked it. The *chunk* and *whoosh* and *hiss* filled the room as the back wall rumbled up into the ceiling.

After they marched up the hallway to the lab, they found Susan, Frankie, and Sid gathered around the meeting table, which was covered in blueprints pinned down at each corner. The light above the table threw a dramatic orange glow that cast shadows on everyone's faces.

"Good evening, my young friends!" Sid said spiritedly. He readjusted the goggles on his forehead and said, "I assume the Leftybike suits you well?"

"It's perfect," Herman replied. "Thanks, Sid."

"How are you feeling about tonight?"

Herman slid a glance at Cassie. "A little nervous. We don't know exactly what we're up against."

"I'm not worried," Cassie said.

"Of course," Sid replied. "Now, Mr. Chan, tell us what you learned about Alpha Master's hideout."

"We just know where it is," Frankie said, pointing at the blueprint. "It's the old abandoned hospital on the north side of town. Susan and I went crimefighting the other night after Herman's aunt came into town and managed to squeeze the information out of Nikki and Chet. That's all we could get before the cops showed up."

"So, we don't know if there's anyone guarding the compound," Susan said with folded arms. "Alpha Master could be tucked away in there all alone, or the hospital could be heavily guarded by more of his goons. We just don't know."

"That's why we need to be strategic about this," Frankie said. "Did anyone hear from Tyler?"

"He's not coming."

Everyone turned to Herman. Susan cocked her head and said, "You're sure?"

"Yeah," Herman said. "He said he'll come if things get crazy, but that's it. He doesn't care about what we're doing."

Frankie frowned. "Wow. He doesn't care about a cure?"

"Nope."

Everyone deflated. Sid shook his head. Cassie didn't say anything. Susan rolled her eyes. Frankie sighed and said, "Well, let's hope things don't get too crazy, but at least he can be our backup."

"So, what's the plan, then?" Herman said.

Sid straightened his goggles again and leaned over the table, shrouding his face in shadow. "We don't know precisely where in the hospital Alpha Master is hiding. We are also unaware of what kind of precautions he'll take, assuming he's expecting you. The main entrance and the emergency room entrance are on opposing sides of the building—north and south. I recommend that we decide on an entrance immediately and designate which one to enter as a team. It's better to have all of you together in case of heavy reinforcements."

Eyes hopped around the room to each other. It sounded like a good enough plan. If they split up, they might be able to cover more ground, but the team would be weaker. The best thing they could do is stick together in case there were loads of goons.

"When do we leave?" Cassie asked.

"Sundown," Frankie said. "We'll take the Leftybike and the minicopters. Hey, Sid, when are the rest of us getting something like a motorcycle?"

"I don't need one," Susan shook her head.

Sid blinked. "I thought your Bludgeoning Stereo Playback Performance Device was quite enough. Why do you need a motorcycle?"

"Well, Herman's got one."

"You have an automobile," Sid explained. "Everyone here has their own mode of transportation excluding Mr. Fitzgerald. If you've forgotten already, Mr. Fitzgerald is in this very predicament because of a serious car accident—"

"Okay, sure. But could you, like, soup up my car or something? It would be awesome if it had an electro-gun or something."

"Absolutely not, Mr. Chan!" Sid frowned. "The Leftybike is a mode of transportation constructed specifically for an individual with a physical limitation! The thought of installing advanced weaponry on your vehicle on a whim of unbridled masculinity is absolutely preposterous—"

"Fine, sheesh!"

"I'll let you ride it sometime," Herman said.

"Yeah, but it only works with your hook."

"Oh, that's right."

"*As I was saying*," Sid said. "Shall we enter through the emergency room entrance or main entrance?"

"Emergency room," Cassie said without hesitation. "Look. The emergency room entrance leads to a lot of tightly-packed operating rooms. We can sweep these rooms as we go by. Avoiding bigger rooms like the main entrance will make us harder to spot."

Susan, Herman, and Frankie exchanged glances before agreeing in the affirmative. At that, Sid nodded in approval and his finger starting darting across the blueprints.

"The emergency room entrance is on the south side," he said. "Like Ms. Copland said, there appears to be a large cluster of confined operation rooms nearby, so be careful. The hallways don't look too narrow. However, these patient rooms would be excellent opportunities for Alpha Master's associates to surprise you. The hospital is only one floor, so it shouldn't take too long.

"In the middle of the compound, there's an atrium. It has a large sunroof that can be accessed by this staircase and elevator just outside the room, so this can be an emergency pickup point if necessary. I'll monitor your locations and keep the minicopters at the nearest exit at all times."

Herman asked, "But I and one other person will still have to get away on the Leftybike?"

Sid scratched his head. "I only have two minicopters. They take a while to build."

"Okay," Herman said as he looked around. "Guess we just need to watch our backs."

"Are there any questions?" Sid asked with both hands on the table, gazing around his crew.

"I feel like this plan has a lot of holes in it," Susan said dryly.

"I know," Sid replied. "But we don't have much to work off. We're doing the best we can."

"If we managed to catch this Alpha Master character," Herman said. "Then what?"

"Our goal isn't so much to capture him as it is to confirm his whereabouts," Sid said. "If we can confirm that Alpha Master's base of operations is at the abandoned hospital, we can send the word on to Citytown Police and they can apprehend him."

"Okay, but the police aren't exactly doing a bang-up job right now," Frankie said as he put his hands in his hoodie pockets. "Maybe we'll have to capture him ourselves. Fight fire with fire— our powers against his. Then once we got him, we can take him to the police. That'll get the Green Juice off the streets sooner, too."

"You do have a point, Mr. Chan," Sid said, clapping his hands together and pointing them at Frankie. "If you find yourself in a position to confidently capture Alpha Master without repercussions, take that course of action. Does anyone have any questions?"

"So, it's a definite no on the electro-gun?"

"*Indeed.*"

"I feel like we're prepared as we're ever going to be," Herman said. "How much longer until we go?"

Frankie looked at his watch and said, "Sundown isn't for another few hours."

Everyone exchanged glances, the silence of the lab echoing off the walls. It was at that moment that a smile spread across Sid's face.

"Have you all seen the motion picture adaptation of *Death Soldier?*"

*

Herman didn't feel the wind snapping at his face as he sped through the lit streets of Citytown. The helmet fastened on his head (which Cassie insisted on not wearing) shielded his skull from the gale. Cassie's hair, however, bounced and waved in the wind as she held on tightly to Herman's torso. They careened through the streets, the Leftybike's engine roaring against the night. Herman kept his eyes peeled for police cars which, thankfully, were very few.

Overhead, the faint outlines of two minicopters were barely visible due to the cloaking software programmed into their systems. Herman and Cassie could hear both Susan and Frankie in their ears, though.

"Just passing over downtown," Frankie said. "We should be there in about seven minutes."

Over time, the skyscrapers disappeared and gave way to smaller apartment buildings, then those disappeared, and a derelict industrial area of Citytown materialized. Some of the warehouses and factories were still in use, but for the most part, the chain link fences and bleached asphalt parking lots gave the impression these buildings had been abandoned years ago. Herman scrunched his eyebrows as he glanced at the lot of them.

Graffiti riddled every vertical surface. No one was out walking the sidewalks. Trash filled the gutters. Herman constantly had to watch for unfilled potholes.

After a couple of minutes, Herman and Cassie found themselves on the south side of a massive single-story complex. A glass dome could be seen that bubbled out of the center of the building—the atrium. Before their eyes, a massive red cross was mounted above a sign indicating an emergency room entrance. Like all the other buildings in the area, the perimeter was guarded by a chain-link fence, but that didn't stop vandals from spray-painting every wall of the building.

The Leftybike slid to a stop. Herman and Cassie shielded their faces as two invisible minicopters descended from the sky, sending out heavy gusts of wind. In the usual coat of blue sparkles, the cloaking devices lifted and the minicopters appeared. The bucket seats landed neatly next to the Leftybike. Susan and Frankie unbuckled their harnesses and hopped out without much of a word, each toting their weapons.

Herman clicked his hammer into place before swinging his leg off the Leftybike. Once he was off, he turned to the Leftybike and said, "Stealth mode."

The Leftybike beeped, then its surface rippled like a mirage of blue sparkles before it disappeared into thin air. Susan and Frankie did the same to the minicopters. Not far away, a large tear in the chain link fence was wide enough to squeeze through.

"You guys ready?" Susan said.

Nods all around. Frankie pushed on his headphones and clicked a button on his Bambox.

The fence jingled quietly as every member slipped through, cautiously treading through the parking lot. By the emergency room entrance, three rusting ambulances with flat tires were stationed—two of which were turned on their side. Herman straightened his jacket.

"How long has it been since this hospital has been abandoned?" He asked.

"Sid's blueprint was from forty years ago," Frankie replied quietly. "It's been at least a couple of decades since someone has worked here. There was something about an airborne virus outbreak and they had to quarantine the entire building. A lot of people died."

"You don't think that virus is still floating around, do you?" Herman asked, the hair standing up on his neck and arms.

"It's definitely gone," Susan said as she marched with her soccer ball by her hip. "There are other things in there that probably want to kill us instead."

Their feet crunched on the asphalt as they crept up to the entrance. Herman took a peek inside the ambulances as they lurked around. Their back hatches were wide open, but their walls were bare of any medical supplies. One of the ambulances had a sleeping bag and some empty cans strewn around the inside.

"These probably belong to a hobo," Frankie said.

The door to the emergency room was a closed sliding door. However, all the windowpanes had been shattered, leaving nothing but a pool of broken glass on the floor—nothing from keeping them outside. Everyone tiptoed through the broken doors, being careful not to let their feet crunch too loudly on the glass.

It was like a hurricane had gone through the emergency room. Most of the chairs were overturned. Old posters peeled off the walls, which were also riddled with graffiti. Two rats scurried across the laminate floor. The whole place reeked of dust and mold.

A set of double-doors led into the rest of the building. They all inched toward it, tense, with weapons at the ready. All was still.

The double doors made no sound as they pushed through, and immediately they were met by a hallway lined with doors. Everyone agreed to carefully try each door, opening and closing each one, checking for traps. Every door revealed a room with an operating table, empty drawers scattered across the ground, broken glass, and discarded surgical equipment, but no goons. After every room was checked, the team regrouped before moving on.

"Nothing… everything has been really easy so far," Frankie whispered.

"Don't say stuff like that," Cassie said. "That's the kind of stuff idiots say before—"

Chhhk!

A loud hissing blared through the hallway, causing everyone to jump and bring up their weapons. The hissing was caused by the intercom system, which only crackled for a fraction of a second. Then, a man's voice, smooth and dark, echoed through the hall.

"You started cold," he said. "But you're getting warmer."

Chhhk.

Just like that, the voice was gone. Everyone looked at each other.

"He's expecting us!" Herman said. "This is a total trap. Should we just turn around?"

"And then what?" Cassie shot. "Come back another time when he's had a chance to prepare something else?"

"Yeah! And that would give *us* time to prepare something else, too!"

"Not necessarily," Frankie shrugged. "He might move after this. Besides, I think Sid has made us all the crime-fighting gadgets we need. No electro-guns or motorcycles…"

"Dude, you gotta let that go."

Chhhk!

"I have no desire to harm any of you this evening," Alpha Master's slick, dark voice echoed through the hall again. "Why would I destroy such incredible specimens? You'll find my lab on the opposite side of the atrium. I look forward to speaking with you all."

Chhhk.

There was a brief silence before they all exchanged. looks again. Susan was the first to speak up.

"Seriously, we should go back and just report that he's here," she whispered.

"I agree," Herman said.

"Or it could be that he actually, genuinely, sincerely wants to talk to us," Frankie said brightly.

"Are you serious?" Herman said firmly. "This whole place has 'trap' written all over it."

"That's not what the graffiti says. That tag looks like a—"

"Sid, move the minicopters near the atrium," Cassie said as she touched her ear.

"You got it," Sid sounded in everyone's earpiece.

Cassie looked at everyone. "There. Alpha Master's lab is right by the atrium. If it gets too heavy, we can make a break for it. We'll be fine."

"I'm telling you, this is a mistake," Susan said firmly. "We've got what we came for. We know he's here. Let's *leave* and report him."

Cassie was already moving deeper into the hospital. Herman followed her closely, looking around, wary of anything that could jump out at her. Frankie followed behind Herman, but not without turning to Susan to shrug apologetically. Susan rolled her eyes and shook her head with a clenched jaw. She stormed behind the rest of the pack.

Worn-out signs on the halls indicated directions for different places in the hospital: the cafeteria, the intensive care unit, and the atrium, among other things. The trail that led them to the atrium was cluttered with dirt, discarded wrappers, and used syringes. They leered at every doorway they passed through, but nothing jumped out. The only thing that kept them company was the eerie silence of a dusty abandoned hospital, rife with vandalism and trash.

At length, they crossed the entrance to the atrium. It must have been magnificent decades ago. The center of the room was a sprawling garden with dead trees reaching their dry branches to the half-dome sunroof. However, the soil was completely dry and cracked—the remains of other shrubs and plants had disappeared long ago, and the tree bark had a ghostly pale glow in the moonlight.

The team edged their way around the atrium, scanning other entrances carefully. Nothing moved. Just them.

"*Listen!*" Susan hissed angrily.

Everyone's heads swiveled about. Her foot was over her soccer ball, pinning it to the ground as her eyes burned. Last of all, her hands stuck to her hips like a scolding you-know-what.

"Do any of you remember why we're here?" she whispered.

Frankie answered timidly. "To get Alpha Master?"

"Right! And how do we do that?"

"We confirm his location and report it to the police," Frankie continued just as timidly.

Susan tossed a hand in the air. "So *why* are we doing this? We *know* he's here! If we keep going, we're playing into his hand. I guarantee he's got a trap waiting for us. We have to go or one of us is going to get seriously hurt."

"We decided to capture him and bring him in ourselves," Cassie said. "Remember? At the lab?"

"We said we'd bring him in ourselves we *could*," Susan was still whispering. "We don't know if we can. We don't know what he has in store for us. Are you seriously willing to take that chance?"

"Yes," Cassie said.

Their heads jerked to Frankie and Herman. The two boys' blood went cold.

"Ghetto Blaster, come on," Susan said. "Let's get out of here. We've got what we came here for. Let's go call it a night and put *all of this* behind us for good."

Frankie's eyes darted around. He moved his headphones and scratched his head. "Uh... I'll go with whatever Hammerfist decides."

Both Cassie and Susan reared on Herman. He swallowed.

"I know you agree with me, Hammerfist," Susan said. "You said it yourself. Let's go."

Cassie took a step forward and put her hand on Herman's shoulder. "We can do this. We can handle him."

Frankie watched silently, his eyes wide.

Herman swallowed again, shifting his gaze from Susan to Cassie. Susan was being completely reasonable. But Cassie's emerald eyes were much closer to him. Looking at him. And her hand was on his shoulder, holding it gently. He cleared his throat as he gazed into Cassie's face.

"I think we'll be okay," Herman said. "We've got our communicators and Tyler said he'll help us if things get too crazy. With him, we can get out of this place without a problem. Let's bring Alpha Master in ourselves. Okay?"

Susan's jaw hung down. Then she pursed her lips together, shook her head, and kicked her soccer ball into her hand. Cassie's eyes sparkled with satisfaction and she strolled around the edge of the atrium.

Moving forward, Susan put her hand on Herman's shoulder and leaned over to whisper in his ear.

"Remember, Hammerfist, we're not invincible," she said. "All of us still have families. We have people who are waiting to see us in the morning. I hope that nothing happens to anyone here tonight."

She squeezed his shoulder and walked away. In her wake, Herman shuddered.

As they edged their way around, they noticed a dim orange light flickering on the opposite side of the atrium. They all knew that had to be where Alpha Master was broadcasting from. They edged closer and closer to the light, and as they did, the sounds of clinking glass and small footsteps became clearer.

Herman nudged the others and pointed out the ladder ascending to the top of the atrium. His hand motions said, *Hey, we can use that if we need.* The others nodded and kept walking.

They emerged into a hallway with loads of doors on either side, but just one door was open. From that room, the orange light seeped into the hallway. The sound of clinking glass was now accompanied by bubbling liquid, and a smell like rubber and burnt cabbage percolated through the air.

Herman nudged the others again as he noticed a door to their left with a staircase sign on it.

Everyone crept closer to the light. Now they could hear wistful humming from the room. Cassie extracted the brick from a pouch on her back, levitating it in the air. Herman cocked his hammer, Susan readied her soccer ball, and Frankie turned up the volume on his Bambox.

They turned the corner. There, a long recovery room that must have housed two people once stood. Now, the entire room was wallpapered with old sheets containing formulas, graphs, and schematics. Much like Sid's lab, jars and beakers populated tables that were pushed against the walls, containing fluids of various colors and odors. The only difference was that this lab didn't look futuristic at all—the tables, shelves, and chairs were all secondhand.

And there was a man. On the far side of the room, with his back to the crew, he heard them approach. He perked up like a dog at the sound of a whistle. His lab coat swished as he turned around. Under the lab coat, a vibrant teal sweater covered his torso. His soft face adorned a dazzling smile and a perfectly parted haircut.

Herman's jaw fell and his eyes widened. He knew this face, but it wasn't that of a supervillain. Alpha Master clasped his hands behind his back and said:

"Welcome, my friends, to my private lab!"

14

"*Mac?*" Herman bellowed as he pointed his hammer. "Mac the bus driver? *You're* Alpha Master!?"

"Herman!" Mac smiled jovially. "My favorite passenger! I had suspicions that you weren't really at that arcade!" He laughed. "Out fighting crime, you little rascal! And these are your friends? Hello! Pleasure to meet you all!"

Everyone was too dumbfounded to speak. Herman felt as though someone had taken his own hammer and smashed him in the face. Mac the bus driver? Alpha Master? Green Juice? And he was all behind it?

"You look confused," Mac said as he placed his hands in his pockets. "I'm sure you have many questions. To begin, allow me to introduce myself properly. My full name is Doctor Malcolm McMasters—former chemist for The Genesis Corporation and the father of Compound Z24. Please, have a seat."

He motioned to four metal folding chairs off to the side of the entrance, waiting for them. No one moved.

Doctor McMasters deflated. "You have no reason to be nervous. Look!" he turned out all of his pockets and spun around. "I'm completely defenseless! And even if I did have a weapon on me, I wouldn't be any match for you four. Please sit down."

The four tensely exchanged glances. Naturally, Cassie was the first one to sit. Her brick rested on her lap, ready to strike out at any moment if need be. The other three cautiously slid into their seats, not taking their eyes off Doctor McMasters.

Meanwhile, Herman was still reeling.

"Mac, *why are you doing this?*" Herman couldn't keep himself from shouting. "Why are you driving all of these goons to commit crime and steal things? This doesn't seem like you at all!"

Doctor McMasters frowned. "I never compel them to commit crime. I'd prefer that they didn't. But they keep buying the Compound. How they choose to carry out their evenings is no business of mine."

"Then just stop making it!" Herman said. "Cut them off! How can you go on producing something that you know hurts people? How do you live with yourself?"

"Herman, you must calm down," Doctor McMasters said. He slid into a swiveling task chair not two feet from where he was standing. "Lots of consumable goods are produced daily that do more harm than good—tobacco, alcohol, refined sugars. I never force my clients to take the compound. They can stop coming to me at any time. I'm just a simple man running my own little enterprise, no different from any other shop in Citytown."

"Yeah, I'm like, nintety-nine percent sure you're not paying property taxes, though," Frankie said as he looked around.

Doctor McMasters laughed. "Well, you got me there!"

"But why this?" Herman said sternly. "You could be doing anything else."

"I do it because this is my life's work," Doctor McMasters said earnestly. "I've dedicated my entire life to formulating compounds that improve people's lives. It would be death for me to see it go to waste."

"Well it's almost been death for us, literally," Cassie said coldly. "Multiple times."

"And for that, I am sorry," Doctor McMasters said. "But again, that is not my doing. Not directly."

"Just indirectly," Cassie narrowed her eyes.

Doctor McMasters teased a smirk like a parent flexing their patience in front of a misbehaving child. He sat up straight, took a deep breath, and crossed one leg over the other.

"My friends," he said. "Allow me to start from the beginning.

"Years ago, I was the top chemist at The Genesis Corporation, an institution commissioned by the United States government to concoct a variety of chemicals for human consumption. I led a team of chemists that were tasked with creating a compound that granted temporary bouts of insomnia, drastically increased energy output, and rapid healing with no adverse side effects. With thousands of tests, we were less than successful."

Herman slid subtle glances to the others, who returned them. Doctor McMasters went on:

"But then we experienced a breakthrough. With the compound, we found that we successfully achieved temporary insomnia, increased energy, and rapid healing... but the subjects experienced superhuman side effects depending upon their DNA structure. These included super speed, telekinesis, manipulation of fire or electricity, and other abilities. We believed we had finally found something special. We dubbed the formula Compound Z24."

Doctor McMasters stood from his chair and clasped his hands behind his back before he began pacing in small circles, his face to the ground.

"I presented it to the executives. They were unsatisfied. They wanted *no* side effects *whatsoever.* The additional superhuman abilities were not deemed acceptable. At the time, the only other thing we had concocted was Compound X, which granted superhuman strength and speed, but was fifty percent lethal to subjects. This didn't satisfy them, either.

"At this point, I had run out of options. I knew the executive team's patience was running thin, so I left the organization. They had no interest in Compound Z24, so I took many of my notes with me. It took ages, but I acquired the necessary resources and began mass producing Compound Z24 privately."

From the desk, he extracted a small vial with a thick green liquid. He held it up to his eyes, twisting it curiously, leering at it with satisfaction.

"The effects last less than 24 hours," he continued. "But the results are consistent. You don't need sleep. You have perpetual energy. You can be pummeled and bludgeoned as much as you like, and you heal before you can recite your ABC's. I concocted a true marvel of modern chemistry—a compound to restructure human DNA for the better."

With that, he gingerly placed the vial back on the desk. The crew watched carefully with furrowed eyebrows and tightened jaws, soaking in everything they just heard.

"So you just sell the compound to whoever can pay?" Frankie said.

"Precisely," Doctor McMasters said. "And it's a very high price, mind you. You've met some of my customers, but certainly not all of them. Many of them are athletes, doctors, lawyers— slaving away for countless hours, in desperate need of something that will help them finish the next surgery or the next case. Compound Z24 breathes life into them. You could say that I have helped serve hundreds of others across the Citytown area. Indirectly, of course." He smirked in Cassie's direction.

Cassie narrowed her eyes again. With arms still folded and brick still levitating, she said, "But your compound is only temporary?"

"Yes."

"Then why have we been like this for over a week?" Susan shot.

Doctor McMasters' eyes flashed. "It's very interesting, isn't it? When I first heard of your escapades, I assumed that somehow, someone had stolen servings of the compound from my lab. But night after night, I saw that my inventory was untouched. Was it possible that one of my buyers was selling to others? Perhaps, but all of them have denied it time and time again. So, let me ask you all one simple question…"

He took a menacing step forward. Everyone bristled. His hands stayed clasped behind his back, and any ounce of jovial hospitality he had was now gone. The following words slithered from his lips.

"…do any of you know a man by the name of *Sidney Saskatoon?*"

Silence. The four were dumbstruck. Upon seeing their reactions, Doctor McMasters' eyes flashed again.

"Ah," he began. "I see."

"What do you know about Sid?" Frankie shot with pointed eyebrows.

"Doctor Saskatoon was an associate of mine at The Genesis Corporation," Doctor McMasters said. "He and I worked closely together on the Compound Z24 project. When he found out I was leaving the company, he was not pleased. I was his leader, his mentor… his friend. But, Sidney was also very clever and slippery. Far more than I ever was.

"He tried to take all my notes and keep them for himself. He wanted to take all that I had done and build upon it so he could take the glory for himself when The Genesis Corporation finally achieved what they wanted. No. I couldn't allow that. I had worked too hard for it. I took everything that I could and destroyed the rest. I can only assume that he's tried to reconstruct the compound from memory since then."

"So..." Frankie said. "You're not the one who put the compound in us?"

"Of course not!" Doctor McMasters threw his hands in the air. "Why would I subject someone to the compound against their will? That's madness! Besides, my version of the compound is *temporary.* You four have suffered from a *permanent* variation of the compound! The only explanation is that Doctor Sidney Saskatoon has done this to you. How he did this to you, however, is beyond me."

More silence. Cassie's voice was small as she stared at the ground. "All of us were in the Citytown General Hospital last week."

Doctor McMasters nodded. "It appears as though you have your answer. He must have gained access to the hospital and subjected you to the compound. It's the only explanation."

Herman's head was swimming. He stared at the ground between his feet. The hammer attached to his wrist, resting on his knee—the product of a man that had turned his life upside down. And for what? The communicator, the tether between him and this man, was still fastened in his ear.

"Sid..." Herman whispered half to him and half to himself. "Why?"

On the other end, no answer.

"Like I said, I have no intention of fighting any of you," Doctor McMasters said. "I know you expected this place to be booby trapped or guarded in some way, but you can see that I am but a lone man avoiding astronomically high Citytown property taxes.

If you have no other questions, you can feel free to be on your way. However…"

Doctor McMasters reached for a small apparatus on his desk. As he pulled it into the light, the four recognized it as a syringe. Its long, sharp needle glistened in the orange lamplight.

"I would very much like a sample of your blood," he said, taking small steps toward the group. "I have no antidote for you, but I could construct one for a price. I must know what Sidney has concocted—a permanent solution to Compound Z24 is a fascinating prospect. Being the father of this compound, I feel as though it is my right to have—"

The four abruptly stood from their chairs. Doctor McMasters shrunk. The greedy flare in his eyes subsided to caution.

"It's a no from me," Herman said.

"Same," Frankie said.

Susan and Cassie both chimed in the affirmative. Doctor McMasters took a step back, pocketed the syringe, and ran his fingers through his perfectly parted hair before clasping them behind his back again.

"Very well," he said. "I'm sorry for what you all have been through recently. I wish you all the best."

He's here, Herman thought. *He's unguarded. He's not going anywhere. Forget Sid—we can go straight to the police and they'll come get him. This is all over after tonight.*

With that, the four began filing out of the room, weapons in hand. Cassie hung back, making sure she filed out last. Before she crossed the threshold, she leaned back and hissed to Doctor McMasters, "You'll stop selling the compound to the Thespian, Nikki and Chet, and Demonspawn. Now. Got it?"

Doctor McMasters nodded politely. "Understood."

Their footsteps echoed dully in the hallway, the only other sound coming from Doctor McMasters' bubbling test tubes.

Cassie wasn't far behind Herman. As he looked back, he caught sight of her hissing an order at Doctor McMasters. He smirked.

As she saw Herman's face, she almost cracked a grin. As she began walking away from Doctor McMasters, a devilish sneer splashed across his face. Herman's smile dropped as quickly as he saw Doctor McMasters' hand dive into a desk drawer.

15

It all happened within a second. Doctor McMasters withdrew a taser in his desk and fired it at Cassie. She howled and collapsed to the floor, twitching and convulsing as the device shot jolts of electricity through her body. Her brick dropped. Doctor McMasters kicked it out of the room. Herman scrambled to her aid, but he was too late. A steel door fell from the ceiling, trapping Cassie inside. The sound of its fall rebounded through the hall.

BOOM!

"*Cassie!*" Herman screamed.

He darted to the door and began slamming it with his hammer. He pictured her body, still convulsing and twitching with the taser barbs stuck in her. He also pictured Doctor McMasters hovering over her, that long syringe in his greedy fingers, sucking the red blood from her fair skin.

He slammed the door harder and faster, the crashing booms echoing down the hallway. He bared his teeth and tried to keep his eyes from misting. The hammer didn't make a dent.

"*Let her go, you bastard!*" He bellowed.

"Hammerfist!" Frankie shouted.

Herman tore his eyes from the door to see a flickering light sparking from the darkness. He had seen that flicker before. He dropped to the floor just as a lightning bolt shot over him, missing him by inches, crashing into the wall behind him and sending a burst of rubble into the air. One of Frankie's blasts shot into the darkness, but the shadow evaded it gracefully, causing another eruption of rubble down the hall.

"O, what a tragic turn!" The Thespian's voice cackled from the darkness.

"We gotta go!" Frankie said.

"*I'm not leaving her!*" Herman shot as he struggled to his feet.

"There's no time!" Susan said. "Look!"

A steel door to the atrium was closing. They only had a matter of seconds. Herman slammed the door one more time. No use. He pressed his face up against the steel and shouted, "*I'll come back for you! I promise!*" With that, he bared his teeth, wiped his eyes, dug his feet in, and sprinted for the atrium.

Frankie hurled blasts into the dark, leaving explosions of debris and rubble. Meanwhile, the Thespian dodged each blow and shot back multiple thunder bolts. Each shot illuminated the dark hallway with a pale blue light. Herman took a blast in the shoulder just before he reached the door. He yelped as the thunder blast seared into him like a hot iron. He bared his teeth again, knowing that the pain would go away in a few minutes. He just couldn't take more hits.

The door was nearly closed. Frankie ducked underneath, along with Susan. Herman slid underneath like a runner between third and home, arriving in the atrium just before the door rumbled shut.

All the other exits were closed with similar steel doors.

"Trapped," Frankie said. "Of course."

"Tyler!" Herman hollered into his earpiece. "Tyler, come in!"

Nothing.

"Tyler, *can you hear me?*"

Smash!

The unmistakable sound of broken glass echoed from above. Everyone's gaze shot up to see Chet, Nikki, and Demonspawn cascading from the sunroof in a shower of broken glass. The three heroes scattered, throwing themselves away from the shower.

Herman rolled out of the way just before Chet's metal fist came crashing into the floor. The impact left a crater six feet wide and the ground shook. Herman slid onto his feet, his blood boiling. He darted at Chet, hammer raised.

Chet caught the hammer with his open fist and raised Herman off his feet. Herman tried to kick his stomach, but Chet caught his foot.

"You looking to cut off my stash, bro?" Chet seethed. "The Green Juice is my best preworkout! I'm gonna smash your—*ah!*"

In the middle of his monologue, Herman jammed his fingers in Chet's eyes. Chet dropped him in a heap, his metal hands shooting up to his face. With that, and Herman kicked at his feet, toppling Chet to the ground.

Meanwhile, Susan battled with Nikki, who was blocking her soccer ball with every attack. The two kicked and twirled like an aggressive synchronized dance, the soccer ball rebounding from person to person. Finally, with a mighty spin and jump, Susan gave the ball the biggest kick she could muster, aiming it directly at Nikki's face. Nikki planted her feet and raised her hand.

Smack!

Nikki caught the ball single-handedly, her arm outstretched.

"I was a state champ goalie," Nikki sneered. "You're gonna have to try harder than that."

Susan sneered and said, "*Shock.*"

On command, the soccer ball's black panels flashed and blue jolts of electricity erupted from its core. Nikki roared as the sparks traveled up and down her body, tightening her muscles and burning her hair. She composed herself for just long enough to drop the ball and launch it at Susan. Susan took it in the stomach, the ball still electrified, sending her somersaulting backward and clutching her gut.

Not far away, Frankie launched one blast after another at Demonspawn, who neutralized each blast with every fiery breath. Demonspawn darted forward, brandishing his katana, metal chain dangling around his baggy black jeans. When he was upon Frankie, he raised his sword.

Frankie deflected the blow with the Bambox just in time. Swing after swing, Frankie narrowly parried the blows. Blow after blow, the Bambox took more cuts until finally, Frankie was too slow. Demonspawn's blade sliced into his shoulder.

"*Aaugh!* You little—"

Blam!

A successful close-range blast sent Demonspawn hurtling through the air, slamming against one of the dead trees, nearly snapping the trunk in two.

A dozen yards away, Herman just landed a generous swing on Chet's face, who staggered to the floor.

"Sid!" He shouted in his earpiece. "We need evac! Bring the minicopters to the floor level! I can't climb the ladder and Ghetto Blaster is injured!"

"Of course," Sid's voice sounded grave. "They'll arrive in twelve seconds."

Above, the minicopters began descending into the atrium. Demonspawn had recovered and spotted the minicopters. He gave a mighty inhale, ready to blow one out of the air. Frankie noticed him just in time and let out a blast.

Smack!

Demonspawn took the blast in the back and pinned him against the tree, then he slumped down, unconscious. Frankie hiked up the Bambox and dashed to the nearest minicopter, which was nearly on the ground.

Across the room, Susan's hands were locked with Nikki's. Chet had just landed a solid punch on Herman's face, shattering his nose. The impact made his face roar with pain and his eyes blurry. He spat out some blood and shook his head, trying to ignore the dissipating pain.

Frankie didn't hesitate—he fired two more blasts at Nikki and Chet, a perfect hit each time. Each of them toppled and rolled across the floor, letting out disoriented moans as they stopped.

"*Come on!*" Frankie shouted. "No time to strap ourselves in! Let's go!"

Susan darted for the minicopter and Herman staggered as he went. As Frankie passed him, he slid under his arm and carried Herman along like a wounded soldier.

"Now we're even, Hammerfist," he smirked. "Hold on tight to me. The minicopter isn't going to move fast with both of us."

As Frankie dropped into the seat and grabbed onto the straps, Herman got a better look at the gash in his shoulder. Blood was caked onto his jacket sleeve and was starting to seep down his shoulder. He grimaced.

"It'll be fine in a few minutes," Frankie said. "I'll heal even faster if I can get some meditative whale song going, but I don't want to change the music until we're in the clear. Your face looks like hell, though. Hold on tight to this other strap, okay?"

Herman planted his feet on the edge of minicopter and gripped the other free strap white-knuckle. His eyes weren't blurry anymore. The minicopter's blades revved up and slowly, it lifted off the ground, swaying unsteadily.

Nikki and Chet had composed themselves. Both of them bolted toward the minicopters, their metallic arms and legs glistening in the moonlight. Susan was already out of reach—her minicopter floated to the sunroof nearly a dozen feet above the others. Herman and Frankie, however, were barely off the ground.

Blam!

Frankie fired a blast as Chet advanced. Chet narrowly dodged it, and the minicopter took the brunt of the blast. The inertia of the blast threw it off course, swaying dangerously as it tried to ascend. Herman's foot slipped off the edge and he struggled to regain balance.

"Hey! Cut that out!" he yelled.

"Then *you* handle him!" Frankie shouted.

The minicopter was about eight feet off the ground. Chet was upon them. He leaped into the air and latched one of his metal hands onto the minicopter, causing the blades to whir and strain. Herman struggled to hold on as he started beating Chet's metal hand with his hammer, but his hammer rebounded off his fist like steel. Chet's fist clamped onto the edge of the minicopter and he started swinging his legs like a pendulum, making the minicopter reel to and fro as it tried to ascend.

It was useless. Herman's hammer wasn't doing anything. He shouted, "*GB!*"

Frankie's head popped over the side of the minicopter and he pointed his open palm at Chet's face. His eyes narrowed and he said, "Wrong move, bucko."

BLAM!

Chet took the full force of the blast to his shoulders and face, ripping his grasp from the minicopter. He shot to the ground, breaking the tile around him and kicking up dust. His nose had shattered and the skin on his face and shoulders peeled from the blast. His head swirled around, bleeding profusely, teetering on the brink of consciousness as Herman and Frankie taunted him a dozen feet above.

"Get wrecked, Chet!"

"Yeah, you suck, Chet!"

"Get a life, Chet!"

"No one likes you, Chet!"

The minicopter ascended quicker without Chet hanging on. Higher and higher it climbed until finally, it had ascended through the sunroof. Susan's minicopter was nearly out of sight, already on its way to Citytown Applied Technologies. Back in the atrium, the goons darted for the south hallway.

"I'm gonna let go!" Herman said. "I've got the Leftybike waiting for me. Get strapped in and I'll see you back at the lab!"

"Don't die!" Frankie admonished.

Then Herman jumped. His legs flailed through the air as he plummeted onto the hospital's roof. He touched ground, rolled out of the jump, and broke into a run.

Herman pumped his arms and legs as quickly as he could as breaths came out in great bursts. There were loads of rooftop entrances and the run to the emergency room entrance was long—Chet, Nikki, or Demonspawn could jump out at any moment. Would they? Are they that fast?

Tyler. He's fast. If he were here, he probably could have saved Cassie. This entire mess could have been avoided. Not only that, if they would have listened to Susan's advice and turned around when they did, none of this would have happened. Herman clenched his teeth, his body trembling with anger.

KABOOM!

Suddenly, Herman shot forward as massive, blazing hot force erupted from behind him. He stumbled and slid to a halt on his face, his ears ringing and his vision blurry.

A bomb! He thought. *They actually planted bombs up here! How many more are there?*

He didn't have time to consider it because the ground beneath him was beginning to shudder and crumble. The structural integrity of the hospital roof couldn't be that strong. Herman felt himself begin to sink along with the roof as he pushed himself onto his feet. He forced himself to keep going. He couldn't stop. It would be him against the three goons if he didn't manage to get out, and he would end up just like Cassie.

Faster he ran. He pumped and pumped his legs, anxiously looking for what looked like they could be mines—flashing lights, small metal boxes. He had run fifty yards before he noticed one right below his feet.

KABOOM!

He flew farther this time, landing in a heap nearly a dozen feet away. Shards of shrapnel miraculously missed his face but lodged in his arms and legs, some cuts being several inches long.

I can't stop, he thought. *Not now.*

The roof was collapsing, but the emergency room entrance was so close. Through the dust, he got back onto his feet and kept running as he agonizingly ripped bits of shrapnel from his arms. He tossed the fragments aside as he ran, and the deep cuts tingled as his body rapidly tried to heal.

With a mighty heave, he jumped off the roof and landed on the side of an overturned ambulance. He looked back just as the emergency room entrance caved in, leaving nothing but a dusty pile of rubble and debris. He ripped out three large pieces of shrapnel from his legs before he jumped off the ambulance.

They probably think I didn't make it, he thought. *They'll be looking for my body for the next little while.*

He touched his face gingerly—his nose was fixed, but he could feel the hot, sticky blood still drying on his lips and chin. He could taste it on the tip of his tongue.

As he turned about, he noticed someone was inside the overturned ambulance. A scraggily hobo sat cross-legged on his old sleeping back, staring at Herman with wide eyes, a spoon in one hand, a can of refried beans in the other. His jaw hung agape and he didn't speak.

Herman sighed. "Sorry." Then he turned away and darted for the fence. "Deactivate stealth mode."

The Leftybike materialized just moments before Herman slipped through the fence. He didn't even throw on his helmet. It wasn't supposed to be for him tonight. He kicked it off the handle, jumped onto the saddle, holstered his hammer, and the Leftybike roared to life.

The tires squealed as he sped away. The blood on his jeans and jacket began to dry in the wind as the wounds on his arms and legs tingled and healed. As he rocketed through the decrepit streets of Citytown, he thought of Cassie alone in that abandoned hospital, subject to whatever Malcolm McMasters had in store for her. He thought of Compound Z24. He thought of The Genesis Corporation.

He thought of Sidney Saskaloon.

16

By the time Herman arrived at Citytown Applied Technologies, Susan and Frankie were there waiting for him at the back door. Their arms were folded and they stared at the ground as if they were at a funeral. They looked up as the Leftybike rumbled up next to them. Frankie stared as he saw Herman's bloodstained jeans and jacket.

"We didn't want to go in without you," he said. "Also, you look terrible."

"There were landmines on the roof," Herman said aggressively as he jumped off the bike. He snapped his hammer onto his wrist and stormed up to the back door, Frankie and Susan following close behind.

He threw the door open with a slam, which echoed throughout the lab. None of them said a word as they stomped into the dim laboratory, waiting to see if Sidney Saskatoon had the brass to show his face.

He did. Sid sat in an office chair, his face down, his hands laced together, waiting.

"Cassie is *gone*, Sid!" Herman shouted as he advanced on the doctor. "Doctor McMasters got her! Does that name sound familiar to you? Malcolm McMasters?"

"Indeed, it does," Sid said.

"Is it true, Sid?" Frankie said seriously. "The compound, The Genesis Corporation... us? Did you do it? Is this all your fault?"

Sid slowly lifted his face to match the gaze of the three superhumans hovering over him. His eyes overflowed with hurt and humility, like an honor roll student sentenced to life in detention. His lower lip tightened as he tried to suppress his emotions.

"It's true."

Herman, Frankie, and Susan all glared at Sid, incredulous. They wanted to erupt into anger, but there was still so much confusion that no one could speak a word. How did he manage to get into the hospital? Why are their conditions permanent? Why did he choose *them*?

"*What's wrong with you?*" Susan hollered, her eyes flaring. "You had no right! We all have lives, Sid! You can't just uproot the lives of five innocent people to live out some sort of superhero fantasy! Look at what happened!"

"I didn't know what else to do!" Sid pleaded. "I know it was awful, I know I had no right—"

"*Then you shouldn't have done it!*" It was Herman's turn to explode. "Now Cassie is *captured*! We have no idea what Doctor McMasters is going to do to her! I was hit by two landmines tonight! Susan was electrocuted! Frankie's arm nearly got cut off! For the first time since I got these powers, I really thought I was going to *die* tonight. What would you say to our families if one of us had been killed? What would that make you?"

Those last words cut like a knife, and it was obvious. Sid's gaze dropped again. He twiddled his thumbs slowly, thinking. Then he raised his face to the others' again.

"I should have done this long ago," Sid said. "I owe you all the truth. The whole truth. Not just what Malcolm McMasters would have you believe.

"He was truthful about one thing—we did work together at The Genesis Corporation. We were on the same team trying to concoct the temporary superhuman compound. I was Malcolm's friend and top chemist by the time we had constructed Compound Z24. We spent many late nights pouring over notes together, comparing formulas, before we reached a breakthrough. But the only person who was truly proud of the new compound was him. We knew that this wasn't what the Corporation was looking for, but Malcolm wouldn't let it go. He thought we had found something better.

"When he presented the compound, the executives were furious. He had gone against direct instructions and sought to place his own ideas above that of the Corporation's and the government. That was unpardonable. Malcolm didn't walk away from The Genesis Corporation. He was unceremoniously terminated."

Everyone was following along closely, not looking at each other.

"That made him enraged after all the work he had done," Sid continued. "He confided in me that night that he had the plans to take his notes for Compound Z24 and privately go into production. He didn't want to see an ounce of his work go to waste. Everything he was setting out to do was terribly illegal—stealing plans from a government-funded project to go into private production on the black market? That's treason.

"I couldn't support it. I tried to take the notes and warn the executives, but he caught me. He threatened me at the end of a gun to leave the notes and walk away, so I did. I couldn't sleep that night. When I went in to work the next morning, the building was up in flames. Malcolm McMasters burned The Genesis Corporation to the ground. Any research Malcolm hadn't taken with him regarding Compound X or Z24 was now ashes.

"From that point, I knew I had to find him. The only question was how.

"I spent ages searching for him while trying to rebuild the compound from memory—thankfully, my resources aren't few. I managed to construct a new compound that was nearly identical to Compound Z24, but it gave permanent effects instead of temporary.

"One night, as I was visiting a pub downtown, I saw him. Doctor Malcolm McMasters. Thankfully, he didn't notice me. He was in the mouth of an alleyway, handing off a vial of green liquid to a man in a suit just outside a law firm. I rushed back to the lab and hacked into the police mainframe. I found reports of multiple burglaries very recently that were carried out in extraordinary ways, but the police were still investigating. It was then that I knew without a doubt that Doctor McMasters was carrying out his work here in Citytown. And I knew that I needed to act fast.

"But what could I do? I had no idea where Malcolm McMasters was hiding, I had no valuable information I could possibly give the police, and I certainly didn't need them snooping around my lab. The only solution I could think of was absolutely ludicrous, but it felt like my only option…

"So, I broke into the hospital. A disguise and a counterfeit clearance badge were not hard to construct. I administered the compound to the first five people I could find—all of you. I took down all your information and contacted each of you soon after your release. I gambled that maybe, *maybe* you all would be open to cleaning up this city if it meant an antidote to your conditions or exorbitant amounts of cash. Amazingly, I was right.

"I sent you out to work with the help of my gadgets and communication because I knew that fighting these villains would eventually lead us to Malcolm McMasters. And when that happened, I could report his whereabouts to the authorities and bring him the justice he deserves. But it appears as though his new friends are protecting him and their access to Compound Z24, and the local police don't have the means to confront them. That leaves you."

Sid stood from his chair, mustering all the courage he possessed.

"Yes, Miss Copland has been captured, but we can find her. Every day, Doctor McMasters sells more of the compound. Certainly, there are plenty of normal people in this city—but how many more monsters is he going to create? More Nikkis, Chets, or Thespians? What will happen to this city when there are too many of them? How long will that take, and who will stop them when that time comes?"

Herman, Susan, and Frankie were all silent, letting that last question hang in the air.

"You could be wrong about creating more villains," Frankie mumbled.

"And if I'm not?" Sid said.

More silence. Herman could barely believe his ears. So much had happened in the past couple of hours. So much had happened in the past *week*. And what kind of say did he have in any of it? Not much, if any. The powerlessness was maddening, and in such dire and absurd circumstances.

"You've thrown this whole conflict on all of us and kept us in the dark," Susan said severely. "That's not okay, Sidney. That's a villainous thing to do. You should have taken the compound and done this yourself."

"I've been a coward," Sid said. "I know I have. And I know I've asked far too much of you all. But I'm asking you to stay in the ring for one more round. Doctor McMasters will likely have found a new base by morning, then we can find one of his goons and squeeze out his new location—"

"No," Susan said. "*We* will, while you sit here comfortably and safe, out of harm's way."

At this, Sid had no comeback. His voice was soft as he continued on.

"When we find his new location, we can confront him and capture him and rescue Cassandra. I feel personally responsible for her capture, so I will do everything in my power to make sure she's brought back to safety. I swear it."

"What good are your promises to us now, Sid?" Herman said quietly.

Sid didn't reply. A hand that had wrapped itself so tightly around Herman's heart, and it wasn't loosening up. The feeling of betrayal was palpable. Herman wanted to believe they'd want to find Cassie. He wanted to believe she could be rescued. But after tonight, they knew exactly what they were dealing with, and it was bigger than any of them imagined.

And for what? A few dollars in his pocket? Inwardly, Herman cursed himself for his recklessness and desperation.

"I don't know what you both think," Susan said as she turned to Frankie and Herman. "But I want no part of this. I'm done. I've been had my fill of lies."

With that, she dropped her soccer ball at Sid's feet. It bounced a little before coming to a rest between Sid's loafers. Sid couldn't help but stare at it—a symbol of abandonment. Susan didn't immediately turn away, however. She took a step closer to Sid, eyeing him like a hawk.

Susan's next words were venomous. "You already have the antidote... don't you?"

Sid said nothing. Instead, he defeatedly crept over to a table and came back with three small vials. The vials weren't even three inches long, but they each contained a rich purple liquid. Sid held his hand out, his palm up, with the three vials resting inside.

"There is one for each of you," he said lowly. "I haven't had the chance to test them yet, but I'm ninety-eight percent sure that this will cure your conditions completely. You'll likely experience very sudden fatigue and a raging appetite. I recommend that you wait until you're home before you take it."

Susan snatched one of the vials and thrust it in her pocket before she flipped on her heels and marched away. Before she made it halfway to the door, Sid called her name.

"Susan."

Her hair swished as she jerked her head, her eyebrows pointed and her jaw tight. The next words from Sid's lips were soft and earnest.

"I'm sorry. For everything."

Susan's gaze didn't change. She stormed out of the lab, and with that, she was gone into the night.

Sid sighed. "I've been awful to you all. Just *awful.* I understand if the two of you want to take the antidote immediately as well. I wouldn't blame you. But what will become of Cassandra if you do?"

Instantly, Herman thought of her trapped by Malcolm McMasters again, alone and abandoned. She had struggled with neglect and worthlessness all her life—and to be discarded at her greatest need?

Herman and Frankie both reached out to take their respective vials. Herman held the vial up to his face, twisting it between his fingers, glaring at the particles that floated in the tiny purple reservoir. He also saw the reflection of his face—still caked with blood, but no scars or cuts, just a pair of blue eyes that were very angry and confused.

And the image of Cassie kept resurfacing in his mind, captured forcefully by Malcolm McMasters just a short hour ago. The steel door, the long syringe, her body convulsing from the taser barbs.

That's when he felt it. The need. The need to bring her back. The need to show her she wasn't disposable or abandoned. The need to put Malcolm McMasters behind bars and punish him for his crimes. The need to set this all right.

"I'm going to take this," Herman said. "But not now." He put the vial in his pocket. "Cassie comes first. When she's safe and Doctor McMasters is behind bars, I'm kissing these conditions goodbye."

Sid wanted to smile but couldn't bring himself to. His gaze reverted to Frankie. Frankie's eyes were glossy as he rolled the vial around in his hand. The gash on his shoulder was completely healed, but his hoodie was torn and badly stained with blood. He put the vial in his pocket too.

"I'm with Herman," Frankie said. "We're gonna find Cassie and take these goons down. After that, I'm over this."

At this, Sid's eyes became glossy and his lower lip tightened. Without warning, he threw his arms around Herman and Frankie and pulled them in tightly. Herman gasped to breathe. Doctor Saskatoon was surprisingly strong for such an old man.

"Thank you," he said. "Thank you both. I never meant for any of this to happen. I just wanted to make some good for the world." A pause. "Let's bring her home."

17

"So how are you feeling about everything?" Frankie said.

"Awful," Herman said.

"Yeah. Me too."

They were on the top of Herman's apartment complex, sitting with their feet dangling over the edge just like he and Cassie did a couple nights ago. The sun was out, and a sweltering heat covered the city that rose up from the asphalt and cement. Frankie had a new hoodie free from bloodstains—something he picked up from a thrift store shortly after the run-in at the abandoned hospital.

"Have you heard anything from Susan or Tyler?" Herman asked as he scraped his metal hook into shapes on the cement.

"No," Frankie said. "I left a couple of messages on Susan's communicator, too. No answer. She's probably taken the antidote by now. I think she's done for good."

"Well, I haven't heard anything from Tyler," Herman said as something flared darkly inside him. "I left a pretty pissed-off message on his communicator—filled him in on everything last night from the hospital, even Sid and the antidote. If he would've had the balls to come with us Cassie would probably be fine. His power makes everything so *easy*."

"Yeah. I'm mad that we didn't listen to Susan, for real," Frankie said. "She said we should have turned back way earlier and we didn't listen. She's always been the smartest one."

"Okay whatever," Herman retorted. "But Tyler said he'd be on call if we needed him. We needed him *badly*, he blew us off. Period. Now Cassie's gone. This is his fault more than anyone's."

Frankie rubbed his legs anxiously. "Yeah, maybe. But it's too late now. We need a new plan."

Herman paused as he continued to scrape shapes into the cement with the blunt hook. He couldn't stop thinking of Tyler, with his luxury car and his perfect smile and his other priorities. The thoughts made Herman's insides squirm. He looked at his watch and realized it was just the right time to be at the soup kitchen.

He stood up from the edge and said, "Come on. Let's go."

"Where are we—"

"We're gonna go visit that lazy traitor, Tyler. Are you coming?"

Frankie didn't argue. He pushed himself from the ledge and followed behind Herman as they descended down the fire escape. In less than a minute, they were both on the back of the Leftybike. Frankie held on tight as Herman gunned the Leftybike to life and peeled out of the parking lot.

As the wind whipped around his face, Herman let the anger stew inside him. It swirled and bubbled as recent memories piled on top of each other: Cassie's suicide confession, Tyler saying he would be on call, Cassie's capture. He scowled and gripped the handlebar tighter.

After several minutes of traffic, the two of them pulled up to the First Baptist Church of Citytown. A line of homelesss gathered around the one side of the building just like they did days before. Before Herman could put his kickstand down, he noticed Tyler's freshly-washed luxury sedan just a few parking spaces away. He frowned.

Frankie hopped off the Leftybike and stared at the spectacle, his eyes scanning the stone church and the legion of homeless people that were lined up to get chili.

"He works here every day," Herman said as he killed the bike's engine. "Let's say hello."

Herman and Frankie made their way to the back entrance— the one leading to the basement. Frankie didn't make much sound as they went, and he had to power walk to keep up with Herman's fuming stride.

Herman threw open the door and they crossed through the threshold, their eyes scanning the scene. Frankie soaked it all in —the hair nets, the aprons, the florescent lights, the thick smell of chili wafting through the air. He blinked.

"A soup kitchen?" he asked.

"That's right."

"Have you two come to volunteer?"

The sweet old lady with horn-rimmed glasses and a hunched back strolled over to them as she gave the two a big, toothy smile. Herman's face remained hard. He said, "We need to talk to Tyler Calvin."

"Oh, Tyler is almost always here," the sweet lady said as she turned and pointed out to the common area. "Looks like he's wiping the tables right now."

Sure enough, there he was. Just across the room, wearing a hair net and a plastic apron, Tyler Calvin leaned on a table laughed it up with a small gaggle of hobos while clamping a dirty rag in his hand. The raggedy urchins listened to Tyler delightedly as he yammered on, waving his hands and smiling broadly as he unwound a story for them. A celebrity among his fans.

Herman tried not to grind his teeth.

"*Tyler!*"

Herman's bark made half of the congregation turn and stare, including Tyler. As Tyler's dark chocolate eyes found Herman and Frankie at the mouth of the kitchen, his smile quickly faded. He excused himself from his friends and dropped his rag on the table before marching to the exit. Herman's eyes followed him with every stride. Tyler didn't return the glare.

When Tyler finally reached the two, Herman held open the door. Tyler marched outside, and the other two followed. The door slammed shut. The three of them stood in a circle just outside the soup kitchen entrance, the cathedral and the Citytown skyline looming just above them.

Tyler folded his arms. "Did you come here to apologize?"

Herman was dumbfounded. His face and ears went scarlet and the fire inside his chest blazed even hotter.

"*What?*" he bellowed.

"Hey, Herman, take it easy," Frankie put his hand on Herman's shoulder.

"*No,*" Herman swatted Frankie's hand away. "You deserved to hear every freaking word that I left on your communicator last night, you coward! You said you would be there if things got heavy. And where were you, huh? Just doing homework, like you do every night when you should be out with us instead?"

"Yeah, that's right," Tyler said as his eyes narrowed and he nodded his head. "I left my communicator in my backpack and forgot about it. I had a physics exam."

"You *forgot* about your *communicator?*" Herman echoed. "After you said you'd keep it on? You don't just forget about something like that!" At this, he advanced on Tyler, putting his nose inches away from his. Tyler didn't budge. He stayed rigid, his arms folded, his eyes filled with just as much heat as Herman's. Herman's next words were soft but venomous.

"Maybe you really do want to be a hero… but you want to be seen for it. That's it, isn't it?"

Frankie's eyes got wide. Tyler didn't say anything. Instead, the heat in his eyes overflowed until he launched a fist at Herman's face.

It was quicker than a blink of an eye and it threw a strong gust of wind in every direction. Herman's face cocked back and he staggered, clutching his nose with his free hand. A dribble of blood seeped down his lip.

Frankie caught Herman and helped him right himself. Herman gasped and wiped the blood from his lip, glaring at Tyler with eyes like lightning. Tyler's jaw tightened.

"Insult me again," Tyler seethed. "I dare you."

"So you'll help these people, but not your own?" Herman wiped more blood from his lip.

Tyler's eyes narrowed again. "*My own?* I didn't ask to be a part of this little group of freaks! I didn't ask to have these powers!"

"*None of us did!*" Herman shot. "But here we are, aren't we? And while your nose was in a book last night, Cassie got captured. You remember Cassie, right? Red hair, green eyes? Yeah? *Gone.* Kidnapped. We don't even know if she's still alive. And guess who could have stopped it? You. But you weren't there when you said you would be."

Tyler tightened his lips. "You think I'm proud of that? Don't be stupid. I messed up and I get it."

"Then *do something about it!*" Herman shouted.

"Herman, come on…" Frankie said gently.

"*Shut up, Frankie!*"

"No, he's right," Tyler said while nodding at Herman. "I should do something about it. But rolling up on a guy while he's with his friends and shouting at him is hardly a way to ask for favors."

"I'm beyond asking for favors," Herman said. "I'm telling you how this is going to go. Cassie was captured because you royally effed up. This is on you."

"Is it, though?" Tyler's head cocked sideways. "Or are you just taking your anger out on me because you were too slow and stupid to do anything about it yourself? Four superhumans against one scientist and one still manages to get caught? Pathetic. It looks like you're the leader of this little group, too, so this one is actually on *you*, Hammerpiss."

Herman pushed the next sentence through his teeth. "If I had my hammer I'd beat your cocky little face so hard."

"You couldn't hit me, and you know it," Tyler hissed back.

"*Guys, guys, guys!*"

Frankie finally wedged himself between the two of them, but Tyler and Herman's gaze remained locked on each other. His eyes darted from person to person as he spoke.

"Here it goes: Cassie is captured and we're going to make a plan to get her back. Tyler, you screwed the pooch last night. But you know what? *We all did.* We had the chance to turn around and we didn't, like a bunch of morons. So it's on you. And it's on Herman. And it's on me. But standing around playing the blame game isn't helping anything, so can you guys *cool it for five seconds*?"

With that, Frankie dropped his arms. Both Tyler and Herman decompressed. Tyler put his hands on his hips and stared at the ground for a hard second, taking in a deep, meditative breath. Without raising his eyes, he tightened his upper lip and muttered quietly:

"Sorry I punched you."

The cauldron in Herman's chest began to simmer. Tyler admitted he dropped the ball last night, but Frankie was right. At this point, pointing fingers wasn't helping Cassie. Herman took a deep breath, exhaled, and said, "It's fine. You know it'll heal."

"So, you guys don't have a solid plan yet?" Tyler said calmly.

Frankie shook his head. "We're going to get started on it asap. But first, we need to see who's on board. We've got us, and you, if you're in. We're going to try to reach Susan, too, but she might have already taken the antidote already. If that's the case, she's useless."

Tyler nodded, still not making eye contact. "Let me know when you have a plan. I like having a plan. Just looking around for a fight feels… reckless."

Frankie shrugged at Herman and said, "He's got a point."

Herman slid Frankie a disapproving scowl.

"Look, I'm sorry," Tyler said. "I shouldn't have said that stuff to you and I shouldn't have called you Hammerpiss. Have you guys been back to the hospital since last night?"

"No," Herman said.

"It's the one on the edge of town, right? With all the graffiti?"

"That's the one."

In a gust of wind, Tyler was gone, leaving nothing in his wake but a hair net floating in the air. Frankie and Herman flinched and stared at the hair net floating to the earth like a brittle, falling leaf. Before it could reach the ground, Tyler was back with another gust of wind, his plastic apron nearly torn completely from his body. He scooped the hair net out of midair and placed it back on his head.

"Well, whoever Doctor McMasters is, he's gone," Tyler said while panting conservatively. "No trace of life anywhere at that hospital—it's like he was never there. Probably wanted to find a new base, especially after half of the building caved in."

"Great," Herman said. "Now we have to track him down *again.*"

"Hopefully we can run into one of his goons tonight," Frankie said hopefully. "Squeeze some more info out of them."

Herman turned to Tyler and said, "Are you going to join us?"

Tyler looked at the ground, then looked at Herman. "Not tonight. But I promise you guys, when you hatch a plan to get Cassie back, I'm all in. Cool?"

Herman looked at Frankie. Frankie looked at Herman. Herman looked at Tyler. Herman nodded.

"Great," Frankie said. "I think it'd be appropriate if you two hugged this one out."

"*No,*" Herman and Tyler said in chorus.

*

On the eastern district of Citytown, just beyond the Citytown State University campus, several suburbs for upper middle-class families sprawled across the landscape. The neighborhood that Herman and Frankie found themselves in was populated with perfectly manicured lawns, kids riding bikes, and stuttering sprinkler systems. Every house belonged on the cover of a magazine, or at least the setting for an award-winning sitcom.

The Leftybike rumbled through the winding, picturesque streets before it came to a stop directly in front of a white colonial style home. Herman inhaled the crisp smell of freshly-cut grass while Frankie scrunched up his nose.

"It's too perfect," Frankie said. "I hate it."

"It fits Susan and Clint, though," Herman said as he swung his leg off the bike. "They do kind of look like an Instagram power couple."

"It's these people that have something to hide, Herman," Frankie said as they strolled up the walkway to Susan's front door. "For all we know, Clint is hiding bodies in their basement or poking his secretary. Or both."

"*Or* you're just watching too much TV."

Ding dong

Herman and Frankie heard the doorbell echo in the home's interior, followed by the sound of footsteps. Within a matter of seconds, the faint clumping of footsteps sounded closer and closer until they came to a stop just on the other side of the thick oak door. The peephole went dark. A loud sigh. Then, the door swung open.

There, Susan Terry stood with one hand in her pocket. She had obviously just gotten home from work, seeing as she had removed her makeup and had nestled into a pair of sweats and a t-shirt. Her glower, however, was thick with impatience, as if she had opened the door to traveling salesmen or missionaries.

After a dramatic sigh and a probing stare, she said, "If you're wondering if I've taken the antidote... I haven't yet."

Herman and Frankie didn't say anything. Susan brushed her fingers through her flawless hair and defeatedly said, "Come on."

The two stepped into the house and Susan closed the door behind them, leading them into the living room. The parlor was bathed in light from a crystal chandelier that hang a dozen feet overhead, and beneath them, freshly-finished hardwood that creaked as they stepped. To their right, the living room was decorated with contemporary furniture, a zebra-patterned rug, abstract artwork, and a grand piano nestled just in front of a bay window.

Frankie whistled. "Your home is *nice*, Susan."

Herman slid him a look. *Wasn't he the one saying this whole neighborhood looks too perfect?*

"I know," she said.

Herman and Frankie plopped down on the couch while Susan sat in an armchair just across from them, separated by a glass coffee table covered in design magazines. Herman couldn't help but look around a little bit more, taking note of the bamboo plants in the corners of the room and a bookshelf stuffed with leather-bound novels. Frankie, however, couldn't help rubbing his hands on the sofa and throw pillows. The material was obviously very expensive.

"Did you have something important to tell me?" Susan asked with her hands clasped together. "Maybe something like 'We should have listened' or 'We're sorry'?"

"Both of those things," Herman said as he rubbed his hook with his thumb. "If we would have listened to you, Cassie would still be here, and Malcolm McMasters would be behind bars. We screwed up hard."

Susan sighed, satisfied. "I agree. And I accept your apology."

Herman shot Frankie another look, then fixed his eyes on Susan. "Uh—so… you haven't taken the antidote yet?"

"If you think if I'm going to go back to *fighting crime every night*," Susan whispered those words. "You're mistaken. I don't take well to being lied to. I'm surprised you two are still on board with all this."

"We just want to get Cassie back," Herman said. "Then we're done with Sid and these powers for good. That's the plan."

"What's the next move then?"

"Well, we just visited Tyler," Frankie said. "He and Herman almost got in a fistfight. It's good that Herman backed down when he did because Tyler totally would have—well, you definitely weren't asking for more. Anyway, Herman only has one fist anyway so even if Tyler didn't have his powers—dude, calm down, I didn't mean anything by it—"

"So *what?*" Susan interjected.

Frankie swallowed, then cleared his throat. "Tyler went and checked out the old hospital. McMasters is gone, along with everything else. We don't know where he is now."

Susan's tone dropped. "Along with Cassie?"

Herman looked at the space between his shoes and nodded. Susan leaned forward in her chair and rubbed her arm. She was silent for a second, as if her mind could picture Cassie suffering all alone—just like Herman had pictured so many times today.

She asked, "Herman?"

He looked up. Her brown eyes were fixed on him in a very maternal way, like how Aunt Josie used to look at him after a bad day at school. She asked, "She means a lot to you, doesn't she?"

Herman's eyes became glazed as he remembered the night that they talked together on the roof. He also remembered when she came into his room and sat next to him, how she sat so closely, staring into his heart with those emeralds that radiated with the pain of the past. The things that she had done because she had felt disposable—like no one cared.

Herman nodded.

Susan rubbed her hands together dipped her head again. "I haven't stopped thinking about her all day. When I left last night, I was going to take that antidote as soon as I got home. I planned on it. I got home, parked the car, uncorked the vial... and I just couldn't do it. Because all I could think of was how I'd feel if that were one of my kids that got captured by that lunatic. And who's looking after Cassie? As far as I know, only us."

There was a brief silence before Susan's face got harder. "No matter how upset I am at that lying snake Sidney Saskatoon, I couldn't stop thinking about that." She looked up. "We've got to do something about her."

"Susan," Herman said. "Frankie and I can track down where she is. But when it comes time to rescue her, we're going to need all the help we can get. We need you."

"You've got me," Susan said seriously. "But just to get Cassie. That's it. Then I'm drinking that antidote, too."

Suddenly, the patter of small feet came scurrying up to the living room entrance. Alex, Susan's son with the wavy black hair, stood in the archway fully-suited for soccer, except from the knees down.

"Mom, I can't find my cleats!" he said.

"Did you look under your bed?"

"Yeah."

"Are you *sure*?"

Alex paused. Then he darted away. Within seconds, Alex's distant voice said, "Found them!"

Susan smirked at Herman and Frankie. "Do your families know? Mine still doesn't."

Herman and Frankie replied in the negative.

"Then we better make sure we do this right, shouldn't we?" She said.

18

It was nighttime in Citytown. But in this area of town, people were still out and about. This was the arts district, a place for concerts, clubs, and five-star steak restaurants.

Frankie and Herman climbed up some cement steps to a massive theatre with marble columns and stone lions. The theatre's presence felt a lot like the cathedral where Tyler volunteered—a classic dash of the past nestled amidst a population of modern architecture. Dozens of other people were climbing the steps too, all sporting suits and ties and dresses and designer handbags. As Herman looked around, he suddenly felt very self-conscious in a wrinkly button-down shirt and a clip-on tie with the tag still on it.

"Why are we doing this again?" Herman said as he adjusted his tie. "This doesn't really seem important to our situation."

"Because you and I both know none of the goons are going to be out until later tonight," Frankie replied. "And this won't take much of our time. We'll be out before nine. Is that a clip-on tie?"

"You ever tied a tie with one hand?"

"Right. Sorry."

Herman shot more glances at Citytown's upper class as they all congregated to the theater. Several of them stared at his hook as they caught sight of it. Sometimes, Herman stared back just as hard so he could make them uncomfortable in kind.

"Were the tickets expensive?" he asked.

"For us? Nope," Frankie said with a smirk. "My mom gets free tickets to these things all the time."

"So why aren't your mom and dad going instead of us?"

"Mom's grading papers for summer semester. Dad's working on model trains. That's his free time thing."

As they reached the top of the stairs, a box office to their right was congested with people hoping to get seats. Just ahead of them, ushers stood at the door ripping people's tickets and welcoming them to the venue. As Frankie and Herman shuffled through security and handed off their tickets, the usher glanced at them both and said, "Thank you, and welcome to the Citytown Central Theatre."

Herman couldn't help but gawk at the foyer as they made their way inside. Two sets of magnificent stairs ascended to an upper floor which then led to the balcony. Giant oil paintings of past owners hung from the walls and an enormous antique chandelier dangled from the ceiling dozens of feet above. Frankie meandered through the crowd, unimpressed. Obviously, he had been here many times before. The only thing that didn't impress Herman was the maroon carpet. He followed on Frankie's heels.

"Wait, what are we watching tonight?" Herman said.

"It's a collection of movements from Franz Joseph Haydn," Frankie replied. "Eighteenth century composer, Father of the Symphony. His compositions were mostly light and bouncy, kind of flamboyant, which I think reflected his personality. He was really popular and outgoing in his home of Austria—"

"Okay, I asked for what we're watching, not a history lesson."

Frankie smirked. "I grew up around music, man. This is my best chance to flex on you."

The two wandered down the aisle, weaving through Citytown's silk-garbed and perfume-splashed upper class, then found their seats. As they went, Herman's head swiveled about his shoulders, taking in the auditorium.

It was magnificent. The entire structure of the auditorium seemed to bow out from the stage, most definitely for acoustics. Columns lined the edges of the hall. Behind them, an ornate balcony with brass railings and intricate edging hung below the ceiling, looking down on the stage from a bird's eye view. Hundreds upon hundreds of cushioned seats were rapidly filling. And, of course, several spotlights pointed at a red curtain that was drawn over the stage.

"Real talk," Frankie said as he leaned back and loosened his tie. "We're kind of here for my benefit. You know how music affects me in different ways? Classical relaxes me." His voice died to a whisper and he leaned in. "It was nice before I got my powers, but *now*?" A scoff. "When that music starts playing, it's like a warm cloud of sparkles just wraps me up in a bear hug. It's next level."

Herman tightened his lower lip, which turned into a half-grin. "Well if there's anything we haven't had in the last week, it's relaxation."

"Amen, brother."

Frankie extended his fist, and Herman gave it a little punch. At that moment, the buzz of the auditorium began to die down. The lights dimmed. The people of Citytown began to settle in their seats. In a swoop, the curtains retracted, revealing a fully-outfitted orchestra that filled the stage. As the conductor marched out to the middle of the stage, he took a bow and everyone applauded.

"Hey," Frankie whispered through the white noise.

Herman leaned over. Frankie said, "We're still going to hang out after all this is over, right? Like, when we lose our powers and go back to normal?"

This time, Herman extended his fist. "Sure, dude."

Frankie grinned and gave Herman's fist a little punch. Then the orchestra struck their first chord.

For the next couple of hours, the people of Citytown were graced with the jubilant compositions of Franz Joseph Haydn. There were a handful of Scottish folk songs that were sung by guest artists that arrived and departed as their songs came and went. Herman didn't listen to a lot of modern music, let alone classical, but he found himself enjoying Haydn for the most part.

But not as much as Frankie. Throughout the duration of the performances, Frankie was leaned fully backward in his seat, his arms folded, his eyes half-closed, smiling ear-to-ear.

On occasion, the orchestra got a break and some pieces were performed by just a quartet of string players. This didn't make the music any less potent or effective, however. It made Herman think about their super team—they had operated as a quartet for a while, each member bringing different strengths to every fight. Cassie's telekinesis, Frankie's musical abilities, Susan's agility and dexterity with a soccer ball, and Herman's—

His eyes fell to the blunt metal hook protruding from his shirt sleeve. The hook's dim silver hue reflected oil smudges and finger prints in the dull light. Clear flashbacks of the car accident reverted in his mind—the car, the eighteen-wheeler, the hospital.

Tyler said I'm the leader, Herman thought. *But how could I be? I'm the least special by far. Have I really brought anything important to the table?*

The thought hung in his mind for the duration of the show as Frankie sat to his left, racked with bliss. At length, the orchestra played its final movements and the audience stood for a rousing ovation. The applause carried on for a long while. Herman had to clap his left hand on his right forearm. The man to the right of him couldn't help but shoot glances at it.

As they exited to the foyer, Frankie stretched as if awakening from a glorious nap and said, "*Man*, that was nice."

"Do you have any of that tuned into your Bambox?" Herman asked.

"Nah," Frankie said. "I've got songs for blasting and songs for faster healing, but that's it. Everything else is just weird—like making me float or giving me monster farts. I found out about the classical thing when my mom put on some old classical records. I almost went into a trance when she played Mozart."

They crossed through the doors into the night. Immediately they were greeted by the typical neon lights of Citytown. The buzz of footsteps, car horns, and chatter filled their ears as they walked. Scores of concert goers dispersed into the streets in search of their parked cars or the nearest bus stop.

Amidst all the people pouring out from the theatre, there was one figure that stood at the bottom of the stairs. The figure was garbed in all black, from the hoodie to the sweats to the sneakers. Its hands were in its pockets and its head was down so they couldn't see its face. It just stood there, facing the theater but not looking up.

Frankie nudged Herman and said, "This looks sketchy."

"Yeah," Herman said. "Bet it's got our names written all over it. I don't have my hammer, though."

"And I don't have my Bambox."

The figure didn't move from its place. Its head lifted for a second, but the two still couldn't get a good look at the face. It seemed to acknowledge them both, then, satisfied, dipped its head down again. Herman and Frankie looked at each other again before cautiously descending the stairs.

Their steps were small as the two reached the hooded figure. Herman and Frankie hunched down to try to get a look at the figure's face, but as they did, the figure flipped around, turning its back on them both.

"He's at an abandoned warehouse in the south industrial district," the figure said. "The old HyperFizz Cola factory. That's where you'll find him."

The voice was familiar. It was trying to sound deeper than it actually was, but they both knew they had heard the voice before. Frankie and Herman exchanged stony expressions.

"Who are you?" Herman said with squinted eyes.

"I am a shadow that lurks in the night," the figure continued. "I am the face of justice reborn. I am—*hey!*"

Frankie shot his hand forward and yanked the hood off the figure's head. Before the figure could throw it back on, Frankie grabbed him arm and flipped him around. The greasy black hair and pale skin was unmistakable. The figure's adolescent eyes stared daggers at Frankie and Herman, trying to hide a recent dash of shame.

"What are you doing here, Demonspawn?" Herman commanded.

Demonspawn threw the hood over his head and pulled hard on the drawstrings, covering his face and ears. With that, he thrust his hands back in his hoodie pockets and didn't make much eye contact from that point on.

"What does it look like I'm doing?" he said. "I'm telling you where Alpha Master is. He moved."

"Yeah, we already know that," Frankie said. "But why are *you* telling us this?"

Demonspawn shrugged before he said, "I don't want to be the bad guy anymore."

"Bull," Herman said.

"I'm serious!" Demonspawn insisted. "Look! Do I have my sword? No. And I couldn't breathe fire on you even if I wanted to. I'm done with the Green Juice and Alpha Master and everything." He sighed. "I don't know why I started off. I think I'm just mad at my dad. He's always working at night and when he's home, he doesn't give a crap what I'm doing. Maybe I just started taking the Green Juice and stealing stuff because I wanted some people to hang out with. And because I hate my dad."

"How do we know you're not lying to us?" Frankie said.

Demonspawn shrugged again. "I don't know. But you won't be seeing me anymore. I'm done. I just wanted to help."

With that, he turned around and dragged his feet away. He had hardly moved before he turned to Frankie and said, "Sorry about your arm. My real name is Collin, by the way. Collin Axewielder."

Herman and Frankie's eyebrows popped. But they didn't say anything. The boy formerly known as Demonspawn kept his head down and his feet dragging all the way down the block. Frankie and Herman didn't move until he was out of sight, disappearing behind another building.

"That little twerp almost made me feel sorry for him," Frankie said coldly. "Even after he nearly chopped my arm off."

"I bet anything he's Detective Axewielder's son."

"Oh, for sure."

"Do you think he's telling the truth?"

Frankie shook his head. "I don't know. We could ask Tyler to go check it out. It should only take him a minute."

"It could be a trap."

"I don't think there's a trap fast enough to catch Tyler."

"Maybe," Herman said. "I don't know. If he's lying to us, we'll find out soon enough."

19

"Did you find anything?" Herman said as he touched the communicator in his ear.

"It looks like Collin Axewielder could be telling the truth," Tyler's voice was tinny in the communicator. "The factory was mostly empty except for some tables with some glass bottles and vials, but no one was there."

It was nearly midnight. Herman and Frankie lurked through the alleys of downtown Citytown, armed with their hammer and Bambox. The cars were relatively few where they were, and thankfully, they had managed to evade every police car that drove by. They saw more homeless people than suspicious characters, but they kept their wits about them.

"It could still be a setup," Frankie interjected.

"That," Tyler's voice came again, "or Demonspawn really is done for good. And that means if he's telling the truth, we already know where McMasters and Cassie are. But I don't know. I think it's a good idea that you guys are on the prowl tonight. Getting info from another goon just to make sure is a good idea."

"*If* we can even find one," Herman said. "The streets have been dead tonight. We'll let you know if we find anything."

"Great," Tyler said. "I'm out."

And like that, Tyler signed off. They had already wandered around the most decrepit parts of the city with nothing more than a purse snatching and some public urination. Neither of them really felt the need to bring the heat on someone who got a little drunk, but the purse snatcher was taken care of without much effort.

It wasn't until they had walked down the next street that they noticed something worthwhile. A figure wearing basketball shorts and a hoodie stood over an outdoor ATM, feverishly stuffing money into a pillow sack. The ATM was smashed to pieces, spitting sparks while fragments of its metal frame lay scattered on the sidewalk.

"Not a goon, but I'll take it," Frankie said as he dug his feet down and broke into a run. As they both pelted toward the crook, Frankie shouted, "*Hey!*"

The figure's face jerked towards the two. He scooped up the pillow case and peeled away from Herman and Frankie, but not before throwing a punch.

But this wasn't just any punch. The assailant's fist shot thirty feet forward and snapped back like his arm was made of super-stretchy rubber. Herman narrowly dodged the oncoming fist as it rocketed past him and he could feel the wind flick his ear as it went by.

"*A new one!*" Herman said without thinking. "*A goon!*"

Frankie revved up the Bambox and shot a blast ahead, but the goon darted into an alleyway. As the two turned the corner into the alleyway, Frankie was immediately sucker punched in the face with a rubber fist.

Bam!

He somersaulted backward and landed in a heap, his face to the ground, broken and bloody. A moan slid from his lips as he

223

slowly pushed himself up, gripping tight to his Bambox. Herman sprinted ahead.

The robber spun around as he ran, dropping the sack of cash. It spilled onto the asphalt and Herman jumped over them as he went. The robber threw two fists at Herman.

Clang!

Herman deflected the second fist with his hammer after ducking under the first fist. When the robber's arm retracted, he waved his throbbing fist with open fingers and swore loudly.

Herman's sprinted toward the assailant and shouted, "Try that again, I dare you!"

They arrived at a chain link fence that reached over ten feet high. Nowhere to go. Herman was sure that the robber would give himself up at this point. Nope. With a mighty squat, the robber stooped down and launched himself over the wall with spring-like legs. His shins grew to nearly eight times their length as he hurled over the wall.

Herman's eyes widened. *You gotta be kidding me.*

The robber staggered as his feet touched down on the other side, but quickly regained his balance and sallied forth. There was a padlock on the chain link fence. Herman smashed it with his hammer, then threw the door open and followed in hot pursuit.

I've already lost ground, Herman thought despairingly. *He's gonna get away.*

Then a thought popped into his head. It was a longshot, but hey, you never know.

Herman touched his communicator and said, "*Extract.*"

At that moment, the robber turned around to see Herman still on his trail. He growled and launched a couple more punches. Herman dodged the first one just by his right cheek, but the second one, he took in the gut.

Boof!

Herman stumbled to the ground, clutching his stomach, trying not to puke. It was like getting hit by a cannonball, and all his organs moaned loudly as he doubled over, struggling to breathe. His eyes watered as he grunted and his body slowly healed.

Just ahead, the robber laughed something between bewilderment and relief. But it didn't last long. While he was running backward, the roaring of the Leftybike echoed into the alleyway like an angry lion, heading straight for Herman.

Pow!

The Leftybike struck the assailant in the back, sending him reeling forward in several somersaults before skidding to a halt just a dozen feet in front of Herman. His eyes clear and the pain subsiding, Herman jumped to his feet and darted over the stretchy thug, cocking his hammer back, ready to strike.

The hood had fallen off the man's face. He looked like any guy you'd see shooting hoops at the YMCA—late twenties, moderately tall, no particularly striking features. The hoodie and basketball shorts were both from discount brands and his white tube socks bunched up by his ankles.

By this time, Frankie had caught up to the two and held his open fist over the assailant's head, his headphones still firmly fastened to his skull. Dried blood streamed from his nostrils down to his chin, but his nose was intact—perfectly healed.

The assailant lay on the ground, both hands helplessly in the air. The Leftybike purred just a few feet away.

"Whoa, whoa, hey guys," the robber began. "I swear this was only a one-time thing—"

"Who are you?" Herman shot.

The robber didn't answer immediately, then said, "Gus."

"That's it? Just Gus?" Frankie said with a raised eyebrow. "No clever alias or code name or whatever?"

"No," Gust said, puzzled. "...Why would I do that?"

Frankie sneered. "Something wrong with your bank account, Gus?"

Gus' eyes darted from Herman, to Frankie, to the Leftybike, then to Herman again. He said, "Who are you guys?"

"Hammerfist and Ghetto Blaster, dingleberry," Frankie said. "And I'm gonna call you Stretch because your mom couldn't think of a better name than Gus."

Suddenly, Gus' eyes got really wide and his face leaned in. His voice died to a whisper and he uttered, "*You're* Hammerfist and Ghetto Blaster? Oh, the other guys are really pissed at you. Not as much as they're pissed at that kid, though."

Herman's face got hard and he leaned in closer. "What kid?"

"The kid who used to take the Green Juice!" Gus stammered. "He had one of those code names like you. Devilspawn, or something like that. They said he spilled the beans on Alpha Master's hideout, so they were going to give him what's coming."

Frankie and Herman's eyes became dinner plates. They didn't have to say a word. Both of them darted for the Leftybike and hopped on. Herman revved the engine, but before they peeled away, Frankie pointed his finger at Gus and shouted, "You're done with the Green Juice, got it Stretch? Or you'll be seeing us!"

With that, the Leftybike spewed smoke and roared out of the alleyway, leaving Gus/Stretch laying on the asphalt, alone, scared, and a little confused.

"Sid!" Herman shouted. "Track down the coordinates for Detective Norm Axewielder's house! His kid's in trouble!"

"Working on it," Sid said. There was a brief pause, then Sid's voice came back into their earpieces. "Acquired! He lives on Twelve Butterscotch Avenue. You'll arrive there in twenty-one minutes."

*

Crickets chirped in the warm summer night of Butterscotch Avenue. Resting on a hill, it had a lovely view of the Citytown lights and the sparkling moonlit ocean off in the far distance. All was still. It was nearly one o'clock in the morning, and most of the lights in the neighborhood had turned off.

At Twelve Butterscotch Avenue, only one light was on. The ghostly blue glow of a television screen illuminated the bedroom of sixteen-year-old Collin Axewielder as it flashed images of Death Soldier 5. His gaming controller clacked and clicked with every button press as his eyes fixed unblinkingly on the screen. A half-consumed bag of potato chips rested by his side on the bedspread. The television was muted and a large stereo against the wall played metal music to fill the silence.

Outside, the robust roar of a motorcycle drew closer from the distance until it came to a stop just outside the Axewielder residence. Two figures hopped off and scurried to the door.

Thumpthumpthumpthumpthump

Collin's eyebrows scrunched. He looked at the digital clock by his bedside. 12:52 AM. A frown crossed his face before he pushed himself off the bed and peered through the window. He couldn't see whoever was at the door, just a strange motorcycle with one handle in his driveway. As he pressed the power button to the stereo, the music turned off and he crawled across his bed.

Collin wiped his greasy, sweaty hands on his pajama shirt and made his way to the front door—out his room, down the hall, and down the stairs. Before he unbolted any of the numerous locks on the front door, he closed one eye and peeked through the peep hole. What he saw made the color leave his face and

227

his palms even sweatier. He frantically unlocked every lock and threw the door open.

"Why are you here? I told you I'm done!" he said.

Hammerfist and Ghetto Blaster stood at his door ready to do business. A hammer protruded from Hammerfist's right sleeve and Ghetto Blaster lugged his boombox over his shoulder. Half of Ghetto Blaster's face was covered with blood.

"We believe you," Hammerfist said firmly. "We heard from a different goon today that the others are going to roll up on you tonight. We came to warn you."

Collin's nose scrunched. "Goon?"

"The bad guys," Ghetto Blaster said. "What we used to call *you.*" Ghetto Blaster pointed at him.

Collin swallowed and looked around. The street was quiet. He nodded and beckoned the two inside. Hammerfist and Ghetto Blaster quickly stepped in and Collin slammed the door shut, turning every bolt on the door. When he did, he flipped around.

"So what do we do?" he asked, eyes filled with genuine worry. "We could run, but I don't have a car. And if they don't find me tonight, they'll just come for me another time."

"That's true," Ghetto Blaster said. "Did you give Tyler a buzz?"

Hammerfist touched his ear. "Tyler, we could use your help at Twelve Butterscotch Avenue right now." A pause. "Tyler?" Another pause. "*Tyler?* Crap. The signal was super fuzzy; I could barely hear him."

"Reception out here is really bad," Collin said. "We still have a house phone because of it."

"I hope 1994 is good to you," Ghetto Blaster said. "I guess we're on our own then." Then a lightbulb went off in his head. "*Wait!* Your dad's got guns, right?"

Collin squinted. "Duh. He's a cop. But they're locked up in a safe. I can't get to them."

"I don't like guns, man," Hammerfist said shortly.

"You'd like one more if you had one right now," Ghetto Blaster said matter-of-factly. "Besides, if the goons are really serious about stomping little Collin here, a gun is going to be a lot more help than your hammer. No offense."

Hammerfist frowned. "Doesn't change the fact that we don't have any. So what difference does it make?"

"Okay, okay," Ghetto Blaster sighed. "I guess we're *really* on our own. We should get you out of here for now."

Bam bam bam!

At that moment, three vigorous knocks rapped on the door from giant knuckles. The three exchanged glances. Collin went pale.

"*Hey!*" Chet's unmistakable voice was muffled on the other side of the door. "Open up, kid! We know what you did!"

Hammerfist shot a look Ghetto Blaster a look and whispered, "How did they get here so fast?"

Ghetto Blaster shrugged, worry filling his eyes.

"Don't say you didn't know this was coming!" Nikki chimed in. "You don't just rat out Alpha Master and expect to get let off without a hitch! We know your dad's a cop! If you told him, we're *really* gonna kill you!"

Ghetto Blaster looked at Collin and mouthed, "Did you?"

Collin shook his head.

"*I said open up!*" Chet bellowed as he pounded on the door some more. "I'm gonna give you to the count of three! One…"

Crash!

Suddenly, a metallic fist broke through the door, showering bits of wood and splinters into the hallway. The fist retracted and Chet's orange face filled up the hole that he made. A sick smile slashed across his face.

He said, "Heeeere's Ch—*what!*"

That was the moment that he saw Hammerfist and Ghetto Blaster. His eyes filled with something between shock and rage as he pulled back his fist and launched it through the door with another *crash.* More splinters and wood bits rained into the hallway.

Chet bellowed, "*I'm gonna kill you, you little punk!*"

Hammerfist shot a look at Collin and said, "Go hide." Immediately, Collin made a bee line for his room upstairs. Then, Hammerfist turned to Ghetto Blaster and said, "GB?"

"Kaboom," Ghetto Blaster said softly as he raised his palm to the door.

A blast erupted from his palm. Chet was obviously prepared for it. A huge hole ripped through the door, which was met by Chet's crossed, metallic forearms. He barely budged. With a final punch, the door toppled to the floor, splintered and broken. Chet and Nikki filled up the doorway, huffing and fuming.

Chet broke into a sprint. Frankie fired another blast. Chet deflected it with his forearm, sending it into a wall. A picture frame shattered and the wall burst out drywall and dust.

Herman planted his feet and pulled his hammer back. He thought, *Our communicators are out. That means no Tyler or Sid to come to the rescue. We gotta make this count.*

Frankie rolled out of the way and Herman leapt upon Chet, his hammer raised. Chet deflected the blow. He threw a punch. Herman dodged it and gave his hammer another swing. Chet blocked it with his arm. The two exchanged blows and parries through the hall as Herman backpedaled and Chet advanced on him.

Meanwhile, Nikki and Frankie's spat migrated into the living room. Frankie shot blast after blast at her, but Nikki was so agile that she kicked every blast away. With every deflected blast, a wall or piece of furniture would burst into rubble. Nikki laughed manically as every blast demolished the living room more and more.

Frankie bore his teeth and thought, *Crap. The only attack I've got is long range. I gotta get somewhere where I can isolate the shots. I know! If I guard Collin, they can only get to him through me. Fish in a barrel.*

On that thought, Frankie turned on his heels and darted to the kitchen. Nikki shouted at him and ran after. She tried grabbing at him but caught nothing but air as his feet met the linoleum.

Frankie rolled over the island in the center of the kitchen, stumbling to his feet and peeling past the refrigerator. Nikki soared across the counter with a flying kick, chipping the linoleum with her metal feet as she jumped. Her kick missed Frankie by inches, crashing into the refrigerator instead. The stainless steel door dented brutally and the contents inside shifted and fell in a mess of broken glass.

At the bottom of the stairs, Herman and Chet exchanged blows, each of them with a liberal share of cuts and bruises. Herman managed to land a blow on Chet's head, sending him reeling backward. Chet's scalp bled profusely. Herman popped his shoulders, readjusting his leather jacket, waiting for the counter. The bones in his shoulder felt broken. Chet had landed a punch there.

"You're using a black market Compound for a pre-workout?" Herman jeered. "That's the single douchiest thing I've ever heard."

Chet sneered and wiped the blood from his lip, "At least I'm not a cripple."

Chet launched a fist. Herman ducked, but he didn't see the other one coming. Chet's second fist crushed into Herman's chest, breaking half his ribs and sending him hurtling backward into a closet. Herman crashed through the door and slumped down, out cold, his breathing shallow.

Smiling, Chet cracked his neck and followed Nikki up the stairs.

"*Crap! Crap! Crap!*" Frankie shouted with every blast.

Frankie had lined up his blasts perfectly, but they shot in a perfect rhythm so they were easy for metal limbs to deflect. Nikki and Chet marched farther and farther down the hallway, swatting away blasts, demolishing the walls as they went. The hallway filled with debris and pieces of sheetrock.

I don't know what else to do, Frankie thought despairingly. *All this is doing is blowing apart Collin's house...*

Behind him, Collin literally had his back against the wall. His hands pressed against the stereo system, his eyes wild, his skin ghost-white, and sweat thick on his brow.

Nikki and Chet were nearly in his room. Inwardly, Frankie resigned to the fact that, for once, they had failed to stop a crime.

Behind him, Collin's hand slipped, and with a click, his stereo system turned on.

Everything happened at once. The sound of double bass pedals, overdriven guitars, and barbaric vocals left the stereo speakers, bleeding through Frankie's headphones and into his eardrums. It was like a bolt of lightning shot through him. His eyes popped, he gasped, he dropped his Bambox and threw off his headphones. Tingling like a million hot pinpricks rippled through his body. He bore his teeth.

Nikki swung around and launched a metallic kick at Frankie's face. Frankie lifted his hand and stopped it with a *crack*.

Everything halted. Collin's jaw fell. Nikki and Chet stared at Frankie with wonder, his fleshy, average fist raised in the air, stopping a swinging metal kick inches before crashing into his face. Meanwhile, Collin's metal music played through the stereo speakers.

Frankie's head spun about, his eyes locking on Collin. "*Crank that up.*"

Collin obeyed. His hand jerked over the stereo knob, and suddenly, a bombardment of high-velocity, wailing soundwaves rocked the Axewielder house. Frankie let out a loud whoop as the music filled him, his arms letting off an eerie red smoke. He cocked back his opposite fist and launched it at Nikki.

BAM!

Nikki flew back, perfectly horizontal until she toppled into Chet, sending them both somersaulting backward. Their somersaulting ended when they finally slammed into a wall at the end of the hallway, shaking their heads and staring at Frankie in horror.

"*Woo!*" Frankie whooped as he stalked toward them, his arms fuming. "*Let's go!*"

As they both scrambled to their feet, Nikki pushed Chet forward and retreated down the stairs. Chet brought up his fists, trying to push down the fear that radiated from his eyes. He threw a punch. Frankie dodged. He threw another. Frankie dodged again. He threw a third. Frankie blocked it, grabbed his tank top, spun around, and hurled Chet down the stairs.

Chet tumbled down the stairs like a muscly orange ragdoll and landed atop Nikki in the debris-strewn hallway. Frankie took two generous steps down the stairs then jumped off, falling like a hawk diving for prey. Chet and Nikki just managed to scramble out of the way before Frankie super-stomped them both. Neither of them hesitated to start throwing punches and kicks. Frankie went to town blocking and dodging them all.

Meanwhile, Herman stirred down the hallway in a closet filled with wood pieces and rubble. He winced as he tried to sit up, the ribs in his chest still mending themselves. Through bleary eyes, he peered down the hallway to see Frankie without his headphones and Bambox, but still fighting off Nikki and Chet like a smoky-armed ninja. Aggressive metal music filled the house. Herman forced himself to sit up and he blinked several times to get his eyes in focus.

Bam! Crack! Whap!

Frankie got off a few good hits on both Nikki and Chet, who were both scraped and bleeding. They both shot looks at each other and started to backpedal. Frankie clapped his hands.

"*Come on!*" He bellowed. "*I'm pumped!*"

Nikki and Chet hesitated for a second, then turned on their heels and bolted for the door. They blasted through the empty doorframe and disappeared into the night. Frankie didn't chase after them. Herman was on his feet, clutching his ribs, which felt better with every passing second.

Upstairs, the metal song came to an end. The smoke emanating off Frankie's arms dissipated. And with that, his body drooped.

"I'm not pumped anymore," Frankie breathed.

With that, he collapsed, leaning against a wall for support as he slowly slid down into a sitting position. His breathing came in great gulps and his eyes fluttered like he was on the verge of unconsciousness. Herman limped over to him, pressing his own back against the wall and sliding into a sitting position next to him.

It was at that moment that Collin Axewielder came creeping around the upper hallway. When he saw the coast was clear, he dashed to the bottom of the stairs. He took a look around when his feet touched ground level. It was like a hurricane had passed through the house. The remains of paintings, pictures, furniture, and sheet rock were scattered everywhere. Broken glass crunched beneath his feet. An absolute massacre.

"Look," Herman said as he wiped his face. "We're all for saving your life, but we're not going to be around when your dad comes home."

Numbly, Collin said, "Okay."

"I think you and him need to have a little chat," Herman continued. "About a lot of things."

"Yeah," Collin said.

"Hammerfist," Frankie said breathlessly. "This is the first time I've been tired in over a week."

"That metal song did you in, didn't it?" Herman smirked. "You saved the day, Ghetto Blaster." He slapped his shoulder. ("Ow," Frankie said)

"I never should have taken the Green Juice," Collin said helplessly as he plopped down on the bottom step. "None of this would have happened. All of this—this is my fault."

"No, all of this is Nikki and Chet's fault," Herman said. "*They* decided to come attack you tonight. *They* did this. Don't put this on yourself."

"But this never would have happened if I never took the Green Juice," Collin said, running his fingers through his hair. "I just heard these guys on the streets talking about it and asked them if they could hook me up. Then they got me set up with

Alpha Master. I thought the burglaries and supervillain stuff was sick for a while, but by the time I realized it had gone too far..." He scanned the house and shook his head despairingly. "There's no way my dad is ever going to forgive me after something like this."

Herman paused. Then he said, "I bet he'll just be happy that you're safe."

Collin looked directly at Herman and Frankie before he said, "I'm going to tell him that you guys saved my life."

Herman teased a half-smile. He said, "Stay out of trouble, Collin. GB, you think you're okay to get on the Leftybike?"

"Yeah... I think I'll be okay..."

"We gotta go. Good luck, Collin."

With that, Herman hoisted Frankie onto his feet and helped him out of the Axewielder house. Collin stayed on the staircase, even after he heard the roar of the Leftybike evaporate into the night.

Hours later, an exhausted Norm Axewielder came home to find the interior of his house completely destroyed. He and his son talked for an hour. They embraced, Norman made a couple of phone calls, Collin collected a few things from his room, and they both left to find a hotel. Early that morning, a host of detectives, an insurance agent, and a large cleanup crew arrived at Twelve Butterscotch Avenue.

20

"They know you're here."

"Very well."

"...Very well?"

"Yes, you heard me correctly."

"They'll probably be here tonight."

"So be it."

"You're not worried?"

"No. I'm the father of their powers, including yours. As such, I know them better than they know themselves. Despite their superhuman conditions, they are subject to many of the same injuries as a normal man. I will be prepared."

"You know they're coming for the girl."

"I'm counting on it. Regardless, they won't find her."

"Then she is well hidden?"

"That's not for you to know."

A pause. "She frightens me."

"And you have yet to see her full potential."

*

At Citytown Applied Technologies, five figures huddled around the table. On the table, a crude drawing of a floor plan was labeled "Soda Factory". It included eight giant circles representing abandoned vats of HyperFizz Cola—two rows of four. Between the two rows, a couple of small rectangles were drawn to represent desks where Doctor Malcolm McMasters engaged in his typical operations.

"This is the best I can do after running there a couple of times," Tyler said with his hands on the table. "Sorry, I know it sucks, but it's the best I can do."

"No, this is fabulous," Susan said, pinning her soccer ball under her foot.

"So the main entrance is there on the south side?" Herman said as he pointed at the sketch with his hook.

"Right," Tyler said. "It's a reception room with a few offices attached, but it's all abandoned, dirty, and empty. There are a couple of massive doors on the east side that must have been for loading trucks. I'm not sure which entrance is going to be more discreet."

"Does anyone else think it's weird that Doctor McMasters would set up his work space in the dead center of a factory?" Frankie said while scratching his head. "I mean, why didn't he use one of the office rooms?"

"Beats me," Herman said. "But there's got to be a reason for it. No sign of Cassie then?"

Tyler shook his head. Herman sighed. Everyone else swapped worried glances.

"It might seem simple," Tyler began. "But I think our best plan is for me to run in tonight and assess the building one more time to see what we're up against. They won't even see me. From that point, we can figure out how to infiltrate it. What do you think?"

"I believe that's the obvious thing to do," Sid said as he readjusted the goggles on his forehead.

Herman slid a glance to Sid and said, "Is there anything we should know about this guy? Any weaknesses that might help us?"

Sid sighed. Then he said, "Doctor McMasters will be incredibly hostile. If he had any inclination that you five may descend upon him soon, he will have made necessary preparations to stop you." He paused. "I don't know what else I can do to help you. I've given you every tool at my disposal. If you've made any allies recently that may be able to help with the raid tonight, I recommend that you reach out to them."

Everyone looked at each other. Herman pulled out his cell phone and set it on the table, face up. He leaned over the table like a CEO about to give a pep talk to a fading board room.

"I can think of one person," Herman said. "But it's a longshot."

"We need any help we could possibly get," Sid rubbed his hands together.

Susan said creased her eyebrow. "Who? We've kept these powers secret from everybody we know. Who do we know that —" Her eyes narrowed, then got wide. "Wait…"

"Sierra," Herman said. The phone beeped, readying the search feature. "Call the Citytown Police Department using a private signal."

"Dialing *Citytown Police*," the phone's AI voice repeated.

"Whoa-whoa-whoa, are you *nuts?*" Frankie stammered.

"He's all we've got," Herman said with a shrug. "We did just save his son's life, so that's gotta count for something."

Bbbbbbrrr. Bbbbbbrrr. Bbbbbbrrr—

"Citytown Police Department," the voice of a rushed secretary answered on the other end of the phone. The low noise of shuffling papers, hustling feet, and chatting policemen could be heard in the background.

"I need to speak to Detective Norman Axewielder, please," Herman said firmly.

"May I ask who is calling?"

"A friend of his son's."

"I'll redirect your call."

The police precinct didn't have any hold music. Herman and Frankie exchanged glances again. Susan whispered, asking why they would solicit a person who wants to put them all behind bars. Tyler threw glances to everyone else, confused as to who this detective could be and how in the world Axewielder could be an actual surname. Suddenly, the rough jumble of a corded phone lifting off the receiver came through the speaker.

"Axewielder," the detective said on the other end of the phone. Even his voice sounded like it hadn't shaved in four days. "What's wrong with Collin?"

"Collin is fine," Herman said. "It's Hammerfist."

You could almost hear Detective Axewielder scowl. "What have you done with him?"

"We don't have him. All we want is a favor."

Detective Axewielder didn't answer right away. The receiver gave no sound but the tinny bustle of the police station for a few seconds. Finally, the detective said, "You expecting me to thank you or something? This doesn't change anything. Escaping police custody still makes you a criminal."

"This criminal and another just like me saved your son's life last night, in case you forgot. Remember, we're not really the bad guys here... but we've figured out who is. Do you want to take him down?"

Again, Detective Axewielder didn't reply right away. After a long, painful pause, he pushed out the words, "What do you want?"

"We found out where the kingpin is hiding," Herman said. "And we want to shut him down tonight. We could probably take him on our own, but we want to have some backup just in case. Can you assemble some men for the job? I can give you the time and place."

"What's the catch?"

Herman hadn't thought about this. His head swiveled to the other members of his team. Frankie was the one who made his opinion the most obvious. He put his fists out and pulled them apart like he was breaking invisible handcuffs. Herman got the idea.

"You need to pardon all of us," Herman said slowly. "Whatever charges you have on us, gone."

"Forget it," Detective Axewielder said.

"Detective," Herman said. "With all due respect, you and your team have been outclassed by us and these guys at every turn. You're not going to bring these guys in without our help. Remember, Ghetto Blaster and I risked our necks to save your son last night so you *know* we're on your side. We want to see these goons stopped as much as you do. The only way we're going to make that happen is to work together. But it's up to you."

The tension in the laboratory was thick. Herman surprised even himself with his boldness. For the third time, there was a long pause on Detective Axewielder's end. Surely, he was pacing the floor at the precinct miles away, debating on whether or not he could trust Hammerfist and his little band of freaks.

After a long moment, Detective Axewielder's voice was quiet. "Fine. If we pull this off and we bring in the kingpin, you punks get pardoned. If we don't, I'm taking all of you in. Deal?"

The tone in the lab became grave. What if they *didn't* pull off the operation? What if Doctor McMasters got away again?

Susan's eyes flashed with images of her kids and husband. Tyler thought of those at the food pantries that would be shocked to hear he's arrested. Frankie thought of his parents and Herman couldn't help but think of Aunt Josie. One thing united them, however, and that was Cassandra Copland.

Nods were exchanged all around. Herman leaned in and said, "Deal."

"When and where?" Detective Axewielder said.

"The old HyperFizz Cola factory, eleven o'clock," Herman said. "Be there."

Boop.

The phone shut off. Silence filled the air once more. All eyes were on Herman. He looked around, reading the troubled faces of everyone in the room. Their freedom was now on the line if they failed.

"We're not going to fail," Herman said. "We're gonna find Cassie and put Malcolm McMasters away. Then we can take the antidote as free citizens again. It'll be like this whole ordeal never happened. We got this."

*

But what if you don't? Herman thought to himself. *What if this has all been a huge, astronomical, gargantuan mistake?*

As he sat at his desk, Herman thumped the blunt end of a pencil against his forehead. His heart was in a tight knot and his throat was tight. Around him, dozens of wadded up balls of paper were scattered at his feet. He sniffed.

It was hard to sum up all the feelings he had right now—everything had happened so fast. It was hardly two weeks ago that he was just a normal guy trying to find a job. But now, everything was different. He had been nearly killed or at least pommeled half a dozen times. He had made some new friends. Some new enemies. Felt like he belonged. Felt betrayed.

He threw his pencil down and rubbed his eyes. The digital clock ticked silently at his bedside. The time was 9:40PM. In just over an hour, he'd take the Leftybike to the old HyperFizz Cola factory on the south side of town. In just over an hour, he would have the biggest fight he's had yet.

Shick! Crracckk

He tore another piece of paper from a notebook, wadded it up, and threw it over his shoulder. In time, the city and its police force could be overrun with anarchist goons if Doctor McMasters isn't stopped. A girl named Cassandra Copland was kidnapped days ago and no one knows. The entire city sleeps as a superhuman community grows beneath their noses, and Herman and his friends are the only people that can stop it.

A sigh seeped out of Herman's lips. The time was now 10:01PM. Less than an hour away.

How had all of this happened to *him*? Maybe he should have just thrown away the communicator and the hammer. Maybe he should have never tried to fight crime as some sort of amateur vigilante.

But how would things have been different for this city if he didn't? How will things be different if they fail tonight?

His gaze fell to the metal hook protruding from his right wrist. A frown stretched across his face as he considered the question that had been plaguing his mind for hours. *Is a hammer on my wrist going to be enough for a fight like tonight's? What if I actually... die?*

He stared at the blank page in front of him, thinking. After letting thoughts coagulate for the hundredth time, he picked up his pencil again. The lead scooted between the lines, forming hurried words. He would erase some and write over them with new ones. He would stop, then think, then start again. His eyes stung as the pencil skidded down the page.

After a while, he signed his name at the bottom. Then, after another moment of thought, he signed an additional name underneath his own. He held it up to his eyes as he reviewed the whole thing:

AUNT JOSIE,

A LOT HAS HAPPENED SINCE MY ACCIDENT. IT FEELS LIKE MY LIFE GOT A LITTLE OUT OF CONTROL. AND WHAT'S WORSE IS I HAVEN'T BEEN PERFECTLY HONEST WITH YOU ABOUT IT.

IF YOU'RE READING THIS, IT'S BECAUSE I'VE PROBABLY BEEN KILLED. THE TRUTH IS, THE JOB I GOT HIRED TO DO WAS REALLY DANGEROUS. I GOT SOME CRAZY CONDITIONS FROM MY ACCIDENT, WHICH IS WHY I HEALED SO FAST. AND I BECAME STRONG. AND I NEVER SLEEP. WITH THESE POWERS, ONE WEALTHY MAN WAS WILLING TO PAY ME A LOT OF MONEY TO FIGHT CRIME IN CITYTOWN AND TRACK DOWN SOME BAD PEOPLE. I WAS SUCCESSFUL FOR A LITTLE WHILE, BUT ULTIMATELY, I GUESS IT DIDN'T WORK OUT.

THE WORST PART ABOUT THIS IS THAT I LEARNED I CAN'T PROTECT EVERYONE I LOVE. ONE OF MY FRIENDS GOT KIDNAPPED AND I DON'T KNOW WHAT THE BAD PEOPLE DID WITH HER. AND NOW YOU. YOU'VE ALREADY BEEN THROUGH SO MUCH SINCE MY MOM DIED, AND YOU TOOK ME IN AND RAISED ME LIKE YOUR OWN SON. AND NOW I'M GONE TOO. A PERFECT ANGEL LIKE YOU DOESN'T DESERVE THIS. I'M SORRY.

BUT AS I THINK ABOUT IT, I DON'T REALLY REGRET WHAT I DID. I'VE ALWAYS WANTED TO MAKE THE WORLD JUST A LITTLE BIT BETTER, YOU KNOW? AND I THINK THROUGH THESE INSANE CIRCUMSTANCES, I KIND OF DID IN SOME SMALL WAY. I JUST HATE THAT IT EFFECTED YOU LIKE THIS.

I LOVE YOU, AUNT JOSIE. I'LL LOVE YOU FOREVER. JUST KEEP SWINGING.

YOUR BOY,
HERMAN FITZGERALD
AKA HAMMERFIST

Herman folded the letter into thirds and wrote "Aunt Josie" on the side. His forearm wiped the mistiness from his eyes and he took a look at the clock by his bedside. It read 10:37PM. Time to go.

Herman pushed back his chair and stood up. Briskly, he threw on his leather jacket, stuffed his hammer into his backpack, threw it over his shoulder, and started out of his room. The light was on in Bridger's room, but he didn't make a sound. Herman thought for a second about saying goodbye. He even took a step toward his room, but changed his mind. Adam was gone, as usual. Zach's room was empty.

As he made his way down the hall, Herman's eyes stuck to his shoes. When he crossed into the living room, Zach was there, sitting on the couch, reading a book. He snapped it shut as Herman walked by.

"Hey," he said semi-loudly.

"Hey," Herman said, not taking his eyes off his shoes. "I'm heading out."

"Wait a second."

Zach was suddenly on his feet, striding over to the door. Herman already had his hand on the handle. Zach leaned against the doorframe, eyed him suspiciously, his frame towering over Herman's. Herman's eyes narrowed just a little.

"How's your girlfriend?" Zach asked.

Images of Cassie's wild red hair and emerald eyes flashed through Herman's mind. Then images of her trapped in the clutches of Doctor McMasters flashed just the same. Herman said, "She could be better. I gotta go."

Herman pulled open the door, but Zach's thick arm shot out and slammed his shut. Herman's blood started to boil.

"You want to know something?" Zach said. "I don't think you actually have a girlfriend. You've been acting *weird* lately, Herman Fitzgerald, and I want to know what's up." He leaned in. "What are you really doing every night when you take that backpack out the door? I hear you sneak in here as late as four in the morning. What are you doing? You can't be getting booty every single night. Why so secretive?" Zach's voice died down. "Are you with a street gang now?"

Herman's eyes narrowed more and he shook his head. "What? No!"

"Then what are you doing?"

"None of your business."

"Then it *was* a lie! You don't have a girlfriend!"

Zach slid between Herman and the door and leaned up against it. He folded his arms. Herman clenched his teeth behind sealed lips. Zach nodded and said, "What's in the backpack?"

"*Move*," Herman said firmly.

"Make me move," Zach said smugly.

Herman's hand shot up to Zach's collar, grabbed a fistful of designer polo, and threw him to the ground with a mighty *thud*.

Muffled expletives came from Bridger's room as the floor shook. Zach wasn't angry—he was more shocked than anything. His baffled eyes locked onto Herman as he sat up, looking from his torn polo to Herman's burning eyes.

Herman's fist found the door handle and he pulled it open. He didn't give some snippy remark before his exit. Just a hard, white-hot, unblinking stare. There was nothing to say.

He stepped into the breezeway and slammed the door. He thought to himself, *Well, things are definitely going to be weird between him and I from now on…*

With that, Hammerfist walked into the night.

21

The HyperFizz Cola factory didn't have the chain link fence that the old hospital did. Nestled unassumingly in the southern industrial area of town, it looked like any other metal warehouse if it weren't for the heavily rusted HyperFizz Cola sign above the main entrance. A small parking lot with fading yellow paint was populated by four black SUVs by the entrance. At various locations away from the site, Herman and his friends parked their cars and walked over to prepare for the operation.

Across the street from the factory, the others stood just inside an alley, waiting with their weapons while Herman fastened his hammer and strode up. Susan's soccer ball rested at her hip, Frankie's Bambox hung from his hand, and Tyler stood with his hands in his pockets. All their expressions were grave. They all knew who was waiting for them inside.

"No sign of Axewielder or the police yet," Susan said as Herman arrived.

"They're late," Tyler said distastefully.

Herman was quiet. He took a long look at the factory looming across the street before asking, "How are you guys feeling about tonight?"

Frankie shuffled his feet and said, "I'm nervous."

"Me too," Susan nodded to Frankie.

"I think we'll be okay," Tyler said as he folded his arms. "Just treat this like any other fight. We're the good guys. We'll be fine."

"And what if we get arrested?" Frankie said. "Never thought I'd go to jail for trying to help people."

"Maybe you should've picked a way to help people that doesn't involve assault, trespassing, or destruction of property," Herman said.

"That's what I've been saying," Tyler smirked.

They all gave a hollow laugh, then the laughing died down to silence. Frankie cleared his throat awkwardly. Susan leaned her back against the wall, folding her arms with her soccer ball pinned underneath. Tyler stared at his feet as he shuffled back and forth. Out of the corner of his eye, Herman noticed a hooded figure walk toward them on the sidewalk. The figure was noticeably on the short side and walked with a briskness and purpose that most urban nomads don't have. Instantly, he knew who was under the hoodie.

"Hey," Herman said as the figure stopped in front of them. "Where are all your friends?"

"We've got a sniper on the roof on the north side," Detective Axewielder pulled the hood off his head, revealing his grizzly beard and stone-cold glare. "SWAT team will arrive in three minutes. You all are morons for not wearing a disguise."

"Well, you already know who we are, so," Herman said. "The guy we're looking for is named Doctor Malcolm McMasters. Average height, a little stocky, brown hair with a part in it. He should be inside."

"You sure he's there?" Detective Axewielder said.

"We don't know yet," Herman replied. "Tyler, could you go take a look?"

"One second," Tyler said.

In a gust of wind, Tyler was gone, but he returned in less than the second that he requested. He straightened out his t-shirt and gave puzzled glances to everyone in the circle as the gust died down and the bits of trash settled back onto the sidewalk.

"He's not in there," Tyler said. "No one is. It's empty."

"That's super weird," Frankie chimed in. "Especially considering that there are four black luxury SUVs parked out front. Bad guys always drive black SUVs. Probably mercenaries or dirty lawyers."

"He's not wrong," Detective Axewielder said. "We can wait until the SWAT team arrives and send them in."

"I don't think so," Herman said. "No offense, Detective, but we should probably be the ones to go in first."

The rest of Herman's team nodded in the affirmative. Detective Axewielder frowned.

"Alright then," he said hotly as he pulled an apparatus from his back pocket. It was a small in-ear communication device with a microphone sticking out. It had a long wire that led to a clunky transmitter with a blinking red light. His hand stuck out to give it to Herman.

"Put this on," he said. "The emergency word will be 'Kansas'. When you say the word, the sniper will fire a shot and the boys will go in."

"Try this instead," Frankie said as he reached in his own pocket and handed Detective Axewielder one of Sid's communicators. "This way, you can be tuned in to all of us, including Doctor Saskatoon. He's our eye in the sky—kind of."

"Saskatoon?" Detective Axewielder said, suddenly curious. "Like the Saskatoon family that owns the Picko Company?"

Herman blinked twice. "That's the one. Steam-powered toothpick dispenser and all."

"My ex-wife wouldn't shut up about those products," Detective Axewielder said as he put the communicator in his ear. "Let me know when you're ready."

Herman looked to the others. Frankie clicked a few buttons on his Bambox and music started playing through his headphones. Susan shifted her feet, staring at the ground with her eyes glazed over. Tyler's hands were in his pockets and he gave Herman a nod. Herman swallowed and remembered the note he had written just a few minutes ago.

For Cassie, he thought.

"I guess we're as ready as we'll ever be," Herman said. "Let's go."

Just like that, they marched across the street. Every heart pounded thickly as the group departed from Detective Axewielder, who sunk into the alleyway discreetly. Herman's hand started to get clammy. He shot glances to his other friends as they made their way to the entrance of the factory. Everyone moved forward with caution.

They crossed the parking lot, passing the black SUVs that stood sentinel as loose rocks and gravel crackled under their feet. Frankie pulled the hoodie over his headphones and turned up the volume on his Bambox. Susan spun the soccer ball in her hands. Tyler kept his gaze fixed and his hands in his pockets. Meanwhile, Herman half-lifted his hammer arm, ready to swing.

They arrived at the entrance. Tyler reached out and carefully pulled the door open. The light was on inside. Herman edged his way in and peered around. Just as Tyler said, it just looked like a reception office with cheap tile that hadn't been swept in years. Dead bugs bunched in the corners. The fluorescent light above them flickered. Two additional doors led to a couple of empty offices with no furniture. All was quiet, and the smell of dust and cement made Herman's nose scrunch.

He crept slowly, being careful not to make a sound. Everyone else followed suit. Susan snuck over to the additional rooms and looked around, soccer ball at the ready. She looked back and shook her head. Nothing. The music in Frankie's headphones bled out a little, and everybody could hear faint EDM beats against the silence.

A door lay directly across the room leading into the factory. A tiny glass window was in the door at eye level, and through it, the eight massive vats could be seen. Herman leaned in closer to see that every vat had an elaborate series of conveyor belts surrounding each one, creating a spider web of belts and steel throughout the warehouse. Currently, some bottles were out on the conveyor belts filled with a bright green liquid.

"There's nothing in these rooms," Frankie whispered as he stood beside Herman.

Herman locked eyes with him then looked at everyone else in the room. With mutual nods, they moved toward the factory door and slowly pushed it open.

As the door swung open, chill seeped into the main office. Their footsteps made little sound as they all made their way into the mouth of the cavernous room. All was still.

Herman creased his eyebrows. Above their heads, a catwalk stretched throughout the factory, crisscrossing and pressing the edges of the perimeter. Large windows stretched on the right and left sides of the building. Herman's eyes darted to the left side—the north side. He could see the rooftop to the next building through the glass and silently thought about the sniper waiting for a signal.

"Remember," Detective Axewielder's tinny voice sounded in their earpieces. "The emergency word is 'Kansas'."

Halfway across the room, two foldout desks were propped up with a task chair. One desk was filled with vials, beakers, and

252

jars while the second table was littered with notebooks and loose paper.

Everyone in the crew was in the room by now. Tyler pulled his hands out of his pockets and strode to the head of the group, soaking in the surroundings. With a quick gust and the blink of an eye, Tyler was gone and back. He turned and looked at the group.

"I just did another run through," Tyler said. "Nothing."

BLAM!

A sudden burst like an explosion ripped through the factory. And with it, Tyler collapsed. Several expressions tore across his face in a fraction of a second—shock, anguish, exhaustion. The other three recoiled at the sound, their heads swiveling about, scanning for the source. Herman dropped to his knees and flipped Tyler over.

"Tyler! *Tyler!*"

As Tyler turned over face-up, his eyes were bleary. His t-shirt that read "Mama G's Thrift Store" was quickly staining red, blooming out from a hole shot just above his left lung. Herman's body flushed with ice water. His eyes popped open at the sight and the others got deathly silent.

"He won't heal through that one."

The voice didn't belong to Susan or Frankie, but they all recognized it—smooth and dark. Herman jumped to his feet and reared in the direction of the voice but saw nothing. Everyone was crouched down, weapons at the ready.

Then suddenly, Doctor Malcolm McMasters materialized out of thin air in a veil of blue sparkles, standing by his desks. He wore no lab coat, just a typical sweater and some khaki pants. In his left hand, a small metal device with a large button. In his right hand, a large revolver extended toward Herman and his friends. The barrel was smoking.

"Do you think Sidney is the only one with access to cloaking technology?" Doctor McMasters said smugly. "How wrong you are. Look up."

They did. Dozens of figures materialized around the catwalk —muscular men and women garbed with dark clothing and their faces painted black. Every single one of them was armed with an assault rifle trained on Herman, Susan, and Frankie.

"My latest buyer," Doctor McMasters said, still holding the revolver steady. "They were willing to pay a handsome price for a large shipment of my formula. It's a shipment that you temporarily delayed with your car accident, Mister Hammerfist. Surprise!

"As you can see, there is no point in resisting. You have over a dozen firearms trained on you and the one person who could stop that is… incapacitated. I suppose 'survival of the fittest' isn't always the case."

By Herman's feet, Tyler gasped for air as the color drained from his face.

"You really expect to get away with this, you coward?" Herman sneered. "This place is surrounded by cops! You're not going anywhere! What's your big plan, anyway?"

"The police? Oh no!" Doctor McMasters mocked. "Please. I'm sure Citytown's finest will show their usual incompetent colors tonight. They're the least of my worries.

"As for my big plan, this is it! I already told you before, I have no need to monologue a second time. I'm a scientist and a businessman. Selling my work to the highest bidder is the only reasonable thing to do in my position. This group of talented men and women want a vast quantity of Compound Z24 to do who-knows-what, and frankly, I don't care.

"The transaction is nearly done. I'd love to simply let you all go, but at this point, I'd rather just kill you. And once you're disposed of, we'll carry out with the agreement as planned and I move my operations to a different location. I'm done with Citytown and its filth."

Herman could have ground his teeth to powder. Meanwhile, Tyler was quickly bleeding out. The wound was mending fast, but he was losing blood faster. What to do? They could try to help Tyler, but Doctor McMasters would just put a bullet in him and the others. If they try to pull a fast one and attack, they'll all get blown to bits by the mercenaries. What then?

Doctor McMasters clicked the hammer back on his revolver.

"So that's it, then?" Herman hollered. "Just find a seller and move from one place to another? Where's your next stop, Kansas?"

Susan and Frankie tensed up. Doctor McMaster's face scrunched. Herman held steady.

"Kansas?" Doctor McMasters repeated. "Why would I go to Kansas? There's nothing in—"

BLAM!

A window on the building's north side punctured with a hole the size of a quarter. This time, Doctor McMasters was the one sent reeling. His gun clacked to the floor and he crumpled into a heap, clutching his shoulder. The sniper had missed his vital organs. He was bleeding, but still mobile.

Everyone acted fast. Frankie launched a blast up to the scaffolding, connecting with some rickety cables that held the walk in place. The mercenaries tried to fire their weapons but missed horribly while trying to keep their balance. Susan launched a kick into the opposite rafters, commanding her soccer ball to ignite with electricity before it connected. As the ball slammed into the metal scaffolding, the mercenaries reeled with shock.

Herman crouched down and hoisted Tyler's body over his back as quickly as he could, darting for the door.

"*Man down!*" Herman hollered into his earpiece. "Tyler's been shot! I don't know how long he's going to last, so get him medical attention *now!* I'll leave him just inside the door!"

"On it," Detective Axewielder said in his ear.

"*Hang in there, Tyler!*" Sid's voice also came in his ear.

As soon as Herman had crossed into the reception area, he let Tyler to the ground, leaning his back against the wall. Tyler gasped again and clenched his teeth. The bloodstain on his shirt was bigger than his hand, thick, sticky, and crimson. Herman grabbed Tyler's hand and pressed it against the wound. Tyler winced, his eyes half-closed.

"Stay with me, man! Come on!"

Tyler winced one more time. He exhaled. His hand slid off his shirt, his eyes closed, and his body slumped.

"*Come on, Tyler!*"

It was no use. The body of eighteen-year-old soup kitchen volunteer Tyler Calvin quickly faded. His hands slumped to the ground and his head lolled to his shoulder. Eyes, ghostly and half-open, looked toward Herman Fitzgerald, but not at him.

Herman's eyes stung and his throat tightened. Inside the factory, more gunshots sounded, accompanied with the sounds of shouts and reverberating steel. Doctor McMasters was crawling toward his discarded gun. Frankie and Susan had their hands full with the mercenaries.

Cassie. Tyler. One singular thought echoed through Herman's mind:

Vengeance.

22

Herman sprinted through the doorway, his stinging eyes fixed on Malcolm McMasters. Bullets blazed past him as he tore through the factory, the massive vats of Compound Z24 providing him some cover from the mercenaries. Doctor McMasters noticed Herman quickly advancing on him and crawled faster for his gun, his khaki pants dragging across the factory floor.

McMasters wrapped his hand around the gun, and still clutching his shoulder, raised the firearm to Herman just as he approached. In one swift movement, Herman smashed the gun out of the Doctor's hand.

McMasters recoiled and hollered as he clutched his wrist. The revolver clacked again dozens of yards away, far out of reach. Herman kicked McMasters to the ground, who tumbled backwards onto his feet and scrambled off in the other direction.

"*No!*" Herman roared. "*You're not getting away this time!*"

Herman slammed his hammer into one of the desks, launching it at McMasters and sending all its papers flying. As he ran, McMasters flipped around just in time to see the table hurtling toward him. He ducked just as the table crashed into a giant vat above him with a *boom.* Then he peeled off in a different direction.

There was no way he could outrun Herman. McMasters was a portly scientist with a wounded shoulder and Herman was a superhuman with Compound Z24 pumping through his veins. In just a few more moments, Herman caught up to the sweating, panting doctor and tackled him to the ground. The two tumbled and finally came to a stop with McMasters laying face up, Herman on top of him with his hammer cocked back and his opposite hand clenching McMasters' sticky, bloodied shoulder.

"*Call them off!*" Herman bellowed.

McMasters winced and groaned with Herman's arm gripping his shoulder, but he shook his head. But there wasn't an ounce of fear on his face. It was almost like a child playing 'keep away.' Herman bore his teeth like a tiger.

"I can crack your skull like an egg!" Herman bellowed again. "*Call them off!*"

"You don't seem much like a killer, Mister Hammerfist," McMasters jeered. "That's the difference between you and me."

Shink!

Herman didn't see it, but in the tumble, McMasters pulled out a small blade from his pocket and held it stealthily at his side. At the right moment, he thrusted it into Herman's thigh. Herman hollered and McMasters pushed him off before struggling to his feet. The knife was small, only a couple of inches in length. Herman found the handle at his side and ripped it out, tossing it aside.

McMasters came to a stop several feet away, turning around and facing Herman while still clutching his shoulder. A sick smile remained stretched across his face.

"Don't worry, that won't be enough to kill you," he said. "This will, though."

It was then that McMasters extracted the tiniest vial from his pocket. In it, a fizzy black fluid.

"Remember Compound X?" McMasters jeered again. "Fifty percent chance of mortality, but temporary boost in healing, speed, and strength. If I don't die first, this will heal my wound quickly and give me plenty of time to kill you and your friends. Bottoms up!"

With that, he uncorked it and threw the fluid in his mouth. He swallowed and threw the vial on the ground, shattering it. Nothing happened for a second, then McMasters doubled over, falling to the ground on all fours. Herman didn't wait around to see this transformation complete if it were successful. He bolted to Doctor McMasters.

Herman leapt. As he soared through the air, he pulled his hammer back, ready to slam it into McMasters. For Cassie. For Tyler.

But right as Herman landed to slam his hammer into McMasters, he was stopped. In the blink of an eye, McMasters was on his feet with his hand in the air, clutching Herman's hammer. He stopped it just as he would stop a tossed paper ball. Herman's eyes popped open and a cold rush swept through his body. McMasters smirked.

In a flash, McMasters released Herman's hammer, then threw a punch into his stomach. The force was incredible. Herman flew backwards perfectly horizontal until he slammed into a giant vat, denting it in the shape of a human body. As he slumped to the floor, McMasters was suddenly upon him again, picking him up by a fistful of his hair. Herman grimaced.

McMasters leaned so close that his lips grazed Herman's ear. He whispered, "I'm not going to kill you right away. I think I'll have a bit of fun first."

With that, he hurled Herman into another vat, denting it again. Everything in Herman's body hurt. He couldn't see. His brain pounded. He sunk to the ground, trying to push himself to his feet, but McMasters was already there, launching punches at his face.

Bam! Crack! Whap!

Each blow disoriented Herman more and more, breaking and bloodying his face. Each punch was so *fast* and so *strong*. By risking death, McMasters had given himself Tyler Calvin's speed and the strength of a gorilla. Now, Herman was just a punching bag. His body rapidly tried to heal itself, but it was like putting out a fire with a water gun.

With a final punch, Herman somersaulted backward, landing face-up on the ground. His nose and mouth were both bleeding and it was hard to breathe through so many broken ribs. A cough sputtered from his lips and he gasped, trying to breathe a normal breath. Through swollen eyes, he tried to get grips of his surroundings and force himself onto his feet.

"Your spirit is remarkable," McMasters said with his hands in his pockets several feet away. "Your determination to overpower me compels you even when defeat is inevitable. I admire you, Hammerfist. But alas, you're just a boy with a hammer. And today, you die."

In a gust of wind, he suddenly reappeared where the gun had landed moments before. But now, it was in his hand, pointed at Herman. Herman's eyes focused just in time to see McMaster's smug face behind the barrel of the revolver. But in a second, it was all over.

BLAM BLAM BLAM!

The three rounds ripped through his shoulder, right lung, and stomach. Herman instantly collapsed in a heap. Blood rapidly left his body through the bullet holes. He briefly thought of the note that he wrote for Aunt Josie.

"*Herman!*" Frankie and Susan bellowed in agony.

While Herman and McMasters had been fighting, Susan and Frankie took out the mercenaries. They couldn't avoid every gunshot; they bled from holes in their arms and legs, but their bodies quickly healed in response. They took out the catwalks that the mercenaries had perched themselves on. Now, over a dozen unconscious bodies were strewn across the floor along with their firearms.

Herman's vision was rapidly getting darker and he felt cold. He silently marveled at the feeling of dying—so fast and so dark, like being swiftly carried across a bridge in the pitch black of night. McMasters raised his revolver toward both Susan and Frankie. Both of them froze still, the hair on their necks and arms raised, their clothing bloody and punctured.

"I've got two rounds left," Doctor McMasters said. "One for each of you. Don't try to move. I can kill you even without this if I need, but this is faster."

McMasters' grip tightened on the revolver and a smirk crawled across his face. Susan and Frankie tensed.

Gasp!

Doctor McMasters' face jolted to his left. What he saw made his eyebrows leap and his jaw fall. Hammerfist sat up completely erect, eyes wild, gasping and panting heavily. The doctor stood frozen, bewildered, not sure what to make of the sight. But after a second, he collected himself. He flipped about to point the gun at Herman once more. He fired another shot.

BLAM!

Herman flinched, but everything became as if someone turned on the slow motion for his life's movie. He could see every wisp of smoke erupt from the barrel, the bullet edging out at the speed of a power walk, headed straight for him. Reflexively, Herman lifted his hammer to block it. As soon as the bullet rebounded off his hammer, life zoomed up to normal speed.

Ping! The bullet ricocheted into a metal vat, leaking Compound Z24 onto the cement. Thick sweat formed on Doctor McMasters' brow. He bore his teeth and fired the weapon one more time.

BLAM BLAM!

The same thing happened. The gunhots fired in slow motion and the bullets crept toward Herman, spinning through the air like a horizontal top. Herman moved his hammer to block each one and the bullets rebounded in other directions. At that moment, normal life speed returned. Through it all, Doctor McMasters' dumbfounded face didn't change.

Hammerfist quickly lifted his shirt to inspect the bullet holes, but they weren't there. Instead, a few quarter-sized scars peppered his body, and they glowed an eerie shade of florescent green.

He leaped to his feet, breathing in a mighty breath of fresh air through mended lungs. His shoulder felt great. No hole was in his stomach. However, his hammer arm felt tingly all over. He quickly lifted his sleeve as far as it would go and saw the same green glow all over his forearm. They were shaped as if made by a spray of broken glass, and it was the thickest around his wrist where the hammer connected to his arm.

"Fascinating," Doctor McMasters couldn't help but mutter.

Omigosh, Herman thought. *That's right... the toxic waste during the crash was the Compound. It seeped into me through my arm... and I was exposed to a lot of it.*

With that thought in mind, Herman's eyes narrowed and he said, "I think you're out of shots, Doc."

McMasters smirked. "No matter."

He threw down his empty revolver and dashed at Herman in a gust of wind. The doctor's portly frame slowed down as he was just a foot away from Herman, his fist inches away from crashing into his face. Herman promptly stepped aside, kicking Doctor McMasters' feet from underneath him.

Time returned to normal. Like a missile, McMasters shot into a metal vat with a mighty *clang*, denting it with his own frame. He drooped down to the ground, disoriented.

Herman felt a fresh rush of adrenaline pump through him. He could win. McMasters could be put behind bars. They could rescue Cassie and, with a miracle, Tyler could still be saved.

"*Let's go!*" Herman roared as he slammed his hammer into his hand like a brute cracking his knuckles.

Something fierce flowed inside him, like a caged tiger that was suddenly let loose on an abusive trainer. And that trainer was right in front of him.

Herman bolted toward McMasters. In a flash, McMasters was on his feet, throwing a lightning-fast punch at Herman. Time slowed down. Herman blocked the punch. He swung his hammer and crushed it into McMasters' sternum. McMasters tumbled backward, his chest healing up quickly. He launched another punch at Herman. Herman blocked.

Meanwhile, Susan and Frankie stood dozens of yards away, staring incredulously as the two superhumans fought at breakneck speed. Every other second, a rapid-fast movement would happen between the two that would end in Doctor McMasters getting walloped. Frankie and Susan looked at each other, astonished.

"I think… we're going to be okay," Susan said.

It was then that a mercenary moaned into consciousness, slowly pushing himself off the floor. Frankie fired a blast at him. He fell back to the floor.

Back in the middle of the factory, Herman thrust Doctor McMasters against a dented vat, holding him by the folds in his neck. His hammer was lifted, ready to strike another mighty blow. Doctor McMasters struggled to breathe through a busted sternum and ribs. Blood streamed down his nostrils. An eyelid hung over a black eye. Both he and Herman panted profusely.

"Compound X is waning," Herman hissed. "You're going back to normal; I can tell." He paused as he pushed Doctor McMasters harder into the cold metal. His throat gurgled. "You're a kidnapper, a thief, an arsonist, and a murderer. Your next appointment is with a prison cell, McMasters. But I got one question for you." Herman tightened his grip and leaned in closer. *"Where is Cassie Copland?"*

Fear returned to Doctor McMasters' eyes. Compound X lost its luster. His broken nose didn't heal and his breathing remained labored. With a cough, he told Herman:

"I don't know where she is—"

"Liar!" Herman bellowed.

Doctor McMasters recoiled and his throat gurgled again. *"I don't, I swear!* She escaped the day after I got her! I don't know how she did it—but she did. I even put a tracker in her arm and the signal disappeared. I thought she'd go back to you! I don't know where she is!"

Herman stopped baring his teeth. His shoulders sagged. Tyler never saw Cassie at the hospital or the factory because by that time, she was gone. Doctor McMasters was telling the truth. With misty eyes, he released the villain from his grasp. Doctor McMasters fell to the ground, sputtering and coughing and massaging his throat as he lay in a puddle of Compound Z24.

Then, a stampede of footsteps moved in from the main entrance.

"Let's go, let's go, let's go!"

Everyone turned around to see a legion of Citytown police offers swarming into the factory, guns and handcuffs in tow. They went to work securing all the mercenaries and Doctor McMasters. As the blue uniforms overtook the compound, Frankie couldn't help but throw up his arms.

"Of course they show up *now!*" he said. "After we did all the hard work!"

"Hey," Susan nudged him. "We're free now. Completely pardoned. Like this whole thing never happened."

A smile spread across Frankie's face. "Yeah, free to take that antidote and go back to normal, just like you." He sighed. "I don't know what I'll be without you, Susan Terry. I'll try to carry on. My heart will always be yours."

Susan laughed. "You're so weird. I'll miss you too, Frankie."

She leaned in and gave him a delicate peck on the forehead before patting his shoulder and walking out the door. Frankie's face burned and he tried to force down a smile. It was then that he noticed her soccer ball, discarded, resting by his side. He bent down and picked it up, brushing the dust off it.

As a pair of officers cuffed Doctor McMasters and took him away, Herman felt the tiger inside him saunter back into its cage. He checked under his shirt. The scars from the bullet holes didn't glow anymore, and neither did his arm.

A sigh escaped his nose. Cassie was gone. But where? And why didn't she tell him or the others? Is she close? What if she's not?

"Hammerfist."

Herman turned around to see Detective Axewielder standing in full uniform, his badge glistening in the florescent light of the warehouse. His thumbs were in his belt loops and he stared up at Herman with softer eyes than usual. The rest of his face was just as stony and rugged as always.

"That's it," he said. "All of you are pardoned. No charges. You okay?"

Herman twisted his arm. "I got shot three times, but we got him. I guess I'm doing well. Is Tyler gonna be okay?"

"We don't know yet," Detective Axewielder said. "He lost a lot of blood. They're going to do everything that they can." He was silent for a long moment, then said. "So now what are you going to do?"

"Take the antidote for my conditions," Herman shrugged. "Go back to normal life."

"You sure about that?"

Herman frowned. "Why wouldn't I be?"

Detective Axewielder breathed deep, then said, "It sounds like a large portion of Doctor McMasters' shipment was already sent out earlier today—that Compound Z-three-five or whatever you call it. That means it's still out there. If it's still in this city, that means we're still going to have freaks running around."

Herman didn't say anything. His eyes shifted from the ground between his sneakers to the hammer attached to his wrist.

"Think about it," Detective Axewielder said with a shrug. Then he turned around and walked away.

It was then that Herman was left to himself. Around him, the metal vats of the HyperFizz Cola factory were all dented horribly, with one leaking the Compound to the ground. The sound of police officers scurrying about was dying as they rounded up the last of the mercenaries. Herman took a look at himself—a bloodied-up t-shirt with bullet holes and a leather jacket that had been through multiple shards of shrapnel and three gunshots.

He held his jacket up to his eyes and muttered, "That's the second one this week."

23

Tyler Calvin's funeral was held one week after the incident at the HyperFizz Cola factory. The family was blessed with a beautiful morning, a soft summer breeze wafting through the thick, rustling trees of the Citytown Cemetery. The grass swayed between the headstones that peppered the green. The pastor of the Calvin family's church recited words about returning to dust while black-garbed volunteers from multiple soup kitchens dabbed their eyes with handkerchiefs.

The police told the family that Tyler had been wandering the street that night and got shot by a street thug. It was partially true, but only partially—that's why Herman and the others couldn't bring themselves to participate in the proceedings. They knew what really happened, but the Citytown police thought it would be better that the family didn't know about Doctor McMasters and the Compound. They would try to keep that under control as much as possible.

Herman and the others knew the truth, though. Tyler Calvin lived his life looking out for those who could hardly look out for themselves. He lived as a hero even before the Compound was pumped into his body. But the city couldn't know how much of a hero he really was. At least not today.

*

The sun was almost over the horizon as it cast golden sparkles over the ocean to the west. Above it, a sky painted with brilliantly thick shades of purple and orange hovered over Citytown. Nighttime was almost upon the city, but Herman Fitzgerald wanted to savor the stillness of sunset before the insanity of neon and darkness fell.

The gentle breeze from Tyler's funeral today didn't let up. It was even more refreshing up here, on the mountain overlooking the whole city. The motorcycle ride up here wasn't long—maybe half an hour if you take the scenic route. The trees that sandwiched the switchbacks provided shade the whole way, and when they opened up to the view, it was breathtaking.

The Leftybike was parked just a few yards away in a small dirt parking lot that marked Lookout Point. Usually, this would be a prime location for teenagers to sacrifice their innocence, but Herman lucked out tonight. Not another soul was up here—just him and the sunset. He sat with his legs crossed, his eyes scanning the Citytown skyline.

He couldn't help but think of Cassie. An entire week of Frankie's reassurances weren't that helpful, either. She's a tough girl. She'll be fine. She might just need some time for herself. The unanswered questions left nothing but a hollow spot in Herman's chest. He let out a deep breath as he picked at some grass.

Gradually, the sound of a car engine became louder and louder as it ascended up the mountain switchbacks. Eventually, it pulled in next to the Leftybike and the car rumbled to a stop. Herman turned around and instantly recognized the car but didn't stare. His eyes returned and locked onto the city.

The car door opened and shut and the footsteps moved toward him. After a minute, Sidney Saskatoon sat down next to Herman, imitating his cross-legged position. He wasn't wearing his lab coat as usual. This time, he wore a hideous Hawaiian button-down shirt with jean shorts and flip-flops. Herman pulled some more grass out of the ground next to him.

"That shirt is disgusting," Herman said.

"Really?" Sid said, genuinely surprised. "Katy said she likes it. She says I need to add a bit more fun to my wardrobe."

"Not like that."

Herman turned and smirked at Sid. Sid smiled back.

"Herman," Sid began as he looked out over the sunset. "I could never apologize enough to you. What I did to you and Cassandra and the others was horribly wrong. I'm so sorry—so sorry. I did the only thing I knew without regard to how it would affect you and your lives. I was so eager to stop Malcolm and so desperate that I—well, you all paid an astronomical price for my poor judgment. Especially Tyler and his family."

Herman didn't reply right away. The image of Tyler's shocked face as a bullet ripped through him would be branded in his brain for the rest of his life. He scrunched his eyebrows and pulled more grass from the ground.

"I just—" Sid continued. "I just hope someday that you'll be able to forgive me. That's all."

"Oh, I've already forgiven you, Sid."

Sid turned and looked at Herman, his face soft. Herman didn't make eye contact.

"Tyler did pay the ultimate price," Herman said. "There's no replacing him. He was an awesome kid—one in a million. But he knew the risks just as well as all of us did when we decided to go after McMasters. He could've pulled out at any time, but instead, he stepped up to the plate. I hope more people know that someday."

Sid didn't say anything for a second. Then he said, "I hope so, too."

"So, what's your plan now?"

"Must there always be some big plan?"

"For you, there should be."

"I want to keep innovating ways to help you and Frankie," Sid said. "I'll continue to utilize whatever resources I can to track down the rest of Compound Z24 and be sure it never falls into the wrong hands." He paused. "Are you sure you want to continue on with this? You know you can take that antidote at any time. Susan did, and she seems very happy."

Herman reached into his new leather jacket and pulled out a vial. Its rich purple hue glowed against the sun, swirling thickly inside its tiny tube.

"I will," Herman said thoughtfully. "But right now, there's still a little work to be done."

"Have you thought about looking for Cassandra?" Sid suggested.

Herman locked eyes with him. Then he looked back to the sunset. "Every day. I'd like to, but I don't know if she wants to be found. At least not right now. Otherwise, she would have come back to us."

"Whenever you change your mind," Sid said with a caring grin.

"*Hammerfist!*"

Detective Axewielder's voice sounded suddenly in Herman's earpiece. Herman pressed his finger to the ear and said, "What's up?"

"The corner of seventh and third street," Detective Axewielder said. "You should probably come take a look at this. We might have another goon on our hands. Maybe two. I've already radioed Ghetto Blaster and he's on his way."

Herman looked at Sid. Sid looked at Herman. Herman said, "Got it. Be there soon."

Quickly, Herman jumped from his spot and went to the Leftybike. He rammed the key into the ignition and turned it, roaring the bike to life. Before he turned out of the parking lot, Sid called for him.

"Herman!"

Herman lifted up his head, trying to hear Sid over the rumble of the engine.

"You'll find her again, Herman!" Sid said. "I'm sure of it!"

Herman half-grinned and gave a little nod before he gunned the throttle and rocketed away, hurtling across the mountainside.

At that point, Sid turned again to the sunset. The sun had nearly dipped over the horizon. With it, another night. And what would another night bring? More shadows that creep through alleys in search for a target. More dark deals to be brought into the light. More corruption to be exposed and repulsed. As the sun sets and shadows grow, the plans of those who do wrong grow in kind.

But just as the shadows grow, there are those that shine a light through the darkness—that pierce through the murk. Citytown wouldn't be alone during these nights. Not anytime soon. Who will be the one to shine that light?

You already know the name.

ABOUT THE AUTHOR

Aaron N. Hall is the author of the fantasy epic *Foreordained* and the moderately funny superhero satire *My Name is Hammerfist.* His friend Adam says he dresses like a dad who still listens to blink-182. He lives in Utah.

Visit **aaronnhall.com** for updates on future books

Made in the USA
Columbia, SC
06 September 2020